One Imperfect Christmas

Library of Congress Cataloging-in-Publication Data

Johnson, Myra, 1951-
 One imperfect Christmas / Myra Johnson.
  p. cm.
 ISBN 978-1-4267-0070-5 (pbk. : alk. paper)
 1. Guilt--Fiction. 2. Christmas stories. I. Title.
 PS3610.O3666O54 2009
 813'.6--dc22

                                            2009014260

Printed in the United States of America
1 2 3 4 5 6 7 8 9 10 / 14 13 12 11 10 09

One Imperfect Christmas

by

Myra Johnson

Abingdon Press fiction
a novel approach to faith

For Jack,
my husband, my best friend,
whose love and support keep me going on this journey,
and for our daughters, Johanna and Julena,
who never stopped believing in their mom!

§ Acknowledgments §

To the founding members of "Seared Hearts," my former critique group, who guided the early stages of this story: DiAnn Mills, Kathleen Y'Barbo, and Martha Rogers.

To all the anonymous contest judges who helped me hone and polish the manuscript.

To my award-winning critique partner, Carla Stewart, for sharing her friendship, writing advice, and nursing expertise.

To the fantastic ladies of Seekerville: Audra, Camy, Cara, Cheryl, Debby, Glynna, Janet, Julie, Mary, Missy, Pam, Ruthy, Sandra, and Tina. Whenever I need a good laugh, a shoulder to cry on, a kick in the pants, or professional insights, you're just an email away.

To the staff, volunteers, horses, and clients of SIRE, Houston's Therapeutic Equestrian Center, for your dedication, courage, and inspiration.

A thousand thanks to my wonderful editor, Barbara Scott. Your patience, honesty, expertise, and friendship have blessed and sustained me through the incredible experience of seeing my first published novel become a reality.

And finally, thanks be to God, with whom all things are possible!

1

Natalie Pearce padded into the kitchen in her new velour robe and fuzzy orange-and-white slippers that looked like little foxes. They were a Christmas present from her husband, Daniel, just three weeks ago. The gift tag had read: "To one foxy lady!"

First thing in the morning, straw-blonde hair still tangled from sleep, she felt anything but foxy. Still, her cheeks warmed as she considered inviting Daniel back to the bedroom for a few more minutes of snuggling. Then she remembered this was Saturday—her day to play "coach's widow." After nearly fifteen years of marriage she still hated her husband's erratic schedule. On Christmas Eve her parents had celebrated their forty-eighth wedding anniversary, a legacy of love Natalie hoped she and Daniel could emulate. But was such a dream even possible when the two of them seemed to operate in different time zones?

She paused at the breakfast table and set her hands on her hips. As usual, he'd left the newspaper in shambles, the comics pulled from one section and the sports page decimated after he'd clipped all the articles covering Putnam Middle School's athletic teams.

Daniel breezed into the kitchen, sneakers squeaking on the ceramic tile floor. "Hey, hon, sorry about the paper." He planted a toothpaste-flavored kiss on her parted lips. "I'd sort it out for you, but I'm already running late. I'm meeting Carl at Casey's Diner to carpool to the tournament."

Natalie fought to keep her smile in place as she gave him a playful punch in the stomach. "What's new? Get out of here before I decide not to let you go at all."

"Promises, promises." He wiggled his dark eyebrows.

"Seriously, before you go . . . ," she said in her sexiest voice. She clutched the lapels of his red Putnam Panthers jacket and pulled him toward her.

With a seductive grin, Daniel drew her into his arms. "Sweetheart, I told you, I'm already running late."

She chuckled and bit his ear. "Sorry, Coach, I just wanted to ask you again what time your parents will be here."

"Woman, you break my heart!" He slammed a hand to his chest as if he'd been shot. "Ah, now I get it. You want to know exactly how much time you have to clean the house."

So she wasn't the world's greatest housekeeper—one trait she *didn't* inherit from her mother. Who cared about a little clutter on the kitchen counters, or last night's pizza pan still soaking in the sink? So what if she hadn't dusted since Thanksgiving? Hard to do with Christmas decorations covering every flat, dusty surface in the house.

Daniel seemed to read her thoughts. He tilted her chin until she reluctantly met his gaze. "Next weekend. Promise me, okay? The Christmas decorations need to come down."

She pushed out her lower lip. "Only if you stay home and help. It's depressing to do it all by myself."

"I'll check my schedule." He gathered up his car keys and canvas briefcase and then slicked a hand through ash-brown hair still damp from his shower. "Mom and Dad won't get here before three at the earliest, so you've got plenty of time to enjoy your coffee." He glanced at his watch. "And I don't. I'm out of here, sweetie. With any luck, I'll be home in time for dinner."

"That'll be the day."

The door to the garage banged shut behind him, sending a puff of wintry air into the kitchen. Moments later Natalie heard the ancient green Bronco grumble a couple of times before starting up. The poor thing must have nearly 200,000 miles on it. How Daniel kept it running, she hadn't a clue, but what with paying the mortgage on their dream home and keeping their thirteen-year-old fashionista daughter in designer jeans, replacing a vehicle wasn't in the budget. She sent up a quick prayer for Daniel's safety on the road and hoped the weather held. The last she'd heard, the predicted snow wouldn't arrive until tomorrow morning.

Her chest caved. Much as she enjoyed the visits with Daniel's parents, Alice Pearce was an even more meticulous house-keeper than Natalie's mother. No way around it—the cleaning had to get done. Maybe Natalie could bribe her daughter into helping. After all, half the mess was Lissa's school books, art supplies, and discarded shoes dropped haphazardly between the kitchen door and her bedroom upstairs.

So much for getting back to the watercolor landscape Natalie had begun last weekend. At least her freelance graphic design assignments had tapered off now that the holidays had passed. The extra income supplemented Daniel's small-town coaching salary, but Natalie dreamed of making her living as a fine artist—thanks to her mother's teaching and inspiration. She'd much rather pursue her own creative visions than those of her finicky clients.

She poured a glass of orange juice and a mug of coffee and then dropped an English muffin into the toaster. She'd barely sat down to spread the muffin with her mother's home-made apricot jam when Lissa flounced into the kitchen, her long blonde hair pinned up with mismatched butterfly clips. Natalie suppressed a laugh and lifted her hands in mock surrender. "Is this the part where you say, 'Take me to your leader'?"

"Oh, Mom, how juvenile!" Lissa swiped her finger through the jam jar and licked off a sticky, amber glob. "Have you seen my pink sweater—the one with the gray stripe across the front?"

Natalie sipped her coffee. "Did you check the laundry hamper?"

"Yes, twice."

"The floor of your room?"

"Mother!"

"How about the closet? Any chance you actually hung it up?"

Lissa clenched her fists. "Mom, I need some *help* here. Jody and her mom are picking me up in twenty minutes."

Natalie gave her daughter a blank stare.

"Earth to *Mo*-ther." Lissa rolled her eyes.

"Oh, rats, the youth group skating party." No help cleaning from Lissa today. With a sigh, Natalie bit into her English muffin. "Sorry, honey, but I have no idea where your sweater is. Can't you find something else to wear?"

The ringing telephone halted whatever sarcastic retort Lissa was about to spit out. She squinted at the caller ID on the kitchen extension and grabbed the receiver. "Jody! Did I leave my sweater over there when I spent the night last week-end? Great! Bring it with you. I'll put it on in the car." She hung up and dashed through the den, yanking clips out of her hair and tossing them on the sofa.

"Lissa!"

"Sorry, Mom. I'll get them later, I promise!" Lissa's bedroom door slammed with finality.

Right, when pigs fly. Sure, Natalie could insist Lissa pick up after herself before leaving for the party, but a battle of wills with a headstrong preteen? No-brainer—it was guaranteed to ruin the entire day for both of them. She made a promise to herself, though, that one day very soon she and Daniel would sit down with Lissa and lay out some ground rules—*before* Lissa's adolescent self-centeredness got completely out of hand.

Natalie refilled her coffee mug and carried the remains of the newspaper to the den. Fifteen more minutes and she'd have the house to herself and maybe a little time to work on that watercolor before she got serious about cleaning.

Lissa had been gone barely five minutes when the phone rang again. Natalie, settled in the recliner under a snuggly fleece throw, was tempted not to answer it—probably another of Lissa's perky seventh-grade friends calling to ask what she planned to wear to the party.

Then the answering machine picked up, and after Natalie's recorded greeting and the beep, she heard her mother's voice. "Hi, Natalie, just me. Guess you're out running errands. I'll call later—"

Natalie shook off her annoyance and jumped up to grab the kitchen extension. "Hey, Mom, I'm here."

"Oh, good, glad I caught you." Her mother's cheery voice turned cajoling. "It's that time again, sweetheart. Can I twist your arm to help?"

Apprehension propelled Natalie into the nearest chair. Her mother didn't even have to speak the words. "Oh, Mom, does it have to be today? Taking down Christmas decorations is my least favorite chore in the world. Daniel's already on my case about ours." She gave a weak laugh. "You know me. I'd leave them up year-round if I could." Someday she'd do just that and hire someone to come in and dust them off once a month.

"I know, and I'm sorry to even ask." Mom sounded genuinely sympathetic. "But your dad went to that horse auction, and it's my turn to host the church ladies' book club tomorrow afternoon."

"Did you try Hart and Celia?" Natalie's brother and sister-in-law lived just a few miles from the farm.

"Hart went with your dad to the auction, and Celia's taking Kurt and Kevin to their basketball game." Mom paused. "I'll make apple dumplings and hot cider."

"Bribery—that is so not fair." Natalie patted her stomach. "I already need to sweat off at least five pounds of Christmas goodies."

"Lifting Christmas boxes is good exercise."

Obviously, Mom wasn't going to give up. Natalie stared out the bay window. She needed to come up with some logical reason why Mom should postpone this depressing annual chore. Her gaze settled on the bank of gray snow clouds looming on the horizon. She shivered just thinking about venturing out on this frosty January day.

She offered an idea. "Think of how much the ladies would enjoy the decorations. It wouldn't hurt to leave them up a little longer, would it?"

"Natalie, the tree is completely dry and dropping needles all over the carpet. It really must come down today." A note of apology tinged her mother's voice. "I should have asked your father to help me earlier in the week, but the time got away from us."

"You know I'd do anything for you, Mom, and if it were any other weekend—" Yes, come to think of it, she had a ready-made excuse. She tried not to let the rush of gratitude creep into her tone. "Remember I told you Daniel's parents are driving over this afternoon? Daniel's at a tournament in Fielding to scout basketball teams, and Lissa's at a skating party. I need to clean house and shop for groceries before they get here."

Not that she actually intended to do all that much. If her mother had asked her help for anything else—rearranging furniture, washing windows, even shoveling snow off the front walk—she'd have driven out to the farm on a moment's notice.

But taking down Christmas decorations?

Her mother gave a wry laugh. "It's okay. Don't worry, I'll manage by myself."

Mom's disappointment tarnished Natalie's brief glow of triumph and raised a moment of concern. Her stubborn mother would "manage" all right. She'd take on the whole project by herself, arthritis and all. Natalie pressed the phone against her ear. "Now, Mom, don't you try to carry all those boxes out to the barn. You'll aggravate your bad wrist again, and you won't be able to paint for a week."

"Natalie—"

"I mean it, Mom. Stack the decorations out of sight in the downstairs guestroom, and I'll come by one day next week to help you pack everything away."

After eliciting her mother's assurance she wouldn't take on too much, Natalie said good-bye. Just a few more days to psych herself up for the end of the holidays, that's all she asked. Shrugging off the last twinges of guilt, Natalie snuggled into the recliner to finish her coffee.

Around ten, she finally talked herself into exchanging her comfy robe and those adorable slippers for paint-stained sweats and grungy sneakers. Like it or not, she needed to do a cursory cleaning before her in-laws arrived. She'd just finished loading the dishwasher and returned from the garage with the sponge mop when the phone rang again.

This time it was Daniel's father, calling to say the winter frontal system had already hit their part of the state. With two inches of snow on the ground and more expected, they'd decided not to chance the drive.

A crazy mix of relief and disappointment flooded Natalie. Daniel didn't get to see his folks that often, and Lissa had been planning an after-Christmas shopping trip with her grandmother ever since they'd first mentioned coming. But an excuse to postpone housecleaning? Definitely cause for celebration. Natalie loaded the stereo with her favorite Christmas CDs, set up her easel and paints in front of the bay window, and settled in for her version of the perfect Saturday.

Hours later, she was adding the finishing touches to a winter landscape when the phone startled her. The paintbrush skittered across the canvas, marring a stately pine with aquamarine streaks. Natalie mumbled a few choice words and glanced at the mantle clock as she wiped her hands on a paint rag. Five already? Where had the day gone? Daniel and Lissa would be home soon. She needed to wrap things up and figure out something for supper. Mentally sorting through the freezer contents for a quick and simple meal, she picked up the kitchen extension.

"Natalie?" her dad's voice sounded ragged—choked with panic. "Come to the hospital right away. It's your mother."

Her stomach plummeted. She pictured her mother at the bottom of a ladder amidst a pile of Christmas decorations. "What happened? Is she okay?"

Sprained ankle? Broken hip? *Oh, Mom, why couldn't you wait?*

"Just . . . get here." Her father clicked off before she could press him for details.

Dread coiled around her heart. She threw a parka over her sweats and grabbed her purse and keys off the counter. When she gunned the engine to back out of the garage, her trusty silver Saturn screeched in protest. The side mirror nicked the doorframe, and she barely missed taking out the mailbox and the neighbor's trash can. She drove like a maniac to Putnam General, all the while berating herself for ignoring Mom's request for help. After everything her mother had sacrificed for her, she could only pray these new injuries wouldn't cripple her mother for life.

Natalie burst through the ER entrance and scanned the faces in the congested waiting area. A mother holding an ice pack against her son's forehead. An ashen-faced woman dozing against an elderly man's shoulder. Whimpering babies. Frightened children. Anxious parents.

She spotted her father's silver-gray head across the room, where he paced in front of a set of double doors. Her brother, Hart, stood close by with his hands tucked into his blue-jeans pockets, rocking on his heels.

Natalie rushed over and touched her father's arm. "Dad, how's Mom? Tell me it's not serious."

Her father turned and looked at her—looked through her. "They think it's a stroke." His face crumpled as his thin veneer of strength collapsed. He pressed a fist to his mouth and pulled her to him, squeezing her so tightly, she could hardly breathe.

Natalie struggled away and stared at him, not comprehending. *A stroke?* Ice-cold terror crackled through her veins. She spun to face her brother and seized his wrist. "Hart?"

"It's bad, Nat. Real bad." He drew her into his arms, and she felt her brother's fear in every tense muscle of his body.

A tall, bearded man in hospital greens pushed through the double doors. "Mr. Morgan? I'm Dr. Wyatt." He indicated a frayed blue sofa, the only empty seat in the waiting area. "Why don't we sit down."

Natalie blocked his way. "Just tell us, how is my mother? She'll be okay, right?"

"I wish I had better news." The doctor glanced at the chart he held.

"But there's stuff you can do for a stroke these days. I saw it on TV."

"It isn't that simple. Please try to understand." Dr. Wyatt attempted to explain her mother's condition, tossing out phrases about blood clots and clot-dissolving medications and something about a three-hour time window before irreversible brain damage set in.

A sob tore from Natalie's throat. "Are you saying she got here too late? That there's nothing you can do?"

"We'll continue to do all we can to minimize the damage, but under the circumstances . . . " The doctor gave a one-shoulder shrug. "I'm sorry. I'm so very sorry."

2

Natalie ran a thumb across the misshapen knuckles of her mother's hand as it rested quietly in her own. More than two weeks had passed, with no significant improvement. To see her mother hooked up to all those tubes and monitors, to realize she might never wake up, much less speak or hold a paintbrush or even recognize her family again—how could Natalie ever forgive herself for letting this happen?

One phrase slithered through her thoughts, accusing her, condemning her: *If she'd received immediate treatment . . .*

"Good morning, Mrs. Pearce." A plump nurse in scrubs the color of Pepto-Bismol breezed into the room and patted her shoulder. "Have you been here all night again?"

Natalie bristled. "Where else would I be?"

"How about home with your family?" A pitying smile quirked the nurse's lips in a look Natalie had come to despise. "Seriously, there's nothing you can do here. Get some rest. Eat a decent meal." After another condescending shoulder pat, the nurse inventoried her mother's vitals and monitor readings.

Rest? Eat? The woman had to be kidding. A king-size cup of industrial-strength cafeteria coffee, on the other hand, *might* get her through the morning. She looped her purse over her shoulder and trudged out to the corridor.

When the elevator doors slid open, Natalie almost collided with her father as he stepped off. His accusing expression mirrored the nurse's. "Natalie Rose. Have you been home at all since I saw you yesterday?"

She held up one hand. "Don't start on me, Dad."

He frowned, fatigue etching deep lines around his eyes and mouth. She thought of all her father had to deal with—the farm, the horses, not to mention all the things around the house Mom always took care of.

She followed his sagging form to her mother's room. When he paused outside the door, she hooked her arm in his and rested her cheek on his corduroy sleeve. "Daddy, how are you doing? Do you need anything from the supermarket? Any help with the horses?"

He shrugged. "Celia keeps me supplied with meals. Hart and the twins have been pitching in with farm chores."

Natalie swiveled and sank onto a nearby bench. She should be doing more to help her father, but she couldn't bring herself to leave her mother's bedside. A shudder raked her body. Her mind flicked around the edges of a memory with the hesitance of a tongue probing a sore tooth. *Lightning flashes. Blowing rain. A frightened mare's whinny.*

She pulled herself away from the strobe-like images as Dad settled onto the bench beside her. His thin, callused fingers gripped his lean thighs. "I just spoke with the doctor. They want to move your mom to a long-term care facility."

A blackened thumbnail on her father's left hand drew Natalie's gaze. "Long-term care. For the therapies they want to try, right?"

Dad's chest rose and fell. He rubbed his eyes. "They'll do what they can."

"How soon will they move her?"

"A few more days, once they're sure she can hold her own." He stood and moved to the door. "I'm going to sit with her awhile. Go home, Natalie. Spend some time with Dan and Lissa."

At the mention of her neglected husband and daughter, her heart lurched. They'd been carrying on as usual, or trying to. Daniel had taken a full week off from school right after Mom's stroke, but his personal and sick days were dwindling fast. Lissa had to keep up with her studies or risk failing grades.

She rose and peered through the partially open door. Dad hunched on the chair next to Mom's bed, his frayed work shirt stretched across his bony spine as he clutched her hand. The pink-clad nurse hovered nearby, checking monitors and typing notes on a bedside computer terminal.

An ache, thick and spreading, welled beneath Natalie's heart. Okay, she'd leave for a while and get some fresh air to clear her mind . . . and pray.

꧁

Daniel Pearce paused behind the desk in his cramped coach's office, one hand gripping the back of his chair. He felt as if he'd been praying nonstop ever since he returned from his Saturday scouting trip to find Lissa home alone and Natalie nowhere to be found.

Minutes later the phone had rung—Natalie, calling from the hospital to say her mother had suffered a devastating stroke. Their lives hadn't been the same since.

"Hey, bro." Head coach Carl Moreno nudged open the office door with a meaty forearm. "You headed home?"

Daniel grabbed his jacket off the coat tree. "After a stop at Casey's Diner for another take-out order. I swear, if I eat one more French fry, I'm going to turn into one." Not to mention the food would be cold and soggy by the time he drove home from Putnam to Fawn Ridge.

"Meant to tell you, Marie's sending a casserole tomorrow. Hope your family likes shepherd's pie."

"A home-cooked meal? You bet!" Daniel's mouth watered in anticipation, although Natalie would probably eat at the hospital again, if she ate at all.

The rattle of the janitor's cart echoed in the corridor, a reminder Daniel needed to be on his way. He gathered up a stack of basketball stats and the history reports his fourth-period students had turned in and stuffed everything into his canvas briefcase. With a slap on Carl's shoulder, he said good-bye and ambled out to the parking lot.

He turned into his driveway just after six-thirty. When the garage door lifted, he saw Natalie's car in its spot. His heart rose with a happy thump and just as quickly stuttered and fell. If she'd left the hospital, it must be bad news. Nothing else would draw her from Belinda's side.

The greasy odor of Casey's burgers and fries turned rancid in his nostrils. He shut off the Bronco's engine and sat in silence as the garage door creaked shut behind him. Hauling in a shaky breath, he collected his things and sent up a hasty prayer before heading into the house.

The door opened onto a view of the kitchen table set with a floral tablecloth and their white wedding china. A smiling Lissa poured ice water into crystal tumblers. Natalie stood at the counter stirring a sizzling concoction in the red-enameled electric wok. Something Asian lingered in the air, spicy and flavorful.

A stupid grin creased Daniel's face. He held up the greasy Casey's bag. "Guess we won't need these burgers."

"You could always take one for lunch tomorrow." Natalie's smile didn't quite match her teasing tone. She adjusted the temperature knob and continued stirring. "Liss, check the rice cooker, will you?"

Daniel frowned at the bag and dropped it into the trash can. Laying aside his briefcase, he came up behind his wife and encircled her waist with both arms. She smelled of peach-scented shower gel. Her pale yellow hair felt satiny against his cheek. "I didn't expect to find you at home."

A tremor shook her body, and something told him it had nothing to do with their closeness. Slipping out of his arms, she reached for a bottle of teriyaki sauce. "Mom is being weaned off the machines. They'll move her to a nursing home soon."

"That's good news, isn't it?" He spied a bowl of carrot sticks on the end of the counter and helped himself to a couple. The sweet crunch satisfied him in a way no soggy French fry ever could.

When he glanced at his wife, her lips were drawn into a thin white line. Tears threatened beneath lashes already spiky with wetness. His chest swelled. He tossed the last bit of carrot onto the counter and took her in his arms seconds before she burst into sobs. "Hey, hey. What's wrong?"

"Why didn't I just go out and help her? How could I have been so selfish?"

"It's not your fault, honey. You know it's not your fault." Over Natalie's shoulder Daniel watched Lissa draw into herself—her face a twisted mask of confusion and fear. She replaced the lid on the rice cooker and huddled against the refrigerator.

A knot of urgency squeezed Daniel's chest. Somehow he had to salvage what was left of the first semi-normal evening his family had shared in nearly three weeks. He stroked

Natalie's back. "Please, honey, you've made this fantastic dinner. Let's sit down and enjoy it."

She pressed her fists against his shoulders and pushed away, her head shaking as if she couldn't quite clear it. "I can't do this. I thought I could, but—" She spun away and tore out of the kitchen. Seconds later their bedroom door slammed.

"Dad?" Lissa's tiny voice trickled into his jumbled thoughts. He opened his arms to her. "Daddy, I'm scared. For Grandma and for Mom."

"Me, too, pussycat. Me too."

⤬

Natalie edged her Saturn into a narrow parking space. Nearby stood a concrete-and-brick sign partially obscured by overgrown yews. Etched into the concrete was the name *Hope Gardens Convalescent Center.* It had a pleasant ring to it. If only the place lived up to its promise. If only they could make her mother well again.

Natalie clutched the steering wheel and squeezed her eyes shut. *Dear God, please—* Her mind blanked. She'd run out of prayers.

A crisp February wind whipped at her coattails as she made her way to the entrance. Inside, the mixed odors of disinfectant, cafeteria food, and talcum powder assaulted her. She tried not to inhale on her way to room 51-C.

The door opened into a cheery room painted sunshine-yellow and edged with a border of wildflowers near the ceiling. Natalie's gaze fell upon the shrunken woman lost amid carefully arranged pillows and blankets.

"Oh, Mom . . . "

Only the dimmest light of awareness shone in her mother's pale blue eyes. The emptiness behind them tore at Natalie's heart. Sucking in a quick breath, she pulled a chair closer and plopped down. A pained smile forced artificial lightness into her voice.

"Isn't this a pretty room, Mom? Yellow is such a happy color. And the people here seem nice. I know you're going to do great, I just know—"

It wasn't working. A shuddering sigh shook her chest. She sat back and unzipped her laptop case. "You rest, Mom. I'll just sit with you and get some work done."

She'd practically begged Jeff Garner, her friend who owned the local print shop, for all the graphic design assignments he could send her way. For one thing, Mom's care would surely tax Dad's finances to the limit. For another, Natalie craved anything to help take her mind off the unrelenting guilt.

She looked up from the computer screen, her vision blurring as she recalled the watercolor she'd left unfinished the day of her mother's stroke. Agonizing shame shredded her already raw emotions. Until her mother walked out of here whole and healthy, Natalie vowed never to touch a paintbrush again.

3

Valentine's Day arrived, bleak and cold and somber. The staff had decorated her mom's room and most of the nursing facility with red paper hearts, lace doilies, and pink balloons. Stressing over Jeff's advertising projects all morning, Natalie had pushed herself to the brink of a migraine. Only when an aide brought lunch for her mother did she realize how much time had passed. She retrieved the ham sandwich she'd packed and nibbled at it while the aide slipped bites of something puréed between her mother's lips. Even though Mom had been eating well since the feeding tube was removed in the hospital, her continual sputters and dribbles made Natalie look away in anguish.

Her father came to visit after lunch, and Natalie welcomed a couple of hours to escape. She ventured as far as the lobby but couldn't bring herself to go home. Instead, she settled onto a plaid sofa with some magazines and tried her best to avoid the inquisitive looks of the elderly residents.

Around three, she glanced up to see her father shuffling across the speckled Berber carpet. He sank onto the sofa next to her and gave a tired chuckle. "What am I going to do with you, Rosy-girl?"

The childhood nickname pricked her heart. "I'm fine, Daddy. It's you I'm worried about."

"Don't tell me you're fine when I can see plain as day you're not." His knee brushed hers as he shifted to face her. He held out a colorful brochure. The central graphic depicted a middle-aged couple surrounding an elderly man in a wheelchair. "I think we should do this."

She looked askance at the words under the picture: *Surviving Stroke: A Family Matter.* "What exactly is it?"

"A support group for families with loved ones who've suffered a stroke." Dad flipped open the brochure. "See, they meet once a week at Fawn Ridge Fellowship."

"At our church?"

"Al and Betty Grumbacher told me about it. Betty's dad had that stroke two years ago, remember?"

"I know, but . . . " Natalie edged away. Her pain was still too raw—too private.

"Just think about it, okay? I've got to get going." He winked. "Daniel asked a favor."

She didn't have the energy to ask what, and did she even want to know? She gave her dad a hug and kiss good-bye before returning to her mother's room.

Too bleary-eyed to face another siege at the computer, she'd been sitting next to her mother's bed, a year-old gossip rag lying open in her lap, when Daniel breezed in, a bouquet of scarlet roses in his outstretched hand. "Happy Valentine's Day, sweetheart."

She looked up from the article she'd been skimming about some movie star's recent stint in rehab. Only it was old news now. The star had been arrested two weeks ago for driving under the influence. Natalie had watched the twenty-four-minute car chase live on the tiny TV in Mom's hospital room.

The magazine slid from her lap. "Is school out already?"

"It's nearly five." He laid the bouquet on the bedside table. Taking both her hands, he pulled her to her feet and wrapped his arms around her. His suede jacket smelled of roses and wood smoke. "Honey, you need to get out of here. Let's go to dinner tonight—just the two of us. I made a reservation at Adamo's."

"What about Lissa?"

"Your dad picked her up from school. They're ordering pizza."

The favor. Of course. "I shouldn't leave Mom."

"She'll be fine. It's just for a couple of hours."

Natalie pulled away and fiddled with her mother's pillow. Her gaze fell to her mother's bony right wrist, stiff and misshapen from the arthritis that had set in after—

A shiver ran through her. She'd never forget that terrifying night. *I'll be all right, Natalie. Do what you have to do.*

Daniel came up behind her and slid his arms beneath hers. His warm chest pressed against her back. "You're exhausting yourself, Nat. Come with me tonight. It'll be good for both of us."

Resentment frayed her nerves. How could her husband even talk about celebrating Valentine's Day? She edged out of his embrace. Her thoughts skittered in a thousand other directions, all leading back to her mother. "The Putnam Starving Artist Show is next weekend. Mom should be packing up all her beautiful paintings and pricing them."

"Celia said she'd take over a few. Maybe you could go with her—take some of yours this year. Your mom would like that."

An invisible hand closed around her throat. She should realize Daniel only meant to make her feel better. *He* should realize it wasn't working, and she wished he'd stop trying. The words she'd repeated countless times already slipped out once more. "If I'd been there that day, if I hadn't been so stupid and self-centered—"

"You can't keep doing this to yourself." Daniel paced across the room and swung around. "Nobody blames you for your mom's stroke. You've got to get over the idea that you could have kept it from happening."

She glanced away, too tired to argue. "If you won't try to understand my feelings, then why don't you just leave?"

"Nat, come on. You don't mean it."

"Yes, I do. Go!" Her voice broke on a sob. "Get out of here, and just leave me alone."

"Fine, if that's the way you want it." Hurt and confusion clouded Daniel's eyes. He hesitated, looking as if he expected her to take back her words. When she didn't, he snatched up the roses and stormed out.

In the silence that followed, something in Natalie shattered. Turning to her mother, she brushed a tear from her cheek. "You gave up so much for me, Mom, and look how I repaid you. If it takes the rest of my life, I'll find a way to make you well."

❧

Daniel sat at his coach's desk and proclaimed this year's Valentine's Day the worst on record as he ate another cold burger and fries alone. If only he could figure out what was going on with her. Why the guilt? Why didn't she want to talk about it? A month later and he still didn't have a clue. Trashing the burger, he walked out onto the gym floor just in time for his next class.

"You're zoning out again, man." Carl punched him in the arm in time for him to dodge a poorly aimed volleyball served by a skinny kid in his sixth-period P.E. class.

Daniel chased down the ball and rolled it under the net to the server on the opposing side. "Control, Len. You've got to power that thing straight over the net."

"Marie sent another casserole for you. It's in the break-room fridge."

"Thanks. You guys are too good to us." He checked his watch, relieved to see he'd somehow made it through the hour. He blew a shrill blast on his whistle.

"Time's up, guys. Hit the showers."

Carl lumbered along beside Daniel on the way to their offices at the rear of the gym. "Got time for coffee before you head home?"

"Sorry. Got an appointment with my pastor at four." He scraped a hand through his hair. "Natalie may not be ready for counseling, but if I don't get some perspective soon, I'll lose my mind."

"She still spending every waking minute with her mom?"

Daniel shoved through his office door and collapsed into the squeaky chair behind his desk. "Waking, sleeping, morning, night. And the sad thing is, it's like she's not really there at all. Most of the time I find her glued to her laptop, like she's trying to block out the world."

Carl used his shirtsleeve to buff a smudge off the glass trophy case. "Bummer, man."

"That's not the worst of it." Daniel jammed the heels of his hands into his eye sockets. "When I paid bills last weekend, I discovered she'd made another big withdrawal from our savings."

"What's she doing with the money?"

Daniel lowered his hands. "She gave her dad some money to help with the medical expenses. The other night I found her surfing the Web for anything she could find about strokes. Then yesterday all these books and DVDs arrived in the mail."

"Sounds like she's desperate."

"Which is exactly why I want to get her into counseling. Her dad joined a stroke support group, and Hart and Celia have gone with him a few times. I took Natalie once and she refused to go back."

"You can't force her if she's not ready."

"Yeah, but what do I do in the meantime?" Daniel's gut wrenched. He thrust to his feet but remained hunched over the desk. "I feel like my wife is disappearing right before my eyes."

❧

Natalie paused on the sidewalk outside Garner Printing and Advertising and took a couple of calming breaths. She knew she was on emotional overload, but at least the work Jeff supplied her with kept her from dwelling too much on her mother's illness. Thankfully, Jeff didn't press her to talk about it. All anyone else seemed to care about was convincing her to relinquish the guilt she knew for certain she could never escape. Though people never came right out and said it, the message was crystal clear: Get over it.

And the stroke support group? The worst. How could she sit there and listen to her father and the others talk about feeding tubes, tracheotomies, memory loss, bouts of depression?

At least she'd finally torn herself away from the nursing home. She wasn't sure her mother even knew she was there. Besides, it was better to remember her as she was before the stroke—happy, healthy, and fully alive.

Natalie shifted the strap of her briefcase higher on her shoulder and headed into the shop. The young Tom Cruise look-alike delivery driver stood behind the front counter sorting boxes.

She stepped forward. "Hi, Alan. Is Jeff around?"

The driver slid mirrored aviator sunglasses up his nose and hefted a box. "In the back. Follow me."

Passing through the large workroom, Alan nodded to his right and continued out the rear exit. Natalie spotted Jeff Garner's broad back as he squatted in front of a monstrous printing machine trying to clear a paper jam. "Quite a mess you've got there."

"Hey, Natalie. Be with you in a sec."

The sharp chemical smells of ink and toner invigorated her while she watched Jeff work the ink-smeared paper wad free. He straightened and tapped some buttons on the control panel. Seconds later, the machine resumed its normal hum, spitting out page after printed page faster than Natalie could blink.

Jeff tore a paper towel off a dispenser and wiped his hands. "Let's go talk where it's quieter."

He made a quick detour to grab two mugs of coffee and then joined her in his chrome and fake-walnut office. "Any problems with Mr. Cronnauer's requests? He can be such a fuddy-duddy."

"Under control." She unzipped her briefcase and retrieved the artwork samples she'd prepared. "If these pass inspection, I've got everything on CD ready for printing."

Jeff flicked a strand of auburn hair off his forehead as he perused her samples. "These look great."

She crossed her legs and reached for her coffee. "I aim to please."

"You do way more than that. Businesses around town are specifically requesting you. My layout skills aren't hacking it anymore."

The compliment brought a warm glow to Natalie's heart. How long had it been since she'd felt valued? She smiled her gratitude.

Jeff came around the desk, pushed some papers aside, and sat on the edge. He clasped his hands and leaned toward Natalie, giving her a look that raised the fine hairs on her arms. "I've got a proposition for you."

"A proposition?" Her fingers curled around the padded armrests.

"I'd like you to go into business with me—a full partnership. I'd continue overseeing the business and technical side, and you'd take charge of the design aspects. Graphics, layout, all the artistic stuff." He stood, one hand held out in appeal. "What do you say, Natalie? We could be quite a team."

She pressed a palm to her stammering heart. "Wow! I wasn't expecting this."

"I realize the timing may be bad, what with your mother and all—"

"No, actually, the timing is perfect. Work is the only thing saving my sanity. Except—" Her stomach clenched. Daniel was already furious with her for draining their savings account. "I have nothing to invest in the company. It's costing every spare cent we have to help with my mother's care."

"Not an issue. We'll figure out a fair amount to deduct from your salary each month to buy you into the business."

It sounded exciting and challenging—new motivation to drag herself out of bed every morning. Natalie rose and gripped Jeff's hand in a firm shake. "I'm in. Let's do it."

❦

"Don't do it, Mom." Lissa fought the tremor in her voice as she scraped a plate and set it in the dishwasher. She saw little enough of her mother already. Now Mom would be spending hours and hours every day at Mr. Garner's print shop.

"I need to do this, honey." Her mother whisked a kiss across the top of her head on her way to the fridge with a plastic container of leftovers. The tart aroma of sausage and kraut hung in the air. "You've got school expenses. Your dad's car is in the shop again. And Grandma's medical bills are piling up."

Lissa marched to the table and wrapped her arms around her dad's neck. "Talk to her, Daddy. We need Mom at home."

He cast her a tired glance and flicked to the next page in the sports section. "I've already tried, kiddo. Your mother's mind is made up."

Sucking in short, quick gasps to keep the tears from spilling over, Lissa wrapped her arms around her chest and bolted from the kitchen. Her whole life felt like a roller coaster on rocket fuel, speeding out of control and plummeting toward certain disaster. Mom and Dad were hardly ever home at the same time. When they were, if they weren't arguing about something, they weren't talking at all. It would only get worse with Mom working full time.

4

With Natalie's long hours at the print shop and his school and coaching duties, Daniel hardly ever saw his wife anymore. Not that it mattered. Ever since Valentine's Day, their marriage seemed to be on hold. Life for Daniel had become one long waiting game, waiting for Natalie to work through her guilt, waiting for any kind of change, positive or negative, in Belinda Morgan's condition. Only then could he hope for the return of any semblance of normalcy. It was May. How long was he supposed to wait?

A four-way stop loomed at the edge of his headlights. He applied the brake and glanced in both directions. With little traffic this time of morning, he hit the gas pedal, ready to zip through the intersection. Until the Bronco coughed, sputtered, and died.

"Come on, start, you blasted machine." Daniel twisted the ignition key and jammed his foot on the accelerator, but the engine refused to turn over. Nerve endings screaming, he slammed his fists against the steering wheel and squeezed out a long, pained moan. So much for getting to school early to finish typing up the final exams for his history classes.

After a few calming breaths, he climbed out of the car and gazed up and down the empty stretch of highway between Fawn Ridge and Putnam. Not a headlight in sight. A chilly, pre-dawn breeze whipped at his open windbreaker. He reached into his pocket for his cell phone.

"Nat, it's me. The Bronco died again."

The whoosh of the bathroom shower blunted her disgusted huff. "Where are you?"

"About five miles up the highway." He squinted to read the road signs. "At Connealy Road."

"Okay, I'll be there in fifteen."

She arrived in twenty, give or take five minutes of chewing him out for making her late for her own job.

It didn't end at supper that evening—or the next. Between driving him the rest of the way to Putnam Middle School, arranging for a tow, and then haggling with the repair shop, she made sure he knew exactly how severely she'd been inconvenienced. Once they sent Lissa to bed Friday night, the argument continued behind their closed bedroom door.

Daniel flung his shirt into the laundry hamper. "I can't help it I don't get paid more. You're the one who won't leave Fawn Ridge. You're the one who won't let me apply at a higher-paying school."

"You know what my family means to me. And it's not like I don't contribute. I've been making good money at Garner and Pearce." Natalie yanked her gown over her head and plopped onto the mattress. "Besides, it's your stupid car that keeps breaking down."

"It's not just my stupid car that's eating through our bank account." He tore his belt from around his waist and slung it on the closet floor—right on top of a brand new pile of books and pamphlets about strokes and alternative therapies. Heat seared Daniel's chest. He understood how badly Natalie wanted her mother to get better, but some of the unconventional approaches she'd been reading about were downright ludicrous. Before he could stop himself, he scattered the books with a well-aimed kick. And nearly doubled over as white-hot pain sliced from his big toe straight to his knee.

Natalie glared from her side of the bed. "Feel better now?"

He seethed with embarrassed rage. Every breath scraped his lungs like sandpaper. Without a word, he scooped up his pillow and the chenille throw at the foot of the bed and marched upstairs to the guestroom.

After a couple of hours tossing and turning, he gave up on sleep and went down to the den to boot up the computer. By morning he'd updated his résumé, printed out thirty copies, and addressed envelopes to the highest-rated school districts in three states.

Only after stuffing the letters through the post office mail chute did he pause to consider the possible repercussions. What if he actually got an offer? Would Natalie come to her senses and let go of false hopes about her mother? Would he finally convince her to leave Fawn Ridge with him and start fresh? Or had he just signed his marital death warrant?

⊷⧽

Natalie shuffled in from the garage and dropped her purse onto the nearest kitchen chair. Her keys slipped out of her hand and clattered to the floor. When she bent to pick them up a muscle in her neck cramped. She winced and pressed a hand to the sore spot.

"Hard day at work?" Daniel leaned in the doorway from the den. His tone was anything but sympathetic.

"As a matter of fact." She straightened and glanced around the kitchen, her nose detecting the aromas of pepperoni, tomato sauce, and mozzarella. "Any pizza left?"

"After Lissa had her fill, I finished it off. It's so late, I figured you'd already eaten." Daniel went to the refrigerator and poured himself a glass of milk.

"Thanks a lot." Cactus nettles jabbed Natalie's spine. She shouldn't feel resentful—it was her choice to work late—but she did. She found a can of soup in the pantry and retrieved a saucepan from beneath the range. "Where's Lissa?"

"Spending the night with Jody." Daniel set his milk glass on the counter and folded his arms. "You and I need some time by ourselves."

Her head shot up at his words, and for a millisecond she felt a shiver of warm anticipation. Then she caught the look in his eyes—a look that held not the least hint of romance, not the least hint of love.

A sense of dread curled through her abdomen and quelled the last remnants of hunger. Exhaling slowly, she turned off the burner and stepped away from the stove. "You sound serious. What is it?"

"I can't go on like this, Natalie. The arguments, the blame—when you're here at all, that is."

She hugged herself against a sudden chill. "What are you saying?"

"I'm saying if you can't be a wife to me—a mother to Lissa—then I want you to move out. We need you full time or not at all."

"What?" Natalie spun around, one hand on her forehead. *Move out?* The stove burner still glowed orange beneath the edge of the saucepan. She thought about touching a finger to it. Maybe the shock would wake her from this living nightmare.

A trembling started deep in her core. She crossed to the table and sank into a chair. "You can't mean this, Daniel. Think about what you're saying."

"I have thought about it. Plenty." He stood over her with arms crossed and jaw clenched. "You spend every waking minute either at the print shop or working on your laptop at the dining room table. I go to bed alone; I get up alone. I take care of Lissa alone. It's not fair to me, and it's definitely not fair to our daughter."

Her hands balled into fists. Her eyes burned. She could hardly get a full breath. "You don't understand—"

"That's the problem. I *don't* understand." Daniel gripped the back of a chair. His head wagged like a pendulum. "You've stopped visiting your mother at the nursing home. You won't go with me to counseling. I don't know what else to do."

He turned away, his next words barely audible even as they exploded on Natalie's eardrums. "This is Saturday. Next Thursday is the last day of school. I want you moved out before Lissa and I get home."

⌒◎⌒

"Daniel and I are separating." Natalie rested her forehead on clasped hands and stared at a scratch on her parents' kitchen table—an old scratch, long and wavy and deeper on one end. She probably gouged it with a pencil while doing her homework a thousand years ago.

Silence filled the farmhouse kitchen. A warm gust of air billowed the gingham curtains at the open window beside her. She raised her eyes to meet her father's. "Aren't you going to say something?"

The sadness in his gaze said it all. "It's a mistake, Rosy-girl. And you know it."

"We're only separating—nothing permanent." At least she hoped Daniel would eventually take her back. "We're fighting too much. We need some space. I've already put a deposit on an apartment."

"What about Lissa?"

Natalie rubbed her temple. "She's staying with Daniel for now. This is going to be hard enough on her without making her move out of the house."

Dad rose and strode to the sink. He wet a dishcloth and wiped at imaginary spots on the counter. His shoulders knotted beneath his chambray work shirt. He stopped, leaned over the sink, and pressed his eyes shut. "If your mother knew her illness split up your family, she'd be crushed."

A river of pain flooded her. She swallowed a sob before it could escape. Mom had always done so much for her—selling paintings to help pay for Natalie's art supplies and classes, her riding gear and horse show entry fees, and then . . .

"Natalie, didn't you hear the weather forecast? I won't leave you alone on the farm with a bunch of nervous animals."

On top of all her other sacrifices over the years, Mom had risked everything important to her in that one act of selflessness. Yet Natalie kept making one wrong choice after another.

Now things had gone too far, and she could see no way back. As a tear slipped silently down her cheek, she studied her wedding ring before sliding it off her finger and tucking it into her pocket.

❧

"No problem, Jeff. The Carla's Confections ad will be ready for printing first thing Monday." Natalie snapped her cell phone shut and turned onto Willowbrook Lane. This was her weekend to spend with Lissa, and she promised herself not to spend the whole day working. Maybe by afternoon they'd have time—

Her heart thudded to the pit of her stomach. She'd barely gotten used to seeing the gaudy for-sale sign in the front yard, its red and yellow logo a jarring contrast to the colonial-blue siding and white trim gracing the home she and Daniel had shared for the past three years. They'd dreamed about it together, pored over building plans together, and scrimped and saved together until they had enough for a down payment.

Now someone had slapped a big, bold SOLD sign across the Realtor's emblem. It was over, the dream dying along with her marriage.

After Natalie moved out, it didn't take long to realize they'd have to let the house go. Their combined incomes barely covered the mortgage payment, and now Natalie had apartment rent to pay. The real estate agent assured them that with families wanting to resettle before school started, summer was a perfect time to sell.

The Saturn rolled to a stop in the driveway. Natalie shut off the engine and started up the walk. As she debated whether to ring the doorbell or let herself in with the key she'd soon have to relinquish, the front door jerked open.

Daniel stood before her, looking breathless and worried. "Have you seen Lissa?"

The force of his question knocked her backward a step. "I'm supposed to pick her up, remember?"

He spun around on bare feet, muscles tense and rippling beneath a thin white T-shirt. Natalie chased after him as he shouted Lissa's name—through the living room, the dining room, the kitchen and den, past stacks of packing boxes, and into the master bedroom, the king-size bed neatly made and clearly unused.

They raced upstairs to Lissa's room and through the adjoining bath to the guestroom, which was strewn with Daniel's discarded shoes, shirts, and jeans.

Natalie stood in the doorway and blinked. Half her mind still grappled with the idea that Lissa appeared to be missing. The other half took poignant pleasure in the thought that her husband couldn't bring himself to sleep alone in the bed they'd shared for fifteen years—the bed where their daughter was conceived. *Their daughter.*

Suddenly, her world coalesced into sharp focus. "Daniel. Stop running around like an idiot and tell me what's going on."

Panting, he sank onto the rumpled sheets at the foot of the bed. "When she didn't come down to breakfast, I thought she was sleeping in like usual, but . . . " He gave his head a frustrated shake.

Natalie swiveled and pressed her spine against the doorframe. She clawed stiff fingers through the hair at her temples and tried to imagine things from Lissa's perspective. Poor kid! Selling the house must have screamed the end of her parents' marriage.

Remorse shredded Natalie's heart. She never meant for her mistakes to bleed into her daughter's life. She should have been a better mother. She should have paid more attention.

She clamped her teeth together and inhaled through her nose. "Let's think this through. Did she take anything from her room? Did you look for a note?"

He shot her a look of awed surprise, as if she'd just solved the riddle of the Sphinx. "You know her stuff better than I do. You check her room, and I'll look around for a note."

A quick perusal of Lissa's closet and bathroom revealed missing clothes and toiletries. Plus, Lissa's favorite pink duffel bag wasn't hanging on its usual hook in the closet.

"Found it!" Daniel's voice echoed up the staircase. He met her in the entryway with a crumpled piece of paper. "She stuck it on the fridge under the Pete's Pizza magnet. I should have seen it. Would have if I'd—"

Natalie yanked the note out of his hand. Lissa's rounded, girlish script seemed all wrong for the angry, desperate words she'd penned:

Don't look for me. I never want to see either one of you again!

⋘⋙

Daniel paced the kitchen. Three days and countless phone calls later, Lissa still hadn't been found. Not even her best friend Jody offered a clue—if she could be trusted not to be in on the scheme.

Dear Lord, help! He ought to be out there looking for his daughter, not downing stale coffee and waiting for the phone to ring. But his friend in the county sheriff's department had told him he needed to stay home in case Lissa showed up.

The only upside to the insanity was that Natalie had moved back in. Okay, she hadn't exactly moved in. But she had stayed at the house with him—albeit in separate rooms—while they waited and prayed for word about their daughter.

He poured the last of his cold coffee down the drain and joined Natalie at the kitchen table, where her fingers flew across her laptop keyboard. Dressed in cutoffs and a faded T-shirt, her hair drooping across one eye in a tangled mess, she looked as stressed and anxious as he felt. Yet she kept right on working, working, working.

He banged the table with his fist. "How can you even think about work at a time like this?"

A long, slow sigh whispered between her lips. She leaned back and extended her legs. "If I stop, I'll lose my mind. And anyway, I'm not exactly working."

She swiveled the laptop in his direction. A missing children's website filled the screen.

Daniel's breath snagged. "You don't think—"

The ringing phone sliced through his words. He leapt up to grab the receiver.

"Daniel, it's Bram," Natalie's father said. "You can stop worrying. Lissa's okay. She's here."

"Thank God!" Daniel crumpled over the tile countertop.

Natalie gripped his arm. "Who is it? Did they find her?"

He nodded fiercely. "Hang on, Bram, I'm putting you on speaker."

"Dad?" Natalie looked at the phone and then at Daniel.

"I found her in the hayloft. She's been here all along, sneaking into the house at night to raid the refrigerator and clean up in the guest bathroom." Bram Morgan gave a tired chuckle. "I thought something was fishy when my sandwich fixin's started disappearing."

A gasping sob tore through Natalie. She fell against Daniel's chest. "Thank God, thank God!"

He wrapped one arm around her, relishing the pressure of her body against his. He drank in the smell of her skin, the warmth of her breath whispering across the hollow of his throat. Just to hold her like this: the memory of the long months apart dissipated like dew under the hot summer sun.

Dear God, let this be the end of the bad times. Help us find our way back to each other.

❧

"Forget it. I'm through with both of you." Lissa flounced across Granddad's living room and plopped on the sofa. No way was she giving in and going home—wherever that was anymore—until her parents came to their senses and got back together.

Her dad braced his hands on his hips and gave her *that look,* the one he always used to imply she was being childish.

Talk about childish! Mom and Dad ought to look in the mirror once in a while. When they first tore through Granddad's kitchen door—Mom squeezing Dad's hand like she'd never let go—Lissa felt sure her little scheme had worked. Faced with the fear of losing their precious only child, they'd seen the error of their foolish ways, forged a new bond, reunited for eternity.

Not.

Five seconds after making sure Lissa was all right, they were firing verbal grenades at each other. Mom blamed Dad for not paying closer attention. Dad blamed Mom for spending too much time at the office.

Dad gave a snort. "You can't stay here, Lissa. School starts in less than a month. You can't expect your granddad to keep up with a teenager when he already has plenty of . . . other stuff to deal with."

"Your dad's right." Mom sank onto the other end of the sofa. She leaned forward, her hands clasped like she was praying. "Please come home with me. I've got a room all ready for you at my apartment. With your dad moving to Putnam, you need to be close to school."

"Maybe I'll quit school. Maybe—"

"Lissa!" Mom and Dad burst out in unison. Great, the one thing they had to agree on.

Okay, dropping out was a dumb idea. And if running away didn't scare some sense into them, she'd have to think of something else fast. *Something* had to snap her parents out of this craziness. She laced her arms across her chest and shifted her gaze from one to the other. Which one was the weakest link?

Mom. Definitely Mom. She'd been a total basket case ever since Grandma got sick.

Sky, Granddad's lumbering old Great Dane, padded over and rested his slobbery chin on Lissa's knee. She stroked his head while she came up with a new plan.

"Okay, here's the deal." Heaving a dramatic sigh, Lissa tossed her parents a withering look. "You're both being dorks about this whole separation thing, and now you've sold our house right out from under me."

She sniffled for effect and wiped at an imaginary tear, which really wasn't so imaginary if she thought about it. "Mom, you spend so much time at your office that I hardly ever see you."

"But if you lived with me—"

"Sorry, Dad's earned way more brownie points than you. At least he's usually around when I need him."

Her father straightened and crossed his arms, slanting Lissa's mother an I-told-you-so smirk. Mom just rolled her eyes.

"So if you won't let me stay with Granddad, then I've decided." She skewered her mother with a cold, hard stare, praying her words would hit their mark. "I'm moving to Putnam with Dad."

5

Seated on her secondhand apartment sofa, Natalie hugged her knees and watched the late-August sun climb into the morning sky. The effect lost some of its beauty as seen along the corrugated roofline of the sheltered parking area. Though she should have been dressed and on her way out the door by now, she still lingered in her gray sleep shirt, elephant-print bottoms, and bare feet. Despite the sunny morning, a dreary cloud hung over her—a lethargy of body and spirit—all because she happened to see a bright yellow school bus rumble past the apartment complex entrance, a painful reminder that Lissa started school today in Putnam.

It wasn't fair. Natalie should be the one exulting in the smells of Lissa's new backpack, pencils, and notebook paper. Natalie—not Daniel—should be the one driving her daughter to school, helping with her homework, listening to the endless gossip about her friends and which boy she had a crush on this year and how mean her new English teacher was.

Okay, if she were perfectly honest, she also missed tripping over Daniel's musty briefcase and sweaty sneakers, shoving his endless clippings from the sports pages to the other end of the table, teasing him out of a funk when his team lost a game. She missed all of it.

Across the room, stuffed into a lower cube of her modular entertainment center, she glimpsed the hodgepodge of materials she'd collected on strokes. She wondered why she kept it, why she'd bothered ordering it at all. Half the treatment recommendations were geared toward patients with far more control and cognition than Mom displayed. The other half were so depressing in their descriptions of life after a massive stroke that Natalie couldn't bear to finish them.

A tremor worked its way up her body and culminated in a stifled sob. She felt as if she'd landed on a barren beach at the foot of a rocky cliff, with no way up and no way around. And behind her an angry sea closed in fast. If she didn't find an escape route soon, she would surely drown. She needed help, and it was high time she admitted it.

Uncoiling her legs, she pushed up from the sofa and reached for the phone on the breakfast bar. Her fingers felt heavy and numb as she pressed the number for Fawn Ridge Fellowship. The secretary answered and immediately put Natalie through to Pastor Mayer.

"Natalie, how are you? Everything okay with this week's newsletter?"

"That isn't why I'm calling, Pastor." Her voice sounded distant, hoarse, not like her own at all. "I . . . I need . . . "

Pastor Mayer must have recognized the desperation darkening her tone. "How can I help? Do you want to come in and—"

"No, no, I can't." Until her mother's stroke, she'd prided herself on her optimism, confidence, and self-control. How could she now slice open her heart and reveal its ugliness to someone she'd known for most of her life? "If you could just give me the name of someone. Preferably someone who doesn't know me or my family."

"I see. Yes, give me a moment." A few seconds later he offered the name and number of a Christian counselor. "Dr. Julia Sirpless practices from her home office in Fielding. Is that too far away for you?"

"It's only an hour's drive. Sounds perfect."

If anything in her life could be called perfect. Before she could talk herself out of it, she phoned Dr. Sirpless and made an appointment for the following Monday. Thankfully, the doctor took evening appointments, which would save Natalie the difficulty of explaining absences from the office.

The first few visits went well, with Natalie mostly providing a detached overview of the events that brought her to this point. The petite and professional Dr. Sirpless had definitely mastered the art of smiling and nodding in all the right places. And Natalie had to admit, merely talking through her mother's stroke and some of the arguments with Daniel that led to their separation provided the safety valve she needed to keep from losing it completely.

On her last visit before the Thanksgiving holiday, as the session drew to a close, Dr. Sirpless capped her pen and said, "Tell me how you feel about the progress we've made."

"Good, I think." Natalie glanced around the room, her gaze flitting across an autumn-hued silk flower arrangement on the coffee table, a pine-cone wreath over the mantel. A glass-domed clock on the corner of the doctor's desk ticked off the minutes as the time neared nine o'clock.

"Just . . . good?"

"It's helping to talk objectively about things, but . . . " A whisper echoed in a distant part of her brain, a voice telling her they hadn't yet plumbed the depths of her issues. She lifted her gaze to meet the doctor's. "You think I'm holding back, don't you?"

"I think there are parts of your pain you aren't ready to explore yet. In time, you will be." Dr. Sirpless rose, her signal their time was up. "Try to enjoy the holiday with your family. We'll take this up again next week."

꼭

Enjoy the holiday? She'd tried and failed miserably.

Natalie shoved away from the computer screen and rubbed her tired, dry eyes. Silence cloaked the print shop. A brisk November breeze whisked dead leaves across the sidewalk outside her window. Across the square, an elderly couple she recognized from church strolled into the Hillman House Café, one of the few businesses open on Thanksgiving Day, mainly for the folks who had no one with whom to spend the holiday.

For all the joy this day had brought her, Natalie might as well be one of them. Daniel had taken Lissa to visit his parents. Natalie put in an appearance at Hart and Celia's, but by the time dinner ended and Dad, Hart, and the twins adjourned to the den for a TV football marathon, Natalie had endured all the family togetherness she could bear. She'd intended to go home to her apartment and console herself with another huge helping of the pecan pie Celia had foisted upon her.

The next thing she knew, she'd turned into the empty parking lot behind the print shop. She'd work just long enough to finish the ad layout she'd worked on yesterday—an hour. Two at most. Just long enough to get through the loneliest Thanksgiving she'd ever spent.

Her breath stuck in the upper part of her chest. Her hand crept toward the side drawer and inched it open. She slid out her business card folio and flipped to the last card on the last plastic page. One finger traced the phone number, and she lifted her desk phone receiver.

"Dr. Sirpless? I was afraid I'd get your voice mail. It's Natalie Pearce."

"I saw your name on the caller ID and decided to pick up. How are you, Natalie?" Calm concern laced the woman's pleasantly husky voice.

"Not so good. You're probably celebrating with your family, but—" The tightness in her chest intensified. "I really need to talk."

"Holidays are the hardest, aren't they? I was just heading home. I can meet you at my office in an hour."

"Thank you." Natalie gave a shuddering sniff. "Thank you."

She powered down the computer, flicked off the lights, and slid her arms into her camel-hair coat. Though her hands still shook as she fumbled to insert her car key into the ignition, a tiny glimmer of relief had already nudged its way past the gloom shrouding her heart.

Dusk had closed in by the time she parked in the driveway at Dr. Sirpless's home. She followed the narrow walkway around to the office addition behind the garage. The amber glow of a floor lamp shone through thin curtains. Natalie knocked and entered.

Dressed in slim-fitting jeans and a holiday sweater, her auburn hair in a loose ponytail, the doctor appeared through an inner door. "I've just started water for tea. Chamomile, hibiscus, or Earl Gray?"

"Chamomile, definitely." Natalie smiled her thanks as she laid her coat and purse on a bench by the door. She sank into the depths of a navy velveteen overstuffed chair and inhaled the soothing aroma from a lavender-scented candle.

Dr. Sirpless returned with two tall, white china mugs decorated with Currier and Ives winter scenes. She handed one to Natalie and settled in the matching chair to Natalie's left. "This is your first Thanksgiving since you and your husband separated. I'm sure it raised more than a few memories."

Natalie wrapped her fingers around the mug and let the warmth soak away the stiffness from the drive over. "I miss Daniel. I miss Lissa." Her voice cracked. "I miss my mom."

"Up to now we've only talked around the guilt, the regrets." Dr. Sirpless sipped her tea. "Tonight I'd like you to tell me more about your mother. Not your failure to help with the Christmas decorations. Not the stroke. Just the good things."

Natalie drew in a long, slow breath that shivered past her heart. She set the mug on a ceramic coaster and folded her hands in her lap. Staring at them, she let her mind drift through scenes from her childhood. "She's the best mother ever. Smart. Talented. Devoted to her family—"

Dr. Sirpless gave a low chuckle and held up one hand. "You love her, that's obvious. But no mother is perfect. Is it possible you need to adjust your view of her—allow for a bit more realism?"

Natalie squirmed. She tucked one leg under her and picked at a hangnail. Thunder rumbled in the distance . . . or was it only in her imagination?

"I can take care of the horses, Mom. Go to your art show. You've been working years for this—your chance to be recognized at a major gallery."

"Didn't you hear the weather forecast? I won't leave you alone on the farm with a bunch of nervous animals."

"What are you remembering, Natalie?"

"I'm not sure I can talk about it." Her voice creaked like a rusty feed bucket handle.

"Why not?"

She tipped her head, closed her eyes, and waited for the pain to pass.

It didn't. Instead, it encircled her throat and squeezed. She leaned on the padded chair arm and fixed her gaze on the lamp's golden reflection on the surface of her tea. "It was late March. Mom and I were alone on the farm. Dad had to drive a Friesian mare he'd been training back to her owner, and the round trip would take all weekend."

"And your brother?"

"He was away at college."

"So you must have been . . . how old?"

"Sixteen." Natalie swallowed. "Mom had a huge art showing scheduled at the Dean Gallery here in Fielding. Critics and buyers were expected from all across the Midwest."

Dr. Sirpless gave an appreciative nod. "She must have been very good."

"She'd just finished three new paintings and a sculpture, possibly the best work she'd ever done. She'd planned to add the new pieces to the collection when she drove over for a gala reception that afternoon."

"But something kept her from going?"

"A storm was brewing. The horses were uneasy." Natalie pinched her eyes shut. *Thunder. Wind whistling through the barn rafters. Horses stamping and whinnying.* "Mom didn't want to leave me alone, but I couldn't let her miss her show." She aimed a pointed gaze at the doctor. "I've helped my dad with the horses all my life. I told her I'd be okay."

"But she stayed home with you anyway."

"She could be so stubborn—" A new emotion corkscrewed through Natalie's chest. She clamped down on it before it could find a name.

Dr. Sirpless kept her face impassive as she jotted something on a steno pad. "Go on, Natalie."

"The storm hit around four. Mom had the weather radio on in the house—tornado warnings all across the state. She wanted me to come in from the barn, but I couldn't leave Sunny."

"One of the horses?"

"Our Appaloosa mare. She was with foal, but she wasn't due for another month. Daddy promised me we could keep this one, that it would be mine to raise and train. I could hardly wait." Her heart lifted momentarily. She sniffed and continued. "I got all the horses into their barn stalls, but Sunny wouldn't settle down. I was afraid she'd hurt herself and lose the foal."

The events streamed through Natalie's mind in crystal clarity—rain pounding the barn roof, wind rattling the siding. "Sunny kept pacing and neighing. I could see her sides straining, and I knew she'd gone into labor. Mom called the vet, but he had emergency colic surgery and couldn't come right away."

She pictured her mother, still clad in the chic watered-silk pantsuit she'd planned to wear for the opening. Strands of silver-streaked hair had come unpinned from her French twist and danced around her face. Mom rested her forearms on Sunny's stall door and offered words of encouragement while Natalie stroked the mare's distended belly and tried to keep her calm.

"The mare went down, and I knew she was about to deliver. I checked her and realized the foal hadn't turned yet. If I didn't act quickly, they could both die. I needed help—I couldn't do this by myself—but Mom was the only one there, and she's been uneasy around horses ever since she was thrown as a child."

Dr. Sirpless gave a sad smile. "It must have taken no small amount of courage for her to marry a horseman."

Natalie lifted her chin. "My mother is the bravest person I know."

"Yet you were only sixteen and about to deliver a foal. That sounds pretty brave to me."

Natalie closed her eyes against the undeserved praise. She could still see Sunny on her side, straining and tossing her head. She could still remember how frightened and helpless she felt.

"Go on with your story, Natalie."

"Mom kept insisting I let her do something. She thought maybe she could soothe Sunny and keep her attention diverted while I tried to turn the foal."

She wanted to skim past what happened next—the thunderous clap, the lighting strobe that for a split second lit the entire barn with white-hot brightness. Sunny whinnied and tried to throw herself to her feet. Mom, kneeling at her head, fell backwards, her right wrist striking the rim of a metal water trough with a violent smack.

"Mom? Are you okay?"

"I'll be all right, Natalie. Do what you have to do."

Natalie turned all her attention then to the struggling mare. The full length of her arm swathed in a veterinary surgical glove, she reached into the birth canal, found the foal's forelegs, and guided it into position. Half an hour later, Natalie's little filly Tailwind—"Windy," as she came to be called—made her stormy debut into the world.

"And your mother? Was she badly hurt?"

Natalie lifted her gaze to meet the doctor's. "Her wrist was broken in three places. Only we didn't know it until the next morning when she finally let me take her to the emergency room. Afterward the arthritis got so bad that she could no longer paint for more than an hour or so at a time."

"I'm so sorry."

A rush of fiery passion propelled Natalie to her feet. She whirled away in anger. "If she hadn't been so stubborn. If she'd just gone to the gallery—"

"That's the second time tonight you've used that word."

Natalie dropped her hand from her forehead. She turned to face the doctor. "What word?"

"Stubborn." Dr. Sirpless glanced at her notes. "Twice now, you've called your mother stubborn."

"No, I—" Heat infused her face. She shook her head in confusion.

The doctor rose and rested a hand on Natalie's shoulder. "I want you to think about something, Natalie. I want you to consider the possibility that it isn't only guilt you're feeling. I want you to ask yourself if you might also be feeling anger."

"Anger? Of course I'm angry. I let my mother down."

"I don't mean anger at yourself. I think you're really angry at your mother."

Natalie drew her brows together in disbelief. "Of course not! How can you suggest such a thing?"

Something cracked then—something hard and cold and ugly inside Natalie's chest—because Dr. Sirpless was right, and it hurt too much to admit it.

6

*A*ngry at her mother? Natalie chewed on the idea for the rest of the long weekend. She didn't know which pained her more—the guilt she felt over letting Mom down, or the anger that her mother (yes, her *very stubborn* mother) had gone ahead with the after-Christmas chore Natalie had pleaded with her to postpone.

Not that she could blame the stroke on Mom's putting away the Christmas decorations. But what if Mom had already experienced signs a stroke might be imminent? Natalie couldn't deny her mother's history of brushing off her own health concerns when anything else took precedence.

During her next couple of visits, Natalie allowed Dr. Sirpless to help her explore these thoughts. The powerful emotions they evoked often left her shaken, if not terrified. Still, she sensed she might be nearing a breakthrough, glimpsing a flicker of hope at the end of a long, dark, devastating year.

And then December hit.

"Hart, I'm glad I caught you." Phone receiver tucked against her shoulder, she hammered on the keyboard and then mouse-clicked a Christmas holly graphic and resized it. "I've been thinking about tonight." She swiveled toward the window and inhaled a shaky breath as her gaze fell on the immense Christmas tree near the center of Fawn Ridge's town square. Her heart suddenly felt as cold and hard as the frozen pond beneath the tree's lengthening shadow. Quickly she glanced away. "I'm sorry for disappointing everyone, but I don't think I can do this. Please, Hart, talk to Dad. Make some excuse for me . . . something that won't upset him too much."

"Come on, Rosy-Posey." Her brother's drawl oozed through the phone line like thick syrup.

Leave it to Hart to dredge up her hated childhood nickname. "Hart—"

"Don't argue. It's your birthday. You know how important tonight is for Dad. He's cooking up Grandma Hartley's chili recipe just for you."

Her throat constricted at the poignant image of her father stirring a pot of chili, attempting to follow Grandma's detailed recipe instructions. Dad was usually all thumbs in the kitchen. How had he managed this past year without Mom?

For the hundredth time that afternoon, she brushed aside the limp strand of hair that kept falling across her left eye— one more irritation in her out-of-control life. She backtracked to focus on Hart's annoying reminder of her nickname. "You didn't score any points by calling me Rosy-Posey, you know."

He chuckled. "But Natalie Rose, you blush so beautifully when you're flustered."

And, of course, he knew she was flustered. How could he not know? If there was one day she'd been dreading all year even more than Christmas, it was today. Couldn't her family skip her birthday just this once?

"Okay, then," Hart said, "you rather I call you Nat? How about Nacho? Maybe Nettie, or—I know—Nuttie!"

She slammed her open palm on the desk. "Just stop. Things are crazy enough around here without your juvenile kidding around."

He snorted. "Girl, you need to lighten up. I was only—"

"I mean it, I'm swamped, and I don't have time for this . . . for your . . . " She didn't intend for her voice to break like that. If she gave in to her churning emotions, she'd never get through the day, much less the Christmas season.

She cleared her throat. "All the businesses in town want their end-of-year promos printed and in the mail this week. At this rate I'll never get done."

Stiffening her spine, she wrestled her attention to the computer screen. She adjusted the font size on a line of text and studied the overall effect—just the right blend of whimsy and sophistication. Miss Fellowes at Moonbeams Bookstore should be pleased. She saved the file and password protected it.

Hart broke the strained silence. "You've got to come, Nat. Dad will be crushed if you don't. He's been planning this for days."

"Oh, Hart . . . " The slanting afternoon sun glinted through the fake snow her recently hired assistant had sprayed around the edges of the office window—one more holiday reminder Natalie wished she could have avoided. But Deannie, who also happened to be Jeff Garner's niece, apparently had nothing more productive to do, like maybe helping Natalie get caught up before the holidays.

She mentally shook herself and tried to keep her voice steady. "Please, Hart, don't make me do this."

More silence.

Then, "Ah, I get it. It's because Dad invited Daniel."

Natalie's stomach lurched. Until that moment, the thought that Daniel would be included in the family gathering hadn't even entered her mind. She closed her eyes against the memories—closed her heart against the pain. "Daniel's coming?"

"What did you expect? That Dad would have him drop Lissa off for dinner and leave?"

"No, I—"

"As far as I'm concerned, Daniel will always be a part of this family, whether you two stay married or not."

Tears sprang unbidden. Of course she wouldn't want it any other way. She loved her husband and always would. But the laughter, the dreams, the hopes they once shared—it all seemed so long ago. Could they ever reclaim that happiness, start fresh, and put this whole horrible year behind them?

Her gaze drifted across the desk to a framed school photo, where Lissa's image, a younger version of her own face, smiled back at her. But the blue eyes, fringed by silvery-yellow bangs, held a flat, vacant look. The emotional distance between Natalie and her daughter had only increased after Lissa chose to stay with Daniel. Natalie sometimes felt like a helpless spectator, watching her world crumble around her, piece by precious piece.

"Natalie?" Her brother's tone bristled. "Are you listening to me?"

She swallowed her tears. Somehow she had to make her brother understand—make the whole family understand. "Hart, you know it's not just Daniel. I'm afraid if I go out to the farm tonight, I'll—" The words lodged in her throat.

Hart's voice became gentler. "Do you think it's any easier for Dad? He's trying so hard. Come to your birthday dinner. Please don't let him down."

"I don't want to hurt him, honestly I don't." She locked her gaze on the ceiling in a vain attempt to staunch the pathetic, self-indulgent tears she had no time for. "It seems like Dad's trying *too* hard, like he wants to pretend nothing's changed."

"He's trying to get on with his life, the way Mom would want him to. Don't you think she'd want us to celebrate your birthday and enjoy the Christmas season the way we always have?"

She couldn't answer over the ache in her chest. Dr. Sirpless might eventually help her cope with the massive guilt, and now this anger. But all the therapy in the world would never change the fact that this time of year, a season when the whole world should be joyful and full of love, would never be that way for Natalie again.

"Come on, Nat, talk to me. Haven't you heard a thing I've said?"

Her cracked words came out in a ragged rush. "How many times do I have to say this? I can't deal with it now. Birthday, Christmas, any of it. *Please.*"

"Fine. If you don't want to come to dinner, then don't. Happy birthday, Natalie Rose." The phone slammed in her ear.

Don't you cry, Natalie Pearce, don't you dare cry.

She sucked in a breath and gripped the arms of her desk chair. She had entirely too much work to do, and she couldn't let herself be sidetracked by Hart's disappointment. Blinking several times, she watched the Christmas shoppers bustling in and out of shops along the sun-dappled town square. Despite all the holiday advertisements she'd prepared for clients, she hadn't let herself think about her own Christmas shopping. She should find something for Lissa, at least, but she wasn't sure she even knew what her daughter wanted this year.

Sighing, she allowed Deannie's elaborate Christmas window art to distract her, and once again gratefully transferred her prickling irritation from herself to her capricious red-haired assistant. If Deannie so desperately needed an outlet for her creative energies, she could do something useful instead of wasting office time and resources.

Oh, great, Natalie, you're starting to sound like Ebenezer Scrooge.

Still, picking on Deannie gave her a moment of perverse pleasure. Who could deny that Jeff Garner's niece had grown into the classic underachiever? She'd been a problem child ever since Natalie used to babysit her some twenty-odd years ago. Several years later she and Daniel made the mistake of trusting Deannie as Lissa's babysitter, only Deannie couldn't keep her mind on her duties and off her many boyfriends. She'd taken almost seven years to finish college, changing her major at least that many times, and then flitted from one dead-end job to another, trying to "find herself."

In October, when Deannie expressed an interest in learning the printing business, Jeff had hired her as Natalie's assistant, over Natalie's protests and against her better judgment. Someday, somehow, she'd get back at her partner for this. He owed her. He owed her big-time.

As she toyed with how she could plot her revenge, her gaze settled on Deannie's window stencil of a horse and sleigh. The horse reminded her of the farm, which reminded her of the birthday dinner, which reminded her of Mom.

Face it, Natalie, you've let down your mother. You've let down your husband and daughter. And now you're about to let down your dad.

You can change things, a voice in her head seemed to whisper.

It sounded too easy. Was it even possible that one birthday dinner with her family might be the beginning of a way back?

She pressed shaking hands to her cheeks. For the first time in months, a genuine prayer filled her thoughts. *Dear God, please give me the strength to do the right thing . . . for my family and for myself.*

Summoning her courage, she picked up the phone and dialed Hart's number at the veterinary clinic, but almost changed her mind again as she waited for his receptionist to get him on the line.

Too late. "Hey, Nat, I'm sorry for picking on you. This is a rough time for all of us. If you're not up to celebrating your birthday this year, Dad will understand. We all will."

"It's okay. I'll come. What time?"

A pause. She could picture the satisfied grin accompanying her brother's intake of breath before he asked, "When do you close up shop?"

She glanced at her watch and tried to control the tremor in her voice. "I should be out of here by seven."

"Great. See you at the farm at seven-thirty."

൙

Daniel unsnapped his Putnam Panthers jacket as he sidled into the chair opposite Superintendent Luper's polished desk. "Thank you for making time to see me, sir."

The balding man swiveled sideways in his executive chair and stretched out his legs. "I appreciate the fine job you're doing with the middle-school athletes. Coach Moreno has told me on countless occasions he doesn't know what he'd do without you."

"I think the world of Carl too. When I heard there might be an opening for a freshman coach over at the high school, he told me to go for it." Daniel shifted and cleared his throat. "I realize it wouldn't mean much of a pay increase, but—"

"That's the thing, Pearce." Luper's avoidance of eye contact should have been a warning from the moment Daniel entered the office. "Putnam's budget is so tight that we're not even planning to fill that vacancy. The other high-school coaches will have to take up the slack."

"I see." Disappointment settled like a rock in the pit of Daniel's stomach. He stood slowly. "If something should change . . ."

"You'll be the first to know." Luper rose and offered Daniel his hand. "Great game last night, by the way. You've done wonders with those boys."

Praise but no raise. Why should he be surprised? Shoulders hunched with disappointment, Daniel slogged out to his Bronco. He made it back to school in time to surprise his afternoon history class with a pop quiz, but when his puberty-challenged, seventh-grade basketball team hit the gym floor for practice, he turned the warm-up drills over to the team captain. "Back in fifteen," he said, heading to his office. He needed a few minutes of quiet to get his head back in the game.

Carl found him there. "How'd it go, bro?"

The look in the big man's eyes said he already had a pretty good idea. "Looks like you're stuck with me awhile longer."

"Yes!" Carl pumped his fist.

"Gloating is not allowed. Neither is saying 'I told you so,' even if you did."

"There'll be other opportunities." Carl flipped a folding chair around and straddled it. "You got what it takes, Dan. Brains, guts, talent. One of these days somebody's gonna notice. And then I'll be stuck training *your* replacement." He grimaced. "And I ain't looking forward to it."

"You could do a whole lot better than Putnam, yourself." Daniel shoved a stack of folders aside and rested his elbows on the desk. "Hey, we could promote ourselves as a package deal—two of the winningest middle-school coaches in the central United States. We might even get picked up by the Spurs or the Bulls."

Carl tilted back his head and guffawed. "Brother, when you dream, you dream big!"

"Might as well." Daniel drew a hand down his face, the momentary lightness fading.

Carl quirked an eyebrow. "Natalie problems again?"

Daniel leaned back and laced his fingers behind his head. His gaze slid to the filing cabinet across the room and the framed snapshot of Natalie, him, and Lissa two summers ago at Disney World. Since he realized a few days ago that Natalie's birthday was coming up, he hadn't been able to get her out of his mind. "Today's her birthday. I don't know how she's going to cope."

"First one since her mother got sick. You've told me how that family always had big doings this time of year."

"'Big doings' is putting it mildly." Belinda Morgan had created a mid-December birthday celebration for Natalie that launched the entire family headlong into the Christmas season.

"You gonna try to see her?"

His hands fell limply into his lap. "You honestly think today would be any different from all the other times I've tried to reach out to her? Whatever I do, whatever I say, Natalie's bound to slam the door in my face."

Nope, especially now that they were separated, he couldn't imagine her welcoming his interference. As for joining the Morgans for Natalie's birthday dinner, not even his family status as Lissa's father seemed adequate justification for intruding on what was bound to be an evening of painful reminders for the entire Morgan clan.

A knock on the office door pulled him from his thoughts. Carl slid off the chair and opened it to a sweaty kid in a basketball jersey. "Hey, Jason. What's up?"

The team captain stuck his carrot-top through the opening and sought out Daniel. "You comin' out, Coach?"

Daniel rubbed his eyes. "Yeah, yeah, sorry, Jason. Be right there."

"Stay put." Carl waved a hand toward Daniel. "I'll cover for you. You got more important stuff on your plate." He edged Jason out the door and closed it behind them.

What exactly Carl thought he could do about this "stuff on his plate," he wasn't sure. On the other hand, he couldn't abide the idea of sitting here and doing nothing. There'd been too many months of feeling helpless and "doing nothing" since Natalie had shut him out of her life. Somehow he had to make her understand how much he wanted to be with her today—how much he wanted to be with her always.

An idea surfaced. He tugged open a squeaky desk drawer and searched beneath loose newspaper clippings and random paperwork for the phonebook. Riffling through the Yellow Pages, he found the number of a local florist and keyed in the number on his cell phone.

"I need to order a birthday bouquet. Something really nice. Can you do red roses?" He gave the address for Natalie's apartment.

He heard the youthful clerk slurp something from a straw. "How do you want the card signed?"

He tossed around several alternatives, none of which seemed appropriate, considering how long they'd been apart. The best he could come up with was: *Thinking of you. Daniel.*

Taking advantage of some quiet time in his office, he checked the pop quizzes from this afternoon's history class and entered the scores in the grade book. When the final bell sounded, he gathered up his things and drove around to the front of the school to meet Lissa.

As they drove home, he broached the subject of Natalie's birthday dinner. "About tonight, Liss, why don't I drop you at the farm around six? You can give me a call when—"

He felt her gaze slash through the space between them. "What do you mean, drop me off? Aren't you coming too?"

"Not a good idea, sweetie. I don't want to make your mom uncomfortable—especially today."

"I can't *believe* you, Dad! Mom's birthday, and you're not going? What's *wrong* with you?"

He felt like both his heart and his ego had been run over by a semi. His fingers bit into the steering wheel, and he willed himself not to lose his temper.

"Try to understand, Lissa. You know how easy it is for your mom and me to get into an argument. Why would I want to risk spoiling her birthday?"

"That's just an excuse. You won't go because you're scared."

"I am scared, yes. I'm scared of upsetting your mom when she's already so vulnerable."

Lissa's voice turned shaky. "But Mom *needs* you, Dad. If you would just *try*, I know you could help make her feel better about Grandma, and Christmas, and just *everything*."

He wished that were true. He'd lost count of how many sleepless nights he'd spent agonizing about his wife and his marriage. And these days he couldn't seem to communicate any better with his daughter.

"Don't push it, Lissa," he finally told her as he drove through the ivied entrance to Putnam's Deer Creek apartment complex. Finding himself at an utter loss, he stated his intentions as simply as he knew how. "My decision is final. I told you, I'll drive you out and pick you up afterward, but I'm not staying."

She crossed her arms and glared out the side window. "If you aren't going, I'm not going either."

"Aw, come on, Liss." He swerved the Bronco into a parking space next to building three and jammed the gearshift into park. "Don't do that to your mom. It'll break her heart if you aren't there."

"Like you haven't already broken her heart by staying away?" Book bag hugged against her chest, Lissa flung the passenger door open, slammed it, and flounced up the sidewalk.

Pausing at the foot of the stairs to their unit, she turned, her face contorted. "You guys don't even *try* anymore. All you can think about is yourselves and how you don't want to do anything that makes either one of you uncomfortable." She made a growling sound that made her whole body shake. "Both of you make me sick!"

"That's enough out of you, young lady!" Daniel launched himself from the Bronco and stormed toward Lissa, who immediately hightailed it up to their apartment. Inside, he aimed his index finger toward her bedroom. "Go. And don't come out until I say so."

"Fine. You want to ground me for telling the truth? I'll stay in my room till Christmas. Till *next* Christmas! Till I'm a hundred and five!" Seconds later, her bedroom door slammed, and it felt as if the whole building trembled on its foundations.

Daniel could only stare immobilized and wonder how his world had tilted so far out of balance.

7

*D*ad greeted Natalie at the door with a hug and planted a wet kiss on her cheek. He smelled of aftershave and chili spices. "Here she is, my Christmas Rose! Happy birthday, sweetheart." He linked his arm with hers and ushered her into the warmth of the country kitchen. "How's my little girl tonight?"

"Come on, Dad, at thirty-six I'm not exactly a little girl anymore." Natalie rested her head on his shoulder. The soft brush of warm flannel made her feel momentarily safe. How sweet it would be if she could only make herself small enough again to crawl into her daddy's lap and find shelter from all her troubles.

"Hey, Sis, happy birthday." Hart rose from a spindle-back chair and hugged her, whispering so only she could hear, "Glad you changed your mind. Dad's been cheerier tonight than I've seen him in a long time."

"You were right, I couldn't let him down, but . . . " Biting her lip, she fixed Hart with a desperate gaze. On her way in, she had seen the freshly cut Christmas tree leaning against the house in a bucket of water, the green-and-red plastic boxes of lights and ornaments stacked neatly on the back porch, and finally, the crate containing the ceramic nativity scene, hand-painted and fired by her mother.

How would she ever get through this night without falling apart? How would any of them?

Celia, her sister-in-law, claimed a quick hug, her perky chestnut ponytail bouncing. "Happy birthday, Natalie. Love that sweater. Baby-blue is your color."

Celia stepped aside to make room for Kevin and Kurt, Natalie's lanky teenage twin nephews, who offered awkward, boyish embraces. She held her composure long enough to accept each greeting with as much grace as she could muster and then took a step back and glanced around nervously.

No Daniel. No Lissa. She cast Hart a questioning look.

He ran the toe of his boot across a tear in the yellowed linoleum floor. "Daniel called at the last minute—said they couldn't make it."

So much for her fleeting hopes for this dinner. At the very least, it would have provided the rare chance to spend a little more time with Lissa.

Yet the pressure had lifted. No more worries about staving off the all-too-predictable clashes between her and Daniel. No more worries about disappointing Lissa if this tentative step toward a reunion ended in disaster.

"How come?" she asked through a tight-lipped smile.

"Homework or something." Hart gave an evasive wave of his hand.

Dad forced a laugh. "You know how it is with teenagers."

Natalie caught the regretful look in his eyes. Undoubtedly he, along with everyone else in the family, had harbored visions of getting her and Daniel back together tonight.

Somehow, the flimsy reason given for Daniel and Lissa's absence didn't satisfy her. She knew why Daniel had decided not to put in an appearance. After the many times she'd pushed him away, she couldn't blame him if he'd given up trying. She didn't like herself very much these days.

Her father held a steaming spoonful of chili under her chin. "Here, taste this and tell me what you think."

The aroma usually sent her taste buds into overdrive, but tonight it suddenly filled her with nausea. "Hang on, Dad, I think I left my lights on." She shoved her father's hand away, and the thick, red-brown sauce spattered the floor. "Sorry." She fluttered one hand in a helpless gesture before rushing outside.

Leaning against her car, the hood still warm, she raked in huge gulps of frosty air. Stars shimmered in the clear sky overhead. A sliver of moon peeked over the barn roof. The horses nickered softly in their stalls. The screen door banged, and she looked up to see her brother striding toward her.

"Thought you might need this." He draped her camel-hair coat around her shoulders.

"Thanks." She sniffed away an embarrassed tear.

Hart planted his slim, blue-jeaned hips against the fender next to her. "You okay?"

"Just . . . give me a minute."

"Sorry, Nat. We all knew tonight would be hard for you."

She released a mirthless laugh. "I actually convinced myself I could handle it, at least for Dad's sake. I even dared to hope things might be different between me and Daniel this time. Then you said they weren't coming and . . . "

She looked toward the porch and shuddered. "And seeing the Christmas tree and decorations . . . Hart, it's just too hard."

"The old man's a stickler for tradition, just like Mom. I'm sure he thought it would help the whole family get through this season if some things stayed the same."

"But Mom's the one who made Christmas special. And she isn't here to celebrate with us. It'll never be the same again." She searched the pocket of her coat and found a shredded tissue. Giving several loud sniffs, she drew it roughly across each cheek.

"For crying out loud, Rosy, you talk like she's already dead." Hart pushed himself off the fender and hooked his thumbs in his belt loops. He glared at her over his shoulder. "You claim to love Mom so much, but I bet you don't even visit her anymore. When was the last time you went by the nursing home, huh?"

That was the trouble with big brothers. They never got tired of pointing out your flaws—never let you off the hook about anything. With one simple accusation, Hart could make her feel five years old again. She heard it in her voice as she answered. "I've tried, you know I have. But every time I see her like that . . . "

The ever-present guilt surged over her like a tidal wave. She covered her mouth to stifle a sob. "If I'd only come out that day—"

"Give it a rest, will you?" He spun around. "Dad and I weren't there, either. And Celia turned Mom down, too, remember?"

"But you had legitimate reasons. You and Dad had been planning to go to that auction for weeks. Celia had to take the twins to the game." She let out a tremulous breath. "I could have spared a couple of hours to help Mom, but I scraped around for any excuse I could find."

Hart's gaze pleaded with her. "Come on, Sis, how often have you ever let Mom down when she needed help with something? This was just one time."

Natalie snorted. "One time too many."

"How many times do you have to be reminded? She could just as easily have had her stroke during the week while we were all at work and Dad was out taking care of the horses. The results would have been the same."

Natalie stared at the ground and shook her head. "No, Hart, I'm the one who could have been there, and I wasn't."

"Aw, give it up, Nat. Where's your faith in Mom's love? Don't you believe she'd forgive you in a heartbeat if she could ever speak the words?"

Her voice lowered to a pained whisper. "That's just it. She isn't going to get better. She'll never be able to tell me she forgives me."

"I'm through listening to this garbage." He squared himself in front of her and gripped her shoulders. His fingers dug into her arms until she met his unyielding stare. "You're coming inside, and you're going to put a smile on your face and at least act like you're enjoying your birthday dinner. And afterward we'll put some Christmas music on the stereo like we do every year on your birthday, and we'll help Dad decorate the tree. And then, when we're all done, if you still want to, you can take your pity party home and cry your little heart out."

Grabbing her hand, he all but dragged her into the house.

"Just in time, you two." With sunflower-print oven mitts, Dad set the huge kettle of chili in the middle of the table next to a basket of piping-hot corn muffins. A hint of worry creased his eyes. "Everything okay?"

"Sure, Dad. Hart and I just got to talking, that's all." Natalie's voice rang high and tight, and she doubted even her eternally optimistic father would be fooled by her false assurance. "Mmmm. The chili smells wonderful. Mom would be proud."

With a strained smile she took her place at the table and helped herself to a bowl full of chili, a meal she felt certain she would not be able to eat.

༺๑༻

The bland, boring aromas of lemon-glazed chicken and mixed vegetables—the frozen kind, not home-cooked—wafted through the narrow apartment kitchen as Daniel waited for two microwave dinners to warm. Gazing into the night through the mini-blinds over the kitchen sink, he reflected on a lousy day that had only grown worse. His stomach heaved with a gnawing emptiness far more intense than mere physical hunger.

Nothing made sense to him anymore, no matter how hard he tried, no matter how many times he begged God to help him figure it all out. More and more often, he found himself losing focus on what he was supposed to be teaching in his history class, or, just like today at basketball practice, he'd stare out the gym windows instead of paying attention to the drills he'd assigned.

"You in there, Coach?" one of the boys finally asked, waving a hand in front of his eyes.

Thank goodness Carl was willing to cut him some slack, even cover for him from time to time, as he had today. Anyone else might have fired him a long time ago.

Thoughts of his job brought to mind another prime source of contention between him and Natalie—his goal to move on to a larger school and a better coaching position. When he heard about the possible vacancy over at the high school, he'd taken it as a sign he needed to stay here and work things out with his wife. Until that job possibility went up in smoke too. He might as well admit it. His career had hit a dead end and so had his marriage.

Almost a year had passed since Belinda's stroke, and his marriage had been on shaky ground for nearly as long. How could he hold out hope that things might still get better? How long before Natalie pressed him for a divorce? It was a word he couldn't even bring himself to say aloud, and yet it appeared inevitable. He clenched his jaw. How had things gotten this crazy?

The microwave beeped, and Daniel removed the dinners he had been heating for his and Lissa's supper. He winced as the hot containers burned his fingers. With greater care, he peeled away the cellophane from one dinner and scraped the steaming contents onto a plate. The meager chicken breast and mound of shriveled vegetables made the plate look huge.

"Lissa, supper's ready," he called down the hall. "You can come out of your room now."

The closed door muffled her angry reply. "I'm not hungry!"

Daniel eyed the second dinner hungrily. With a furtive glance toward the doorway, he quickly added Lissa's dinner to his own. He grabbed a knife and fork and the glass of iced tea he'd already poured and started for the living room. No way he could sit down at the kitchen table, hidden beneath Lissa's schoolbooks, his gym bag, a batch of chapter questions he'd barely started grading, and a folder of basketball stats he needed to sort through.

He pursed his lips. Eating meals at the table had gone out with the return of "bachelorhood." Even after Lissa moved in with him, they'd both gravitated toward the sofa with their morning bowls of cereal. Daniel's unimaginative evening meals—usually hamburgers, TV dinners, pancakes, or omelets—didn't inspire table dining, either.

Chomping down on a tough piece of fake chicken, he regretted turning down a bowl of Bram's homemade four-alarm chili for this.

Far more disappointing, however, was missing the chance to spend the evening with Natalie. Maybe they wouldn't have fought this time. It might have been okay . . . maybe. He tried to picture Natalie's reaction when she received the flower arrangement. Would she be touched, angry, or worse, completely indifferent?

Thinking of you. How lame was that? He could have at least signed it, *With love.*

Abruptly, he didn't feel so hungry after all. He set the plate on the coffee table and pressed a hand to his chest, willing away the suffocating emptiness. If he couldn't do anything tonight about his marriage, at least he could try to make peace with his daughter. He walked down the hall and tapped on Lissa's door.

"What?"

"Can I come in?" He opened the door a crack. "I really lost it earlier, and I want to apologize."

He heard the rustle of paper and the squeak of her desk drawer closing.

Finally, Lissa answered with a tremulous, "Okay." As he sidled into the room, she murmured, "I'm sorry too." She lay across the bed on her stomach, chin propped on folded arms, her long blonde hair almost hiding her small face.

Daniel's chest tightened. His normally outspoken daughter suddenly seemed so much younger than her thirteen years. He settled beside her on the edge of the bed. On her computer screen a colorful horse graphic with the look of an oil painting caught his eye. He recognized Lissa's unique artistic style. "You just do that?" At her nod, he said, "Cool."

She grimaced. "Tell my art teacher. She doesn't think computer-assisted art is 'creative.'"

"Bet your mom would disagree." When she didn't answer, he tried another tack. "Hungry yet?"

"Sort of." She rolled over and stared with red-rimmed eyes at the ceiling light. "I still think you and Mom are being jerks."

He winced. "Yeah, you're probably right. What can I say?"

"You could say you and Mom are getting back together." That quaver again.

His own voice shook as he answered. "I hope and pray we will someday. But the decision is up to your mom."

Lissa jerked upright, her gaze accusing. "You could try harder, Dad. You could have gone to her party tonight. You could call her more. You could—"

"Stop right there." Daniel raised a warning hand. "We've already had this argument, and look where it got you."

"Okay, okay." She swung her feet over the edge of the bed and stood. "Can I get something to eat now?"

Daniel could tell it was not "okay," but Lissa's stiff spine as she marched out the door told him their conversation had ended. He didn't know when he'd ever felt so alone and helpless. Even his prayers seemed to bounce off the ceiling and back into his lap.

The phone rang, sending his heart rate skyrocketing. He imagined Natalie on the other end of the line, calling about the flowers. A thousand possible scenarios played through his brain, none of which gave him any peace.

He heard Lissa pick up the kitchen extension. "Dad, it's for you."

If the caller was Natalie, Lissa's tone gave no clue. He stepped into the hallway, palms sweating. "I'll take it in my room." He closed his bedroom door and picked up the phone on his bedside table. "Hello?"

"Coach Pearce, this is Dave Arnell, head basketball coach at Langston High. I have your résumé in front of me."

Daniel's breath hitched. Okay, he'd asked for a sign. Maybe this was it. If Arnell offered him a job, it could mean the time had come to permanently end things with Natalie.

"Yes, sir, Coach Arnell." He tried to mask the trepidation in his voice, but every nerve had gone on red alert. "What can I do for you?"

The other man chuckled. "Son, the real question is, what can I do for you? One of our assistant coaches just announced he's retiring at the end of this school year, and I'm in the market for a new second-in-command starting next fall. Are you still interested in interviewing for a position at Langston?"

<hr />

Lissa had intended to hang up the kitchen phone as soon as her father picked up. She knew it was impolite to eavesdrop, but when she heard the caller identify himself, she couldn't resist the urge to listen in.

The job offer stunned her. If Dad said yes and ended up moving to Langston, he and Mom would never get back together.

With tingling fingers she replaced the receiver as gently as possible. Time was running out. She'd have to kick her plans into high gear.

Her toast popped up. She absently dropped it onto a paper towel and spread it with peanut butter. Thoughts spinning, she carried the toast and a glass of milk to her room and sat down at the computer. She closed the graphic design she'd been working on, logged on to her email site, and wrote:

```
TO: WATERBUG
FROM: LP108
SUBJECT: major bad news
```
I can't believe this. My dad is interviewing for a coaching job in Langston. If that happens, it's over!!!! You know what I've been praying for. Mom & Dad back together by Christmas. And you know I would do anything, absolutely ANYTHING, to make that happen!! If my grandma would just get well, I KNOW everything would be okay again. The idea I told you about has just GOT to work, so don't let me down, okay? Friday, 5:45 a.m., Sixth and Main, just like we planned. Be there, PLEASE????

She clicked the send button and listened to the computerized chime that indicated her e-mail was on its way through cyberspace.

One item checked off her list, one to go. She logged off the Internet, reached for the phone, and pressed a speed-dial code.

"Hello?" said a sleepy voice.

"Hi, it's me. Just making sure we're on schedule."

The voice perked up. "*No problemo*, baby. All systems are A-OK."

8

*N*atalie somehow choked down enough chili and corn-bread to quiet the concern in her father's searching glances, but the birthday meal sat like a wheelbarrow of concrete in the pit of her stomach. Dad and Hart cleared the table while Celia set out dessert plates and lit the candles on the birthday cake. Natalie glimpsed the box on the counter with "Lindon's Bakery" stamped in gold script on the lid. Of course, Dad had ordered one of Maeve Lindon's scrumptious red velvet cakes. They'd always been Natalie's favorite and a longstanding birthday tradition—one she would have gratefully forsaken this year, if anyone had asked.

She had no choice but to sit in awkward silence, a stiff smile pasted across her face, while the family sang "Happy Birthday" and waited for her to blow out the candles before they melted into waxy puddles in the creamy frosting. Celia handed her a knife and dished up generous scoops of vanilla ice cream as Natalie served the cake and hoped no one noticed her shaking hands. Hart and the twins gobbled down second and third helpings, while Natalie toyed with her miniscule slice and watched the dark red crumbs float in iridescent pools of melted ice cream.

Next came the cards and gifts. She dutifully opened each one and gave what she hoped were convincing "oohs" and "aahs." A mint-green knitted cap with matching scarf and gloves from Hart and Celia. A movie rental gift card from the twins. A silver bracelet with horse charms from her dad.

"Thank you," she said, her voice breathy. She stuffed a wad of pastel tissue paper into a silver gift bag and started to rise. "It was all wonderful, but I have to be at work early in the morning. I should really go."

"But, sweetie, we're just getting started." Dad laid a restraining hand on her arm. "With all of us here to pitch in, the decorating won't take long."

"We could do it another night." She lifted her brows in a pleading look. "Maybe next weekend?"

Hart spoke up. "You don't want to mess with tradition, do you? We always do the tree on your birthday."

She cast him a despairing frown. "I know, but . . . "

"It's what your mom would want." The poignant note in Dad's voice stabbed Natalie's heart. "Stay."

She bent to give her father a kiss on his wrinkled forehead. "Okay, Dad, sure."

Her father rubbed his hands together. "You go put your feet up for a few minutes while we clean up in here. Then we can get busy on the decorating."

The kitchen door whisked shut behind her. She settled into her dad's favorite easy chair, its plush velour upholstery comforting her like a familiar hug. Across the room, the wood-stove radiated its warmth, and the subtle, soothing scent of burning oak logs surrounded her. She welcomed the tempo-rary solitude to compose herself for what came next. If only she'd had the foresight to bring up these dreaded birthday traditions with Dr. Sirpless, maybe she could have come away with some slightly more effective coping strategies than "grin and bear it."

She squeezed her eyes shut, one fist knotted so tightly that her nails dug into her palm. *Dear God, for Dad's sake, please let me make it through this night.*

All too soon, Celia joined her in the living room and started some Christmas music playing on the stereo. "Dad set aside a container of chili for you. Be sure you don't forget it."

"Sounds good."

The soft strains of "Away in a Manger" floated toward her from a nearby speaker. Already she could feel what little self-control she had regained beginning to crumble.

"I took the twins by to see Mom after school today." Celia took a seat on the sofa. "Every once in a while I'm sure she actually recognizes us." She gave her head a small shake. "But then the light goes out of her eyes again."

Natalie couldn't respond. She wanted to change the subject, before the mildly pulsating nausea in the pit of her stomach became something much worse. She noticed a tiny chili stain on the front of her wool slacks and self-consciously rubbed at it.

"Well, anyway . . . " Celia's voice took on the rapid, high-pitched timbre of nervous chatter. "I'm glad for your dad's sake that we could get together for your birthday. I'm just sorry Lissa and Daniel couldn't make it. It's such a busy time of year for you at work, I know, so—"

Dad shoved through the door, a stack of Christmas boxes balanced against his chest. "Hey, you two, cut the chatter and give an old man a hand."

"Sure, Dad! Let's get this show on the road." Celia jumped up, the thankful look in her eyes mirroring Natalie's own explosion of relief—anything to put an end to this awkward one-sided conversation.

Hart set the nativity box beneath the antique library table while Kevin and Kurt wrestled the tree through the doorway. Natalie knew from long years of experience that for this stage of the production, she'd be safer on the sidelines. She snuggled deeper in her chair and watched the Keystone Kops-like performance as the men in the family sorted through several containers and planned their attack on the Christmas tree. Dad dug through the boxes until he located the tree lights. By the time he and Hart secured the tree in its stand near Natalie's chair, the twins had most of the light strings untangled and sorted by color and type.

Time to get out of the way. She rose and moved a few steps to one side, leaving Celia to her assigned job of opening and arranging the ornament boxes on the coffee table.

From the stereo speakers, Julie Andrews's lilting soprano poured forth "It Came Upon a Midnight Clear." Natalie hugged herself as memories washed over her—memories as intense as the pungent scent of evergreen filling her nostrils. How she missed Mom! She longed to be anywhere else in the universe, anywhere except this room on this night. As on Thanksgiving, she wondered if Dr. Sirpless would take a last-minute appointment.

Kurt crawled behind the tree to plug in an extension cord and connected the light strands end to end. He and Kevin meticulously checked the strings for burnt-out bulbs as the lights warmed and began to twinkle.

"Looks like everything's working, Granddad." Kevin shoved up the sleeves of his green sweatshirt and carried a strand to the tree.

Celia nudged Natalie's shoulder and cast a disbelieving glance toward the ceiling. "Honestly, they act like it's brain surgery."

Natalie forced a tiny laugh. "No kidding."

The men encircled the tree and fed the lighted strings to each other, beginning at the top and choosing each placement with great deliberation. Finally, Hart stepped back and planted his knuckles on his hips. "There's too many at the top and not enough at the bottom."

Kurt settled on his haunches and moved a branch aside. "It needs more in towards the trunk."

"Look there." Kevin pointed a slender finger. "A bunch of blue ones are all clumped together."

Celia giggled and twisted her long ponytail. "Next they'll be getting out a level and tape measure."

Natalie's father made a few adjustments and turned to her. "What do you think, Natalie? Does it look balanced from that angle?"

Her throat ached. She pressed a finger to her lips and nodded. "It looks fine, Dad."

When the men were finally satisfied with the lights, Celia parceled out the ornaments. She gave Kevin and Kurt the box of starched white crocheted snowflakes, and she and Hart hung the gold and silver balls.

Natalie's father eased his back as he gazed at the remaining ornament boxes on the coffee table. Selecting one from a box of special keepsakes, he came up beside Natalie and held it out to her. "Your favorite," he said softly. "Remember?"

How could she forget? The delicate white globe bore the image of a galloping horse that looked just like Windy, her Appaloosa. Her mother had painted the ornament herself the Christmas after Windy was born. Natalie still remembered how Mom had to ice her wrist every couple of hours as she worked.

"Windy doesn't get ridden much these days." Dad slid his finger beneath the errant strand of hair Natalie could never keep out of her eyes. "She misses you."

"I've been way too busy lately." She turned the ornament slowly in her hands. "Actually, I've . . . I've been thinking about giving Windy away. Last summer I helped design a brochure for a new place in Putnam called Reach for the Stars. It's a riding center for kids with disabilities."

"I've heard of it. Sounds like a wonderful project."

"Don't you think Windy would be a great horse for them? She's calm, steady, and—" She shot her dad a knowing wink. "—not *too* stubborn for a part-Appaloosa."

He cast her a doubtful frown. "Are you sure you could part with her? You raised her from a foal and trained her yourself. Why, you and your mom brought her into the world."

Natalie pressed her cheek against his sleeve, memories clutching at her heart. "I have to face reality, Dad. The truth is I don't have time for a horse anymore—haven't for a long time."

"What about Lissa? She's kind of attached to Windy too." Dad pressed his lips into a tight, sad smile. "Remember last summer? She was practically camped out in Windy's stall."

Natalie shuddered. She didn't want to remember last summer. She didn't want to remember anything about the past year.

She gazed at the delicately painted horse on the ornament she held. "I'm afraid Lissa's outgrowing her interest in horses. Can you even remember the last time she came out to ride?"

Her father wrinkled his brow. "Not since she moved to Putnam with Daniel, I suppose." Shaking his head, he said tiredly, "I've been remiss, my mind on so many other things. I should have made a point of inviting her out to go riding with me."

"It's not your fault, Dad, it's mine."

"Now, Natalie—"

"No, it's true. I don't even know what my daughter cares about anymore. She's changed so much this past year."

"A lot has changed." The catch in Dad's voice almost undid Natalie. He took a deep, harsh breath before laying a callused hand on her arm. "You miss your little girl, I know you do."

She could hardly speak her answer. "Yes. I miss her a lot." She missed Daniel too.

"Then do something about it before it's too late."

After all the mistakes she'd made? It was already too late—far too late.

She moved to the tree on leaden feet. With trembling fingers she selected a branch and carefully attached the Appaloosa ornament. Behind her, she heard her father clear his throat. She turned to see him leaning over the coffee table, peering into the ornament boxes.

"I've always liked this one," he said, lifting out an elegant crystal bell. He rang it gently, and the beautiful, shimmering tone sent chills up Natalie's arms. When she was a little girl, she once asked her mother if that's what angels sounded like when they sang.

"Someday we'll find out, won't we?" Mom had answered. *"What a blessed day that will be!"*

Her mother's faith had always been an inspiration—her love the glue that held this family together. Natalie pictured the vacant gaze in those liquid blue eyes that once held so much joy. How she wished her mom could be here tonight! *Why can't things be like they were?*

Dad placed the bell on a branch and gave the clapper a gentle flick. When the clear, sweet chime died away, he said, "Nothing about life is easy, Rosy-girl, but the good Lord never promised us it would be. All we can do is keep trying and trusting and hoping."

Her father's words rang coldly against the hardened shell encasing her heart. She glanced over her shoulder toward Hart and Celia and the boys, busy with decorations on the other side of the tree. At least they didn't seem to be paying any attention to this conversation. Any more well-intentioned words, sympathetic hugs, or lectures on pulling herself together and she'd implode.

Her father continued softly, urgently, "Don't you think it's about time you and Daniel worked things out? At least try, for Lissa's sake. It's almost Christmas, after all."

She clenched her fists. "Please, Dad—"

Suddenly a blur of black and white dashed past, with Kevin and Kurt in hot pursuit. "Bring it back, Sky." Kurt grabbed for the dog's tail and missed. "Granddad, she's got my Santa ornament, the one I made in second grade."

Her prize dangling from her mouth, the monstrous Great Dane lunged behind the Christmas tree. The whole tree tipped sideways, and Natalie and her father each grabbed for a limb. Ornaments swung precariously on the bouncing boughs. A flurry of pine needles shimmied to the floor.

"Sky," Dad ordered when the tree stopped swaying, "come out of there at once."

Head down, tail between her legs, the dog crept from her place of safety and dropped the slobbery red Santa at Kurt's feet.

"You naughty dog." Kurt smoothed the Santa's floppy cap and yarn beard, a throaty laugh belying the disapproval in his voice. He folded his tall frame to kneel in front of Sky and scratched her behind the ears. As if delighted to be forgiven, she wagged her tail furiously.

But the huge dog stood too close to the tree. The white-tipped tail caught Natalie's cherished horse ornament and swept it from its branch.

"Sky, no!" She made a desperate dive to rescue the keep-sake, only to crack her knees on the hardwood floor and bang her forehead on the corner of the coffee table. A moan of shock and pain burst from her lungs. The sound changed to an amazed cry when she discovered the ornament resting in her open palm. Miraculously, she'd snagged it just before it would have shattered into a thousand pieces.

Natalie felt a wave of vertigo as she knelt there, the small globe cradled in shaking hands. The voices of her family, all rushing over to help, echoed eerily as if from deep inside a cave. The edges of her vision blurred, until she could see only the little painted Appaloosa, stark against the white back-ground of the ornament. Her dizziness intensified, and the whole room seemed atilt on a whirling base. Even the painted horse appeared to be in motion, galloping across a wide meadow glowing green and gold in the sunlight. She imag-ined she saw a rider—a woman—silver hair flowing behind her like a comet's tail.

Mom?

Natalie wavered. She felt strong arms catch her.

"You okay?" It was her brother's voice.

"That was some save, Aunt Natalie," Kevin said.

Celia laid a concerned hand on her shoulder. "You're get-ting a nasty lump on your head. I'll get some ice."

A wet tongue on her cheek, doggy breath in her face, Hart helping her to her feet—a kaleidoscope of activity slowly coalesced into clarity.

"I'm okay, I'm okay." She felt her way to the nearest chair with one hand while the other protected the ornament.

"Let me take care of it for you, Aunt Nat." Kurt loomed over her, his peach-fuzz teenage face filled with concern. "I'll put it on the tree."

She smiled her thanks but stubbornly shielded her trea-sure from his outstretched hand. "No . . . no, I've got it." She waved everyone away and even refused Celia's offer of the dishcloth she'd wrapped around a bag of ice.

While her family looked on in confusion, Natalie dared another glance at the ornament. But she saw only a painted horse again, frozen in mid-stride—no meadow, no rider.

"Hey, Rosy-Posey," Hart said with a chuckle, "you look like you've seen a ghost."

She flung her brother a look of utter disdain. "How many times do I have to tell you? Don't call me that!"

Whether it was his unwelcome use of her nickname or the idea that he'd glimpsed something in her face that hinted at the otherworldly vision she'd just experienced, she suddenly couldn't escape fast enough. She burst from the chair and thrust the ornament into her father's hands.

Tearing through the kitchen, she grabbed her coat and purse on the run and charged out the door. It was a mistake. She never should have come tonight.

"I'm sorry, Daddy," she whispered, jabbing the key in the car's ignition. When the engine grumbled to life, she jammed the gearshift into reverse. Gravel flew as she swung the car around and tore down the driveway. She pushed the speed limit all the way home to her apartment and hoped Dr. Sirpless would answer her call.

Rage burned white-hot through her limbs. If tonight was any indication, the rest of the family hadn't succeeded any better than she at accepting what they themselves had been trying to force upon her for months now.

"A lot has changed," her father had said to her less than an hour ago. About time he admitted it. About time they all did.

No matter how badly she wanted to, she couldn't turn back time. It was useless holding onto the past, holding onto false hope. Somehow she had to find a way to put the past year behind her and move forward. Somehow she had to start living again.

Natalie stumbled up the unlit stairway to her apartment landing and cursed the forgetful maintenance man who had forgotten to replace the burned-out lightbulb. After several unsuccessful stabs at fitting her door key into the lock, she finally got the door open. She slammed it behind her, twisted the deadbolt, and headed straight for the phone on the breakfast bar.

"This is Dr. Julia Sirpless. I'm unavailable to take your call, but—"

Natalie slammed down the receiver. She could never squeeze tonight's turmoil into a fifteen-second voice mail.

Ten minutes later, she stretched out in bed for what she already knew would be a sleepless night. Despite her resolve to stop living in the past, she couldn't let go of the haunting image of her mother on Windy's back, riding alive and free and strong across the sun-drenched meadow.

She flopped over on her side and beat a fist against the mattress. The only way she could imagine Mom enjoying such blissful freedom again would be if she were to leave the prison of her earthly body behind.

Did she wish her mother dead? Silent tears streamed onto the pillowcase. She only wanted to talk to her again, hear her voice, and know that she still loved her . . . and forgave her.

God, why can't you do something?

9

The 6:00 A.M. alarm bored into Natalie's sleep-deprived brain with jackhammer force. She hit the snooze button three times before she finally marshaled enough willpower to heave her weary body out of bed. She felt like a zombie on steroids as she rushed through her morning routine in a hopeless effort to get to work on time. While she waited for a toaster pastry to finish warming, she glanced around for her briefcase and then remembered she'd left it in the car last night.

Rats. All those design projects she'd brought home from the office were still sitting there, no closer to being finished than when she stuffed them in her briefcase. Had she honestly expected to duck out early from Dad's and have any semblance of sanity left to get some work done?

As she stepped onto the landing and turned to lock the door, a splash of color caught her eye. She glanced down to see a bouquet of red and white roses, the edges of the petals limp and blackened from frostbite. The flowers were probably there last night when she got home, only the landing had been too dark for her to notice. Stooping, she lifted the globe-shaped glass vase, careful not to crush the flowers. With a wistful smile, she carried the bouquet inside and set it on the end of the bar that separated the living area from the small kitchen.

Could Daniel have sent the flowers? He knew how much she loved red roses, but . . . She grimaced and shook her head. Maybe Dad. Surely not Hart. She doubted her business partner Jeff Garner would have remembered her birthday. Still, warmth seeped through her veins. No matter how upset she'd been with her family last night, someone had been thoughtful enough to remember her favorite flowers.

She tore open the card. *Birthday Wishes for Someone Special* read the printed verse superimposed upon a background of wispy pink clouds. And beneath it a scrawled signature: *Thinking of you. Daniel.* So he *had* sent the flowers.

Natalie collapsed onto a barstool and pressed a fist to her mouth. She told herself not to read too much into the gesture and tried unsuccessfully to stifle the overpowering yearning to be near her husband again. She could hear his voice, feel his arms around her, and taste his lips on hers.

The phone sat not six inches from where her arm rested on the bar. Daniel and Lissa would have already left for school by now, but she had his number programmed into her speed dial. Her hand crept toward her cell. What could she say to him?

The flowers could mean anything, or nothing at all. After all, it was only a friendly "Thinking of you," not, "Darling, I love you and forgive you and want you back with all my heart." Besides, the left-hander's backward slant and the tiny hearts dotting the *i*'s clearly suggested the card had been signed by a lovesick teenage floral assistant, not Daniel himself. Which meant he'd phoned in the order, probably as an afterthought once he'd declined Dad's invitation to dinner. Obviously, her husband didn't even care enough to go by the shop and sign his own name. Then why send flowers at all? Sympathy, maybe? More likely an apology for not bringing Lissa to the birthday dinner.

Ashamed of her thoughts, she cut him some slack and reminded herself he always phoned in his order. He never had time to swing by a flower shop himself.

"Get a grip, Natalie." How she hated the stomach-churning, roller-coaster ride of emotions.

Still . . . it would only be polite to call and thank him. She lifted the phone and pressed the speed-dial code for his cell phone before she could change her mind. It rang three times before he answered.

"Daniel Pearce."

"Hi, it's me." Shy vulnerability crept into her voice.

"Natalie, hang on a sec. I'm in traffic." A pause, then a muffled, "Liss, turn down the radio, okay?"

"Is that Mom?" She heard Lissa's voice, high and expectant.

"Yeah, talk to her until we get into the parking lot."

She listened to more rasping sounds before Lissa came on the line. "Hey, Mom! How was your birthday?"

"Nice." She closed her eyes, pressed two fingers to her temple. "It was very nice."

"You decorated the tree?"

"Of course."

"I wanted to be there, but Dad grounded me."

Natalie's eyes flew open. Her brows shot together so tightly, it made last night's lump on her forehead throb all over again. "He *what?*"

"Yep, he grounded me because I got mad at him for saying he wouldn't go too."

So the flowers *were* an apology. The warm, fuzzy feeling in Natalie's chest turned to hot anger. How heartless could one man be, refusing to let a child attend her own mother's birthday celebration?

She heard the honk of a car horn, followed by more static, and then Daniel's gruff voice. "Give me that phone."

Natalie was more than ready to give him a piece of her mind. She could feel the adrenaline pumping through her system like steam through a boiler.

"Hey, Natalie."

"Daniel Pearce, how dare—"

"That's not exactly the way it happened. I would gladly have brought Lissa out to your dad's, but when I told her I didn't think I should go along, she threw a tantrum and said she wouldn't go without me."

Threw a tantrum, huh? Daniel always was one to exaggerate. "So, you just decided to ruin my birthday and both of you stay away? Well, thanks a lot."

"No, Nat . . . hang on, let me get this car parked before I have a wreck."

Seconds ticked by as Natalie tried to decipher the various rumbles, crackles, and whines coming over the phone line. She used the moment to rein in her anger and sort out her thoughts before she resumed this little discussion with her husband on the finer points of parenting.

Like she was any expert. Shaking off the accusing thought, she focused on the bouquet of roses, still beautiful and fragrant despite the frost-burnt petals. The image stirred something deep inside her—the hope that something beautiful still remained amid the ruins of her marriage. If she looked past the damage, would she find anything worth saving? Would Daniel? Did he want to?

"Okay, I'm here." Huffing breaths punctuated Daniel's words. "About last night. Things went a little crazy. I lost my temper; Lissa lost hers. I'm sorry."

Tearing her gaze away from the bouquet, Natalie drew the familiar cloak of indifference around her. "It doesn't matter. I really just called to thank you for the flowers."

A sigh. "I hoped your favorite roses would help make up for what I knew had to be a tough evening for you."

"*Roses?*" came Lissa's incredulous shout. "Dad, you sent Mom flowers?"

"Just a second, Natalie." Daniel lowered his voice and spoke away from the phone. "Lissa, you don't need to listen to this conversation. Get going, before you're late for class."

"I'm warning you, Dad." The creak of a car door couldn't drown out Lissa's stern reply. "Don't blow this, okay? I mean it. You'll regret it forever."

"Get to class, young lady, or *you'll* have plenty to regret." The next sounds were a loud slam and Daniel's muttered expletive.

Natalie flattened her lips. Okay, maybe Daniel hadn't been exaggerating about the temper tantrum. Clearly, he struggled as much with parenting Lissa as she ever did.

Daniel cleared his throat. "Um, what was I saying?" She could picture him rubbing his eyebrow with a stiffened index finger as he so often did when distracted.

"The flowers. I was just thanking you for the flowers." She stroked a wilted petal. "And the card was so thoughtful." Had she managed to keep the sarcasm out of her voice? Probably not.

"Yeah, I wasn't sure quite how to say it, but—" His voice cracked. "Nat, honey, I still lo—"

"Oh, gosh, I'm going to be late for work." *Don't say it, Daniel. Not yet. I can't bear it.*

Her heart felt like a helium balloon in her chest, pressing upward into her throat, cutting off her flow of oxygen. "We'll talk later, okay? Thanks again. Bye."

She pressed the off button and bolted for the door.

⊷➋

"Natalie? Nat, are you still there?"

The one thing Daniel couldn't get used to about cell phones was that when someone hung up on you, you just got dead air, not the telltale drone of a dial tone.

And he'd gotten used to being hung up on a lot since Natalie left him. She would sometimes chat with him briefly about how Lissa was doing in school, maybe even fill him in on what Bram or Hart and his family were up to, if he made a point to ask. But the moment he attempted to move the conversation toward deeper issues—her mother, her self-imposed guilt, their marriage—she cut him off.

Stifling a yawn, he swung open the door of his Bronco and started toward the gym. Between worrying about how Natalie was handling the party at her dad's and pondering the call from Coach Arnell about the opening at Langston High, he'd gotten precious little sleep last night. Arriving at his office, he flipped the light switch and blinked as the garish fluorescent tubes flickered a few times before coming to full brightness.

"Dad?"

He jumped at the sound of Lissa's voice and spun around. "Aren't you supposed to be in class?"

"The tardy bell doesn't ring for another two minutes." She chewed her lip and hugged her backpack against her chest. Her voice was barely audible. "I had to know what you and Mom talked about. Did she like the flowers? What did she say?"

He saw the hope in her eyes, and he knew he was about to crush it once again. He circled his desk and plopped into the squeaky and definitely *not* ergonomically designed stenographer's chair, the best Putnam could afford for a middle-school assistant coach's office.

Don't go there, Pearce. You asked for a sign and you got one. If Arnell's offer came through, Putnam's coaching budget would be a nonissue—and so would his marriage.

He picked up a pencil and twirled it, unable to meet his daughter's probing gaze. "It was just a gesture, Liss . . . to make up for skipping her birthday dinner. Don't read anything into it that isn't there."

Lissa sidled over and perched on the corner of the desk. "There could be, if you'd just admit it." She swiveled to face him. "So . . . did she like them or not?"

"Yeah, she liked them. And she called to thank me. That's all." He reached inside his briefcase and pulled out a folder brimming with the dog-eared, seventh-grade history questions he never finished grading.

"That's it? Like, you two aren't going to get together to talk about it or anything?"

"Talk about what?" As if he didn't know.

"You and Mom, of course." Her tone implied his complete stupidity. Then her voice became pleading. "Come on, Dad, it's nearly Christmas. Isn't there something—"

A strident blare echoed throughout the building—the tardy bell. Daniel gave his daughter an "I told you so" look and shooed her off his desk. "How many times do we need to have this conversation, Lissa? When—*if*—your mother ever changes her mind about us getting back together, well . . . we'll take it one step at a time."

Rising, he set a firm hand on her shoulder and propelled her toward the door. "Now, will you please get to your class?"

She turned, another question on her lips and an accusing look in her eyes. "Dad—"

"Not now, sweetie. Go." With a final shove, he ejected her into the corridor and closed the door.

Returning to his chair, he rested his forehead in his hands. How much longer could he hold out hope that Natalie would return to him? And how much more disappointment could Lissa stand if it never happened?

Again, his thoughts returned to last night's phone conversation with Coach Arnell. Langston wasn't that far from Putnam and Fawn Ridge, but it wasn't exactly next door, either. He began to regret his decision to drive up to Langston for an interview on Saturday. If he were to take a coaching job there, Lissa would have to choose once and for all which parent she wanted to live with.

And, of course, the "D" word had to be dealt with. The specter of divorce hung over his head like the blade of a guillotine, ready to sever him from everything he held dear.

❧

Natalie stared bleary-eyed at her computer screen. She'd been working on the layout for Fawn Ridge Fellowship Church's weekly newsletter, trying in vain to manipulate a 400-word Advent devotion into a space large enough to handle only 250 words, unless she resorted to six-point type. She reached for the phone, planning to call the pastor and ask him whether he wanted to edit it himself or entrust her with the task.

"Natalie, you have a phone call."

She almost jumped out of her skin. Catching her breath, she jerked her head up to see her assistant standing beside the desk. The girl had an uncanny way of sneaking up on cat's feet and startling the life out of her.

"Deannie Garner, how many times do I have to tell you? Knock before you come into my office. We do have an intercom system, you know." It was a lot less intrusive than the girl's untimely personal appearances.

Deannie's lips curled into an innocent smile. "I keep forgetting. Sorry." She gave her flame-red curls a toss. "Anyway, it's Mr. Craunauer from The Apple Cart, and he's ranting like a maniac."

"Now what's wrong?" Mr. Craunauer was a stickler for details, and considering what he paid for their professional services, Natalie agreed he had every right to be. A lump of dread formed in the pit of her stomach.

Deannie shrugged. "I couldn't get anything out of him. He'll only talk to you."

Natalie saved and closed the newsletter file and then jotted herself a quick note to phone Pastor Mayer. She steeled herself as she picked up the phone. "Mr. Craunauer, good morning."

"Christmas is less than two weeks away, Ms. Pearce. I expected those flyers to be in my customers' mailboxes long before now. Sales are dying on the vine. Time is money. The early bird catches the worm!"

She cringed at the clichés and adopted her most placating tone. "This is an extremely busy time for us, as you can imagine. The entire staff is working overtime to keep up with all our clients. If you'll wait just a moment, I'll find out exactly where things stand."

She pressed the hold button and turned to Deannie. "What's the status of his order? Please don't tell me it hasn't gone out yet."

"I think Uncle Jeff finally got it printed and folded late yesterday," the girl answered with a naïve smile.

The hard lump in Natalie's stomach swelled to boulder-size. Mr. Craunauer had given the ad copy his final approval early last week, and Natalie had immediately turned it over to Jeff for printing and mailing. She pressed two fingers of each hand to her throbbing forehead. "The flyers should have been at the post office days ago. What happened?"

Deannie rolled her eyes. "Like my uncle tells me anything?"

"Then go find out, *please*."

With a steadying breath she picked up the phone, assuring Mr. Craunauer she'd have an answer for him momentarily. Just then Deannie rushed in, breathing hard. As she started to speak, Natalie made a shushing sound.

Deannie continued in a whisper. "Everything's cool. Alan and Bill are loading the van for a run to the post office. The Apple Cart flyers are in that batch."

Natalie crumpled in her chair. Not good enough! The flyers were stamped for bulk rate, as Mr. Craunauer had originally requested. If they had gone out on schedule, there wouldn't be a problem. But today was cutting it far too close for the Apple Cart Christmas promotion. Bulk mail delivery was notoriously unpredictable.

As Mr. Craunauer's litany of complaints continued in her left ear, Natalie covered the mouthpiece. "Stop the van! Have them leave Mr. Craunauer's order here."

Deannie gave a confused shrug and spun on her heel.

"Yes, Mr. Craunauer, I understand," she said, returning to the conversation. "Your flyers will be mailed today, I promise, and we'll foot the bill for first-class postage. Your customers will receive them before the weekend."

So much for making a profit. Suppressing a tremor of annoyance, she apologized once again for the mix-up and told the partially mollified shop owner good-bye.

She'd barely steadied her nerves after the unsettling conversation when she looked up to see Deannie standing in the doorway, a stack of Apple Cart flyers in her arms.

"You won't believe this," Deannie said, "not in a million years."

"What?" Natalie rose slowly, everything in her rebelling against whatever new disaster she read in her assistant's face.

"I was kind of thumbing through them and . . . " Deannie spread the flyers on Natalie's desk and then folded her arms across her waist.

Natalie lifted an eyebrow and edged closer. With a professional eye she scanned the copy on the top flyer:

THE APPLE CART
The place to shop
when only the very best will do.
Order your gift baskets . . .
Select fresh Florida oranges . . . delicious apples . . .
assortment of candies and baked goods made right here
in our spotless Appaloosa kitchens.

Her mouth dropped open. "*Appaloosa!* It's supposed to say 'Apple Cart.' I *know* I typed 'Apple Cart.'" She stabbed at her computer keyboard, entering the password to bring up the Apple Cart file.

There it was, *Appaloosa*, staring at her from the screen in bold Clarendon typeface. But Mr. Craunauer himself had approved the copy. *What went wrong?*

Natalie sank into her chair, numb with shock. No time for self-recrimination. She had to make the correction, order another printing, and get the flyers in the mail before she permanently lost Mr. Craunauer's business to the bigger, flashier franchise printing company in Putnam.

❧

Long after midnight, Natalie sank into bed, too exhausted to sleep. It had taken the entire day and everyone's help, but the mistake had been corrected and new pre-addressed flyers were printed, this time with first-class postage imprints. At exactly 4:49 P.M. Natalie slammed her trunk closed on two boxes of flyers and began a mad dash to the post office before it closed.

Jeff would fume for weeks about how much her mistake had cost the company, and of course, it would come out of her salary. As much as she wanted to, she somehow doubted she could fall back on her agreement to hire Deannie as a means of deflecting Jeff's wrath.

On the other hand, if Natalie even suspected the girl had anything to do with the delay—or even worse, the proofreading error—it would be a different story. But Natalie and everyone else in the office remained especially cautious about giving the boss's bungling, underachieving niece any task involving more than miniscule responsibility.

No, she thought, tossing and turning through another sleepless night, she couldn't come up with a single shred of evidence to pin the Apple Cart fiasco on Deannie. Still, for the life of her, she could not comprehend how she had made such a glaring typographical error—much less how it had slipped past not only her proofreaders, but also Mr. Craunauer himself. She couldn't even imagine Mr. Craunauer's reaction had the flyers gone out last week on schedule without anyone catching the mistake. She could only chalk it up to everyone's general state of distraction caused by the Christmas rush.

"Appaloosa, indeed." She stumbled to the bathroom for some ibuprofen to stem a fatigue-induced headache before crawling back under the covers.

Too soon, the blare of the clock radio stirred her from a fitful dream. She thrust out her hand to silence the music and lay perfectly still, willing herself to return to that state of dreamy half-sleep. Slowly, the images floated upward through her mind: Windy in the pasture, her mother's hair morphing into a sable paintbrush. Then something about Daniel pushing Lissa in an apple cart. Only Lissa was still a cuddly, smiling baby, not the impulsive teenager she'd become. And starlight. She remembered bright stars in the dream, and a full, shimmering moon, the iridescent light illuminating . . . *what?*

She strained to recapture the image, feeling as if it must be real, as if she should remember something. For a fleeting moment she glimpsed a mental image of her father's barn—the immaculate tack room . . . the brimming storage closet. Something appeared out of place, but she couldn't make sense of what it was. The vision slipped away, this time irretrievable.

Natalie shoved the covers aside, felt around with her feet for her slippers, staggered to the bathroom, and flipped on the light switch. While she waited for her eyes to adjust to the sudden glare, the phone rang. Still squinting, she stumbled to the bedside table. "Hello?"

"Nat, it's me. She's run away again."

10

*D*aniel stood in the middle of his cluttered apartment kitchen and gripped the phone. He pressed his eyelids shut. It sickened him to make this call. Natalie would hold him responsible, and she probably had every right, considering his questionable parenting skills lately.

"Daniel?" Natalie's voice sounded sleep-drugged.

"Did you hear what I said? Lissa's gone again. When I went to wake her for school, she wasn't in her room." He leaned against the refrigerator. A mixed array of magnets holding photos, reminders, and shopping lists dug into his shoulder blades. Unfortunately, unless he overlooked it, none of the magnets held a note from his daughter.

"What do you mean, she's gone? You were supposed to take care of her!"

He stood erect with a shiver that wasn't entirely from the coolness of the refrigerator door. "I can't get through to her anymore. You know how she's been. Ever since she turned thirteen, it's like talking to a brick wall."

"No, I *don't* know how she's been, remember? I hardly see her anymore."

Suddenly, his frustration got the better of him. Words poured from his mouth before he could stop himself. "And whose fault is that, Natalie? Lissa needs her mother, but you've buried yourself completely in your work for months now. You're the one who hasn't been there for her." *For either of us.*

"Oh, like you are?" Her pain and anger stabbed at him through the phone line. "Lissa's had two working parents since the day she was born. At least I was home in the evenings, not gallivanting all over the countryside with a bunch of smelly middle-school jocks."

The well-aimed barb hurt more than he expected. Clawing stiff fingers through his hair, he caught his harried reflection in the black glass of the microwave door.

"Okay." He spoke slowly, forcing a calm he didn't feel. "So maybe we both have a few things to learn in the parenting department. Can't we just focus on Lissa?"

Natalie didn't speak for several moments. Daniel listened to her rapid breathing. Finally, sounding more rational, she said, "Let me call Dad. Maybe this is a replay of last time."

"I doubt she'd try that again. She knows the farm is the first place we'd look."

"Okay, where do we start?"

He pushed a stack of mail off one of the kitchen chairs and sat down. "Actually, maybe I've jumped the gun. This could be another stunt to get our attention, so maybe we don't need to panic just yet."

"Oh, so now 'we' aren't going to panic, are we?" Natalie's voice again dripped sarcasm. "And why on earth would Lissa think pulling another disappearing act has any chance of getting us back together?"

He wanted to say their getting back together was all Lissa lived and breathed lately, that if Natalie only paid a little more attention, it would be obvious how much Lissa was hurting—how much *he* was hurting.

The silence stretched between them, until Natalie burst out, "So what's the deal, Pearce? Has Mr. Head-Coach-Wannabe been too busy with *his* work to keep up with what's happening in his daughter's life? How many résumés did you send out *this* week?"

He flinched as though she had slapped him. "Stop it, okay? We can fight on our own time. This is about Lissa, not us."

"All right, I'm sorry." Remorse took the biting edge off Natalie's tone. "I just get so crazy when she pulls stunts like this."

"Yeah, me too." He rubbed the spot between his eyebrows and tried to clear his thoughts. "I'll start making the rounds here in Putnam, and you get busy in Fawn Ridge. Between the two of us we can hit all her friends' homes in both towns and any other likely spots where she might hide out."

"I'll make a few calls before I leave for the office."

Daniel felt his restraint slipping again. "Our daughter's missing and you're going in to work?"

"I can't be away from the print shop today. Things are too hectic. I've got to keep up with business."

"Your only *business* right now should be your daughter. Call if you find her. I'll do the same." He slammed down the receiver.

He finished dressing, forgetting about breakfast completely. His chin bore stray stubbly patches and a couple of scrapes from a slapdash rendezvous with his razor. He slid one arm into the sleeve of his red Panthers jacket and grabbed his canvas briefcase from the kitchen table. Juggling his car keys and cell phone, he stormed out the door and took the stairs at a run.

Jamming the Bronco into reverse, he played through all the possible reasons Lissa would choose now to disappear. Had she overheard his phone conversation with Coach Arnell? If so, he could only imagine what might be going through her head. Yeah, she'd hate the idea of having to change schools. Any normal kid would feel that way.

But Daniel's real fear went much deeper. Lissa would never forgive him or Natalie if she so much as suspected her parents' marriage was over.

His jaw muscles bunched. He should never have agreed to the Langston interview in the first place. How could he consider a position in another city when his life was in chaos? It would be insane to make that serious a decision until things were settled between him and Natalie, one way or another.

Whatever happened, he had to be certain Lissa could survive the adjustment. After she ran away last summer, he'd taken her to their pastor several times for counseling. Sometimes it seemed to help—mostly not. At least it kept her talking.

If only Natalie would talk to someone, if only she'd continued attending the stroke survivor meetings with her dad. But he hadn't even seen her at church in months. On top of everything else, had she given up on God?

He'd fought the truth as long as he could; maybe no one could help Natalie but herself. Lissa deserved at least one sane parent who could walk with her through the emotional upheaval of her grandmother's illness and her parents' divorce. With or without Natalie, Daniel had to salvage his family.

Now, if he could only track down his daughter!

Natalie stood under the shower for several long minutes. The hot, needle-like spray nipped at her shoulders while the rising steam enveloped her in a fog as thick as the myriad thoughts wrestling for attention.

Lissa, where are you? What are you up to?

Daniel had to be right. This must be another of Lissa's ploys to reunite them as a family. Natalie still remembered the heartbreak in Lissa's eyes when they first told her they were separating.

Okay, maybe she could have held their marriage together. Maybe she could have tried harder for Lissa's sake. But for so long, it felt as if Daniel didn't even attempt to see her side. Every time she tried to make him understand her feelings about letting Mom down, his eyes would glaze over. If her own husband couldn't deal with her emotions—the man who had taken vows to love her for better or worse, in case he'd forgotten—whom could she trust?

At least Dr. Sirpless hadn't called her crazy or told her to snap out of it. Digging through the debris of her guilt took its toll, but knowing Dr. Sirpless was only a phone call away helped Natalie feel more secure. Dr. Sirpless was the safety net under Natalie's emotional tightrope.

She turned off the shower and wrapped herself in a towel. Much as she hated to admit it, Daniel was right about one thing. She *had* become a workaholic. Working late became a convenient excuse when Dad and Hart pleaded with her to "just drop by" the convalescent home.

"Spend a few minutes with Mom," Hart would beg. "She needs to see you, Rosy. You need to see her."

But she couldn't do it anymore. She couldn't see her mother that way, trapped in the tangled web of a stroke-ravaged brain. Her unspoken prayer for her mother to die peacefully in her sleep only compounded her guilt, making her hate herself even more than she already did. Yet in her desperate attempt to protect herself from more grief, Natalie had shut out everyone she loved.

The beveled edge of the bathroom counter cut into her palms as she stared at her reflection in the mirror. She leaned toward the steam-fogged image. *Oh, God, what am I going to do?* Somehow she had to put in at least twelve hours at the office today, or they'd never catch up by Christmas. The clients they'd worked so hard to gain would take their business back to Putnam.

How could Lissa do this to them again, now of all times? Natalie's complaint echoed accusingly through her mind and brought her up short. How could she be so selfish? How had her priorities gone so far wrong?

While her one-cup coffeemaker spit the strong brew into a black-rimmed travel mug, she vowed to inform Jeff as soon as she got to the office that she would have to put the day's projects on hold until she located her daughter. At the shop, she parked near the rear entrance and had just stepped out of her car when Deannie rushed over.

"Natalie, thank goodness. I tried to catch you at home but you'd already left, and your cell must be turned off."

Natalie snatched the phone from her purse. The screen returned her blank stare. "I guess my battery's dead. What is it, Deannie?" Remembering Lissa, her heart lurched. "Did Daniel call? Did he find Lissa?" She couldn't wait to hug her daughter, and she promised God she would try everything to repair their relationship if Lissa would just come home.

"Uh, no." Deannie gave her a confused look. Her mouth dropped open. "Oh my goodness, is Lissa *missing*? That's *terrible*! Have you called the cops? Did you check with—"

The momentary splash of hope dissipated like the light snowflakes melting on the hood of her car. Natalie laid a gloved hand against the girl's fluttering lips. "It's under control, don't worry. I'm about to make some calls." Her voice carried more assurance than she felt. She locked her car and started toward the building.

Deannie's mincing, high-heeled boots sounded on the pavement behind her. "But what I was going to tell you—it's kind of important too."

What else could possibly go wrong today? Exasperation snatched away what little peace of mind Natalie had reclaimed. She whirled around. "Do you not understand that nothing short of a nuclear attack could take precedence over my missing child?" She wouldn't even think about how long it had taken her to realize this for herself. Then she apologized for snapping. "I'm sorry, Deannie. It's not your fault."

Standing there in only her thin sweater, Deannie shivered and hugged herself. "That's okay. But I've got something important to tell you."

Natalie cast her gaze heavenward. "What?" Moonbeams Bookstore? Eleanor's Flowers?

"It's that lady from Hope Gardens, where your mother is. She wants you to call right away." Deannie held out a crumpled pink message form and made a halfhearted attempt to flatten it.

This was not good. Not good at all. Natalie snatched the note and carried it into her office, where she dropped her shoulder bag on the desk and flung her coat across the chair. She started to dial Hart's clinic number and then remembered he scheduled all his farm and stable visits in the morning. She could call his cell, but he'd asked the family to use it for emergencies only during clinic hours.

That left Dad. But if something were seriously wrong, if Mom had become ill or . . . worse . . .

Natalie felt as if an iceberg had lodged in her core. *Oh, Mom, no!* No matter what guilty thoughts she'd wrestled with, she suddenly realized she'd never be prepared for the news of her mother's death—never be ready for that final good-bye.

Yet if it were true, if Mom had passed away, how could she possibly thrust the burden of discovery upon her father? Hadn't he suffered enough already? It wasn't much and would never make up for all the other mistakes she'd made, but placing this call herself might serve as one small act of redemption.

Lips pressed together, she dialed the number. "Mrs. Blaylock, this is Natalie Pearce. You called?"

"Ms. Pearce, I thought you understood." The administrator's clipped tone set Natalie's teeth on edge. "All items brought to the patients' rooms must be cleared by the nursing staff."

Relief flooded Natalie in the brief moment before utter confusion set in. She pressed a finger to her temple. "I'm not following you, Mrs. Blaylock. What items are you speaking of?"

"The Christmas gift you left for your mother this morning, of course. She's made quite a mess."

"Excuse me, but I did not visit my mother this morning." Confusion shifted to annoyance. "Besides, you have instructions to call my brother regarding any problems with my mother's care."

"Yes, I understand, but since it was a paint set, I just assumed . . . ." The woman fell silent.

Slowly, Mrs. Blaylock's statement filtered through. A paint set? Natalie pinched the bridge of her nose. Where could a paint set have come from? She had no reason to think Mom was capable of holding a paintbrush again. If there'd been even the slightest hint of improvement, Dad or Hart would have said something. Unless maybe Dad brought Mom the paints in hopes of stimulating some sort of response. But that didn't make sense, either. Natalie had always been the one holding out false hope.

Giving her head a small shake, she returned her attention to the woman on the phone. "Are you telling me someone visited my mother and no one noticed? Aren't visitors supposed to sign in?"

"Well, actually, with everyone occupied with their duties and all . . . " Mrs. Blaylock's embarrassed tone lasted only a moment before she went on the offensive again. "But *someone* came to your mother's room before visiting hours, which is another policy violation, I might add. A nurse found your mother with torn Christmas paper and ribbon in her lap and this watercolor set and artist's sketchbook. She had the paints open and must have tried to use them. She was soaked with water from her bedside pitcher, and she'd smeared paint all over the sheets. Ms. Pearce," continued the flustered Mrs. Blaylock, "we simply cannot have—"

"Wait." Natalie held up a silencing hand as if the other woman could see it. Her voice shook. "My mother tried to *paint*? And you're upset about it? For heaven's sake, Mrs. Blaylock, it's the most encouraging sign we've had that my mother is still in there."

She slammed down the receiver, pushed away from her desk, and began to pace, feeling oddly hopeful for the first time in months.

"Excuse me." Deannie knocked softly on the doorframe.

"What is it, Deannie? This isn't a good time."

"Even to say your husband just called?"

Natalie froze. *Lissa.* "Daniel called? Did he leave a message?"

Deannie chewed her lip as if replaying the call in her head. "He said not to worry. Lissa's at school, and everything's okay." Then the usually animated assistant fixed Natalie with an enigmatic gaze. "It will be, you know."

Natalie stared in puzzlement. She had to consciously force her jaw shut. "Will be what?"

"Okay. Everything will be okay." Deannie stared at something over Natalie's shoulder. "Lissa painted that landscape, didn't she? Obviously, she inherited your talent." Her mouth twisted in a crooked frown. "I should be so lucky."

Deannie's random remarks always threw her off. Natalie lifted an eyebrow before turning to admire the painting Lissa had done as an art class assignment last year. Yes, her amazing daughter had artistic talent.

Just like I inherited Mom's. An unexpected sense of pride washed over her before regret settled in once more. She hadn't picked up a paintbrush since the day of her mother's stroke.

"Yeah," Deannie said, her tone laced with dejection, "if I'd inherited some of my uncle's business sense, maybe I'd be his partner instead of you." She smiled ethereally and left.

Deannie's comment banished all other thoughts from Natalie's mind, and she could only stare open-mouthed at the empty doorway.

Lissa—the paint set. Of course!

11

*A*n annoyed groan rumbled in Lissa's throat as she used her hip to shove open the heavy glass door of the school office. She glanced in both directions before maneuvering into the stream of students headed toward the main exit—no simple thing with her cumbersome artist's portfolio slapping against her legs. Her art teacher would pick tonight, when Lissa already had tons of homework in other classes, to give a complicated weekend drawing assignment.

Her friend Jody caught up with her on the front steps and grabbed one corner of the portfolio. "Here, let me help."

Lissa puffed out her cheeks, wishing she had a free hand to tug on one of Jody's perky French braids. "Thanks."

She didn't know what she'd do without Jody, whose presence had helped ease Lissa's transfer to Putnam Middle School. The two girls had met in second-grade Sunday school class where their families attended church in Fawn Ridge. They'd been best friends ever since.

Jody nodded over her shoulder toward the school building. "So how much trouble are you in?"

Lissa tipped her gaze toward the slip of blue paper peeking from the side pocket of her purse. It required a parent's signature and had to be returned the next day, or she'd get detention. No big deal, right? And so totally worth it. She gave her head a toss.

"Just another tardy slip. I'm cool."

"With the school, maybe." Jody raised a dark eyebrow. "What about your dad? You were late for first period yesterday too."

"Because I was *talking* to my dad." Lissa grimaced. "I can't believe he missed my note on the fridge this morning. I'm lucky he didn't call out the National Guard. Bad enough Lurking Lattimore nabbed me the second I got here." The students' nickname for the nosy assistant principal couldn't be more fitting, the way he skulked around campus flipping pages in his little notebook. *Get a life, man!*

Jody started down the steps. "When your dad showed up looking for you at my house, I didn't know whether to lie for you or what. And when you weren't in class when the tardy bell rang, I wondered if you really had run away again."

"Run away, are you kidding? My super-dense parents didn't get the message the first time." Reaching the sidewalk, she shifted under the weight of her backpack. "Besides, if I'm not around, who's going to look out for my grandmother? Nobody else has time for her anymore, and those nurses treat her like she's not even a real person."

"How mean! I hope my grandma never has to go to a nursing home."

Lissa bit down hard on her lower lip to keep the tears from spilling over. "Nobody understands, Jody, nobody!"

"Hang in there, Liss, it'll be okay." Jody bumped Lissa's shoulder with her own and beamed a sympathetic smile. "Hey, there's my mom. Call me later, okay?" She helped Lissa get a better grip on the portfolio before releasing it. Walking backward down the sidewalk, she added, "And good luck with your dad."

"Thanks, I'll need it."

Wiping her cheek with her coat sleeve, Lissa scanned the driveway for her father's car. Unless he had a meeting or late practice, he usually pulled around front to pick her up, but today she didn't see the green Bronco anywhere.

"Jody, wait." She trotted after her friend. "I may need to bum a ride with you. Dad must have had a coaches' meeting and forgot to tell me."

Jody slowed and motioned her over. "No problem, if you can handle sitting through my boring piano lesson."

Just then Lissa saw her mother's silver Saturn pull into the drive-through. Chilly fingers of dread tickled her spine. "Never mind. My mom's here."

Jody made a face. "That can't be good."

"Only one way to find out." Lissa waved good-bye to Jody and marched toward her mother's car. She lifted her chin and tried to look as if she couldn't care less, but her insides felt like Jell-O.

Even from five feet away, Lissa could hear Mom's car stereo blasting out a thunderous, heart-pounding symphony. The whole car hummed and thrummed, vibrating the sidewalk beneath Lissa's feet. Yep, definitely bad news. Mom hardly ever tuned to the classical station except when she was really, really upset.

Taking a deep breath, Lissa reached for the door handle. "Mom, what are you doing here?" She had to shout over the music.

Her mother switched off the radio but scarcely looked at her—another bad sign. "I told your dad I wanted to pick you up today. I believe we have a few things to discuss."

"Okay," Lissa said. As she slid her portfolio behind the passenger seat, she purposely swung her hair across her face as a temporary shield against Mom's simmering anger. With a disgruntled huff, she dropped her backpack onto the floorboard and settled into the car. A furtive downward glance revealed a computer disk protruding from the outer pocket of her backpack. Nonchalantly, she tucked it deeper inside and tugged the zipper closed.

She looked up to see her mother glaring at her, brows lifted expectantly. Mom made no move to start the car.

"Wha-at?" Lissa rolled her eyes and fidgeted with the gold metallic clasp on her purse. No way would she come right out and confess about this morning. If Mom suspected anything, she'd have to spell it out.

Mom drummed her fingers on the steering wheel and stared at Lissa.

Lissa made a strangling sound in her throat. "Okay, can we just get this over with? Obviously, you're mad about something."

As if she didn't know what. Dad probably couldn't wait to get Mom on the phone and describe all the juicy details about this morning's little escapade. *Today* he decided he and Mom needed to talk. *Nice, Dad. Real nice.*

Yeah, but talking was talking, right? Lissa slid her right hand down between the seat and passenger door and secretly crossed her fingers. She could survive a whole year of being grounded if it meant getting her parents back together.

Just when she thought the strained silence would suffocate her, Mom finally spoke. "Why would I have anything to be angry about, you may ask. Hmm. How about sneaking out without telling your dad? How about hitchhiking from Putnam to Fawn Ridge and back? How about visiting your grandmother without telling anyone and—"

"First of all, I did not sneak out." Good grief. Adults could be so clueless. She shot her mother an exasperated glare. "I left Dad a note on the refrigerator."

"Oh, like last time?" Mom cocked her head. "How thoughtful of you!"

"I can't help it if he didn't look under the grocery list. And I didn't hitchhike. I bummed a ride from a—" Lissa winced. "From a friend in the high-school youth group." Okay, so maybe she stretched the rules a teensy bit too far with that part. Her parents had stressed to her time and time again never to ride with a teenage driver without their explicit permission.

Mom pressed her lips together. "That issue will be dealt with later. For now, I'd like to hear your explanation about a watercolor set found in your grandmother's room. I caught you-know-what about it from Mrs. Blaylock."

"That witch." The beady-eyed woman gave her the creeps, watching her like she was a criminal every time she visited Grandma, like she'd break a bedpan or something, or run up and down the halls and terrorize the patients, just because she was a kid. She cut her eyes at Mom. "All that lady cares about is bossing people around. She never wants the residents to have any fun."

"From what I hear, the nurse found your grandmother having all kinds of 'fun.'" Moisture filled Mom's eyes. She twisted in her seat and reached across the console to press Lissa's face between her hands. "Honey, you know your grandmother's condition. What on earth were you thinking?"

"Somebody had to do something." Frustration tore at Lissa's heart. She pried her mother's hands away and crossed her arms. Almost under her breath, she added, "Grandma's got to get better by Christmas."

Mom closed her eyes, and Lissa let her thoughts carry her back to that morning. She had arrived at the convalescent center just after six-thirty. She slipped down the deserted corridor and closed the door softly behind her before tip-toeing across the shiny tile floor of her grandmother's room. Grandma appeared to be sleeping, but a soft moaning escaped her balm-moistened lips. Her head rocked gently as if she were dreaming.

"Grandma? Hi, it's me, Lissa." Leaning against the side of the bed, she lightly touched her grandmother's wrinkled hand.

Cloudy eyes flickered open, glanced unseeing for a moment, and then settled on Lissa's face. Something oddly like a smile crooked one corner of Grandma's mouth, and Lissa felt sure that Grandma recognized her.

"Naaaa," her grandmother moaned. Sometimes it seemed like the only sound she could make.

"Lissss-sssa," she enunciated. "Grandma, it's Lisss-sssa. Just try to say it. I know you can."

The lines in Grandma's forehead deepened. "Llllll."

A thrill of hope ignited in Lissa's chest and spread its warm rays down her limbs. "That's right, Grandma, it's Lissa. Hey, I brought you a present." She unzipped her backpack and laid a flat, rectangular package on her grandmother's lap. "Here, let me help you open it."

Grandma's eyes lit up with joy, Lissa felt certain of it. The good hand came around and clutched at the red bow, yanking at it clumsily.

"Good job, Grandma." She loosened a corner of the paper and guided her grandmother's hand to peel it away. She removed the lid from the box and lifted out a sketchbook and an oblong watercolor set in a bronze-colored tin.

"Nnnnaaaa, nnnnaaaaa." Grandma's hands jerked in excited spasms. "Painnnnn."

Lissa's heart soared. "That's right, Grandma, I brought this so you can paint!"

Never once in all the many times she'd visited her grandmother at the nursing home had Lissa seen her so animated. Maybe the drooling, one-sided grimace wouldn't look like a smile to anyone else, but Lissa believed with all her being that Grandma had never been happier or more alive since the day of her stroke. *Oh, thank you, God, thank you!*

A commotion in the corridor snapped Lissa's head around. Every nerve went on high alert. If she didn't leave now, one of the attendants delivering breakfast trays would catch her and report her to Mrs. Blaylock.

"I have to get to school, Grandma, but I'll come this weekend and help you paint something, okay?" She kissed her grandmother on the cheek, edged to the door, and eased it open a crack to peer out. As soon as the two attendants disappeared into another patient's room down the hall, she scurried along a side corridor, through the laundry facility, and out a rear exit, where her high-school friend waited for her in the alley.

Her mission had been a success, which made her want to kick herself for not thinking of it sooner. Why hadn't someone else in the family realized a long time ago that all Grandma needed was to be reminded how to paint again? Mom, of all people, should have thought of it, considering every other crazy therapy she'd made the doctors try. Even if Grandma only recovered a tiny bit by Christmas, it might be enough.

Lissa could only hope the rest of her plans went as smoothly.

Natalie's heart throbbed against her breastbone as she stared through the windshield. With the engine turned off, the December chill quickly permeated the car. She shivered as much from her spinning thoughts as from the cold.

Christmas.

She didn't need Lissa to remind her it was her mother's favorite season of the year. *"You were supposed to be born on Christmas Day, but you came a little early,"* Mom had told her many times. It was the very reason they'd chosen her name. *"'Natalie' means 'the birthday of Christ,' and Christ has been called the 'Rose of Sharon.' So, my darling, you've always been our little Christmas Rose."*

Natalie slowly turned to face her daughter and fought to repress the quiver in her voice. "Sweetheart, you know what the doctors say. How many times have they told us Grandma isn't going to get better?" *Because of me!*

And then that other emotion surfaced, the one Dr. Sirpless made her realize she'd been resisting all these months. She shuddered and stuffed down her anger. It took several deep breaths before she could continue. "Even if Grandma did show some signs of recognition, you mustn't get your hopes up. It might be nothing."

Despite her momentary resurgence of hope after talking to Mrs. Blaylock, as the day wore on and reality set in, she had forced herself back to a state of pragmatism. Now, Lissa must do the same.

Her daughter turned a tear-streaked face toward her. "I don't care what the doctors say," she blurted. "Grandma always told me she promised Granddad they'd have fifty perfect Christmases together. And this is—"

Natalie gasped, her heart sinking. "And this will be the fiftieth Christmas."

How could she have forgotten something so important? Or maybe she hadn't forgotten, just buried it because she couldn't bear the memory. Christmas Eve would be her parents' wedding anniversary, making the next day their fiftieth Christmas as husband and wife. If remembering was hard for her, she could only imagine what a sorrowful, pain-filled Christmas this would be for her father. No wonder he had been trying so hard to keep all those precious family traditions alive.

"So don't you see, Mom? Grandma *has* to get better." Lissa's face contorted. Her voice took on a desperate tone. "She has to paint the star on the manger scene backdrop, the fiftieth little star in the sky over Bethlehem, one for every Christmas she and Granddad have been married. If she doesn't, the promise will be broken, and . . . and . . . " She collapsed into heaving sobs.

In the deepest part of her soul, Natalie understood what her daughter was trying to tell her. If this promise were not kept, this special promise between two people so deeply in love for so many happy years, then nothing was sacred. No vow could be trusted.

As she looked into her daughter's eyes, she realized the promise had as much to do with Natalie and Daniel's future as it did with Lissa's grandmother getting well. How could their marriage vows not mean anything anymore? Didn't they mean *everything* sixteen years ago when she and Daniel pledged their love at the altar? She recalled with convicting clarity the words from Scripture the pastor had read: "For this reason a man will leave his father and mother and be united to his wife, and they will become one flesh. . . . So they are no longer two, but one. Therefore what God has joined together, let man not separate."

Oh, Daniel, I'm so sorry! I've ruined everything, and I don't know how to fix it.

With effort, she finally managed to speak over the lump in her throat. "Honey, I wish with all my heart that things were different. But so much has happened—so much that can't be undone."

Her daughter's voice became harsh. "Just tell me, Mom, are you going to do anything to help Grandma or not?"

Tears coursed down Natalie's cheeks. She shrugged helplessly and drew a resistant Lissa into her embrace. Stroking her daughter's silky hair, she said, "We've done everything possible, Liss. There's nothing else we can do for Grandma. Please try to accept it." She sniffed and searched for some way to bring peace to her tortured little girl and to her own anguished heart.

They held each other for several long minutes before Lissa pulled away and dried her eyes with her coat sleeve. "I need to go home, Mom. I have tons of homework this weekend."

The rebuff stung. Frantic to keep her daughter close for even a moment longer, Natalie thrashed about in her mind for ideas. Something. *Anything.* A fragment of memory from the night of her birthday rose to the surface, and she latched onto it. "Hey, sweetie, I was telling Granddad the other day that you and I haven't gone riding in a while. If you finish your homework tomorrow, we could go out to the farm on Sunday afternoon. You could ride Windy. She misses you, and I know Granddad would enjoy having us visit."

Lissa shrugged. "I may not finish my homework by then."

"Maybe we could do something fun this afternoon. We could stop by that cute boutique you like so much. Would you like a new sweater for the holidays?"

"Can you just take me home now, please?"

The stiff reply dashed the last remnant of Natalie's hopes. She refastened her seatbelt and started the engine.

∽৲৯৲∽

An hour later, still wrapped in disappointment, Natalie parked her car in the employee parking lot behind the print shop. As she shut off the engine, she saw Jeff Garner hoisting boxes into the delivery van and scowling in her direction.

Now what? Why hadn't she followed her instincts? After dropping Lissa at Daniel's apartment, she'd seriously toyed with the idea of taking the rest of the day off. Only the knowledge that she had mounds of projects still waiting convinced her to shrug off the dejection and fall back upon the only thing that had kept her sane this past year—work.

"I thought we were in this together, Natalie." Jeff grunted as he lifted another box. His warm breath puffed small clouds into the crisp winter air. "I can't be responsible for both sides of this partnership. Clients have been phoning you all afternoon."

"Sorry, I had a situation with Lissa."

"So I heard. Glad she's okay." His tone was icy.

Overwhelmed with guilt at disappointing another person, she lowered her gaze and edged toward the door. "Don't worry. I can stay as late as I need to."

"Good thing." His voice resonated with annoyance. "Because I've got family too. I'm afraid you're on your own with this one."

Natalie's heart plummeted. "What do you mean, 'this one'?" Hard work and late hours she could handle. But after spending most of the day stewing over Lissa's little adventure, she was in no frame of mind to deal with another disaster like Mr. Craunauer's.

"Take a look at the box inside the door. It isn't going any-where today." Jeff slammed the rear door of the van and yelled for Alan, the driver.

The young Tom Cruise look-alike strode across the park-ing lot, clipboard in one hand, aviator sunglasses in the other. Natalie almost stumbled as he brushed by her and bumped her arm. Why couldn't Jeff direct his displeasure at Alan just once? How many speeding tickets had the pompous creep racked up, screeching across town in the delivery van like he was piloting a fighter jet?

As Jeff gave Alan last-minute instructions, Natalie stepped inside the building. For long minutes she stared at the box. In black marker across the top she read MOONBEAMS BOOKSTORE HOLIDAY PROMO. And over those words, Jeff's bold scrawl in red: CUSTOMER COMPLAINT—REDO!

Heartsick, she pushed open the lid, revealing twenty-five hundred goldenrod-colored advertising flyers, neatly folded in thirds and banded for mailing. She slipped a flyer from one of the bundles and gingerly unfolded it. At first she didn't see anything wrong. The wording appeared correct, exactly what Miss Fellowes had requested, formatted in the prim English bookstore owner's standard 18-point Tribune, in navy to match the logo—

The logo!

Natalie steadied herself against a worktable. She couldn't—*wouldn't*—have made such a stupid mistake!

The logo for Moonbeams Bookstore had always been the smiling face of the man in the moon, beaming down upon a child sitting cross-legged with an open book in her lap. Natalie had designed the logo herself for Miss Fellowes when the retired school librarian first decided to open her own children's bookstore. In fact, Natalie's design had helped Miss Fellowes decide on the name for her shop. They'd brainstormed several ideas—Sunshine Books for Children, Starlight Dream Shop, Story Time Book Stop—but Miss Fellowes had fallen in love with Natalie's cheery, round man-in-the-moon sketch.

"It's so full of imagination," she bubbled, "mysterious yet inviting."

But here on these flyers, which were supposed to be mailed today in time to announce the January arrival of the latest release by a popular children's author, Natalie didn't see the man in the moon smiling back at her. Instead, she saw one of the earliest design ideas she'd presented to Miss Fellowes, a huge, bright star shining through a window and onto a sleeping child.

Clutching the flyer, Natalie stormed through the shop and slammed open her office door. With flying fingers she typed the password to open the Moonbeams file. She sucked in her breath when she saw the star in the window, exactly as it appeared in the flyer. By some horrible fluke she'd called up the wrong graphic.

"Bummer." Deannie's softly spoken comment startled Natalie half out of her wits.

"Deannie! For heaven's sake!" She slapped a hand against her chest and spun around to see the girl hovering just behind her. "I *wish* you wouldn't do that."

"What a freaky coincidence." Deannie stepped to the side of Natalie's desk. "Miss F just happened by this afternoon. Said she wanted to pay on her account, and why not take a peek at her flyers while she was here?" With a look bordering on self-satisfaction, Deannie drummed her fingertips on her crossed forearms. "Aren't we lucky that she did?"

"Aren't we, though?" A knot of suspicion tightened in Natalie's stomach. Deannie waltzed out of the office as Natalie turned to the computer screen.

Correcting the error was a simple matter of point, click, replace, and resize. Reprinting twenty-five hundred flyers and getting them mailed before the weekend? That was another matter altogether. Once again, Natalie would be eating the costs, and eating her supper out of the snack machine. Once they got through the hectic Christmas rush, she wouldn't be surprised if Jeff decided to dissolve their partnership. Maybe Deannie's dream of going into business with her uncle would become a reality after all.

Natalie chewed her lip, her gaze locked on the empty doorway through which Deannie had just disappeared. *No. It couldn't be. She wouldn't.*

Suspicious as these misprint "accidents" appeared, Natalie couldn't dwell on them right now. She needed to fix the problem. Leaving Deannie out of the loop, she printed out a fresh proof copy of the flyer and had five other staff members verify her corrections—something she thought she'd done the first time around, something she insisted upon with every piece of copy before getting final customer approval and releasing it for printing. There had to be a weak link in her proofreading process. Later, when things settled down, she'd dig out the originals and determine who had signed off on these blunders.

At four forty-five she phoned Miss Fellowes. "All I can do is apologize profusely," she began. "I have a corrected copy ready if you'd like to okay it before we do the print run. I'd be happy to run it by the shop."

"Oh, heavens, no, dear." Miss Fellowes's clipped English accent remained as crisp as ever, even after more than thirty years in the States. "I trust you've taken care of the problem satisfactorily. It was an honest mistake, I'm sure."

Getting chewed out, she could handle. Losing a customer, she could survive. But the one thing she hadn't expected, and suddenly couldn't deal with, was forgiveness. Natalie's chest caved and hot tears welled. "Oh, Miss Fellowes . . . "

"Why, for goodness' sake, it's just a silly advertisement." She said it in the British way, ad-*ver*-tiss-ment. "It's not the end of the world, my dear. You mustn't be so hard on yourself."

"It's just . . . I can't seem to do anything right lately." She reached for a tissue and blew her nose. "Sorry, I didn't mean to break down like that. This isn't your problem."

"Nonsense. I'm sure releasing your frustrations is just what you needed. My dear, I have always firmly believed in divine intervention. Our Heavenly Father always manages to coax us into doing exactly what's best for us, or places us right where we need to be, even if it doesn't make any sense at all at the time."

Miss Fellowes's words didn't make much sense to Natalie, but she thanked the woman for being so understanding and said good-bye.

Divine intervention? Hard to see how not one but two costly printing mistakes could have anything to do with God's purposes. Hard to see how *anything* in Natalie's life these days could possibly be God's will.

12

*D*aniel struggled to keep his mind on the basketball game. Putnam was down 54-22, with less than two minutes remaining in the first half. The varsity's best players had been missing rebounds and throwing away passes like third-string benchwarmers.

"Pearce, wake up, will you?" Carl Moreno's red polo shirt bearing the Putnam Panthers emblem strained across his husky torso. "I put you in charge of the defensive squad for a reason. Now earn your keep." At a referee's whistle, he shot Daniel a warning glance and returned his attention to the basketball court, where another foul had been called on a Putnam player.

Daniel clenched his jaw. Even if he deserved the comment, it stung his pride to be called on the carpet by the head coach. Worse, he hated himself for disappointing his best friend. Carl had cut him too much slack already.

With a determined frown, Daniel focused his attention on the referee's call and checked his roster. Simms already had three fouls. The gangling six-feet-four eighth grader was their best rebounder. Better sit him out for now. He signaled the sweat-drenched boy to the sidelines and nudged the backup guard. "Petrie, you're in."

The team had closed the scoring gap by a mere three points when a blaring horn ended the half. Daniel hustled his squad into the locker room, gave them a chance to gulp their sports drinks, towel off, and then settled them down to review strategy for the second half.

"I can't win the game for you." He smacked a fist against his clipboard. "You know what your job is—keep the other team from scoring. We've practiced the plays a thousand times. You *know* what to do. Now get out there and do it."

Coach Moreno covered the plays for the offense and chewed out the team for letting their opponents get so far ahead. Following a boisterous team yell, he dismissed them to warm up for the second half.

As Daniel marched out behind the players, Carl caught his arm. "You've been zoned out all night, man, even worse than usual." His knowing smile morphed into a probing stare. "Got something you want to tell me, friend to friend?"

"Family problems. What else?" Daniel released a heartless chuckle and raked a hand through his hair. "I know I shouldn't let this stuff get in the way of my job, but lately things have been pretty tense."

Carl sputtered a sardonic laugh. "Family problems. What a relief! I was afraid you were trying to figure out how to tell me you got offered a job somewhere else." He slapped Daniel on the back and headed out to the court.

Daniel grimaced, his earlier guilt surging back with a vengeance. After Lissa's stunt this morning, he'd fully intended to call Coach Arnell and cancel the Langston interview. No way he could even think about making a move like that when his family was crumbling into ruin at his feet. But the day had gotten away from him, and Arnell would expect him to show up on time tomorrow. And now after Carl's comment, he realized breaking that kind of news to his friend and mentor would be almost as hard as telling his own wife and daughter.

The game finally ended as a loss, but at least not the walk-over it started out to be. As they trekked out to their cars through lightly falling snow, Carl flicked his sweat-dampened face towel at Daniel's arm. "Hey, bud, join me for a burger?" Since both were usually too keyed up to eat a decent meal before a game, grabbing something afterward had become a regular habit.

"Sure." Daniel fished the Bronco keys out of his pocket. "The usual place?"

Carl's pickup beeped twice as he punched his remote. "Where else? Meet you there in ten minutes."

They settled into a corner booth in Casey's Diner, each ordering a double cheeseburger with the works. Carl ate with gusto, but after a few bites Daniel pushed his plate aside. He could already feel the rumbles of indigestion, an increasingly regular side effect of the stress he'd been under this year.

Carl took a long swig from his mug of decaf. "Keep this up and you're going to shrivel up to nothing. Baching it does not agree with you, my man."

"You get no argument from me." Daniel picked up a greasy French fry and swirled it through a blob of ketchup. He bit into it and chewed thoughtfully. "Parenting a teenager isn't agreeing with me, either."

"Aha, now we get to the meat of the matter." Carl dipped the corner of his napkin into his water glass and dabbed at a mustard stain on his red shirt. "So what's Lissa up to these days?"

"Oh, sneaking out of the apartment before breakfast, being late for school, the usual." He filled Carl in on the details of Lissa's early-morning venture to the nursing home. "Natalie insisted on picking her up from school, so I decided to keep my distance and stay at the gym until game time."

"I get you." Carl gave him a knowing wink. He and Marie were raising two teenagers of their own. "No fair doubling up on the kid, since I'm sure her mom already let her have it with both barrels."

"Exactly. But I'd love to have been a fly on the windshield listening to that conversation." He took a swallow of iced tea before bracing his forearms on the edge of the table. Coach Arnell's phone call still lay between them, and he might as well get it out in the open. "Carl, there's something else. You weren't that far off base earlier when you made that joke about me getting another coaching job."

"Oh, man . . . " Carl collapsed against the green vinyl seat. "Where?"

Daniel waved a hand. "Nothing's official yet." He paused and inhaled a bracing breath. "Langston High is looking for a new assistant basketball coach for next fall. Dave Arnell wants me to drive over tomorrow for an interview."

His friend gave a low whistle. "This could be your big break. Arnell's not far from retirement."

"Don't think I haven't considered those points. But now that I've had a chance to let the idea sink in . . . I don't know if I could do that to Lissa. She's so messed up these days." Like he wasn't. He lowered his head and plucked at a piece of torn cuticle on his left thumb. "And it would mean a final break between me and Natalie. I'm not sure I'm ready to make our separation permanent. In fact"—his eyes stung—"I *know* I'm not ready."

"I hear you, man," Carl said softly. "I hear you."

The next morning, Daniel poured himself a cup of strong coffee and plopped into his recliner with the cordless phone. One quick call and he could cancel the appointment with Dave Arnell.

But what else are you going to do with another lonely Saturday? No games scheduled this weekend. Lissa had already made plans to spend the day with Jody. As for Natalie . . . *Don't go there.*

Okay, if nothing else, he at least owed Arnell the courtesy of showing up. Besides, he might as well keep his options open . . . for the time being, anyway. If things did finally come to a head with Natalie and she pressed the divorce issue, maybe putting a little more distance between them would be the best thing after all, for Lissa's sake as much as for theirs.

He only hoped his daughter would eventually come around and forgive them both, whichever one she decided to live with permanently—another aspect of divorce that shook Daniel to his core. On top of everything else, how could he bear it if he moved hundreds of miles away and Lissa chose to stay with Natalie? The last thing he wanted to be—not counting being divorced—was an absent, uninvolved father.

His immediate problem, however, was explaining this little day trip to Lissa. Yeah, he could just drive up to Langston and not tell her. But what if she had an emergency? Even if she reached him on his cell, he'd be a good four hours away. He definitely wasn't ready to tell her about the interview, so he'd have to come up with a believable excuse.

"Hey, Liss." He tapped on her partially open bedroom door.

Still tucked under the covers, she gave a sleepy yawn. "What time is it?"

"Just after seven. I forgot to tell you last night, but we need to get an early start. I'm scouting teams for a basketball tournament." It wasn't a complete fabrication; he intended to stop for a few minutes in Carsonville on the way home, where he'd seen in the paper that the middle-school team had a home game.

"Ugh. Jody probably isn't even up yet. Half the world probably isn't up yet." She stumbled to the bathroom and slammed the door. Over running water she yelled, "And what's with the khakis and blazer? You never dress up for scouting trips. You look like you're going to a funeral or something."

He banged his head softly on the wall opposite the door. *Might as well be.*

When he left her at Jody's half an hour later, the suspicious look in her eyes made him wonder if she'd already guessed the truth about his call Thursday evening. After all, she'd been the one to pick up the phone. How long did she listen in before hanging up?

He thumped the steering wheel. Nothing he could do about it now. And no point in agonizing over his daughter's reaction until—or rather, *unless*—the Langston coaching position became a reality.

Four hours later, the Langston city limit sign came into view. He stopped on the edge of town for a submarine sandwich, but by then his nerves were so shot that he barely finished half of it before he tossed the remains in the trash. Back in the Bronco, he rummaged through the glove compartment for his stash of Tums and scarfed down a handful.

He arrived at the high school ten minutes ahead of his one o'clock appointment. The parking lot was deserted, except for a couple of school district maintenance vehicles and a shiny crimson Ford Explorer parked near the side entrance to the gym. He pulled up next to the Ford, swallowed a couple more Tums for good measure, and found his way along a shadowy corridor to Coach Arnell's office.

A lanky, graying man with a butch haircut rose and greeted him with a handshake.

"Coach Pearce? Dave Arnell." He had to be a good six-feet-eight, with a grip like a grizzly bear and fingers long enough to palm a regulation basketball. "Welcome. Have a seat."

Daniel settled into a maroon vinyl chair, its coolness seeping through his khakis. "I appreciate the chance to talk with you and find out more about the opportunities at Langston."

"Well, I hope you'll find them agreeable, because from what I've seen in your résumé here"—he tapped a crisp, white sheet of paper attached to a manila folder—"your qualifications would fit in beautifully at Langston."

The words lit a fire in Daniel's belly. Forgetting everything but his lifelong coaching aspirations, he listened avidly as Arnell described the responsibilities of the job and possible compensation levels. Each enticing detail fanned the flames of Daniel's enthusiasm even higher.

Arnell folded his hands atop his desk. "How's it sounding so far?"

"Good. Real good." Better than he'd even imagined. He did his best to keep a silly schoolboy grin from taking over his face.

Next, Arnell fired some questions at Daniel about his coaching philosophy and background. But when he got around to the subject of future goals, Daniel's excitement fizzled like a dowsed campfire.

"Future goals?" He gave a heartless laugh. "Whew. I thought I knew, but lately I'm not as certain."

"That's not exactly the answer I was hoping for." Arnell shot him a dubious frown. "You know, being the right man in the right place at the right time, you could find yourself in a very sweet position here in another four or five years."

Daniel immediately caught his meaning and sat up straighter. "Yes, sir, don't think that possibility hasn't crossed my mind. It's just that I have some family concerns I need to resolve before I can come to a decision."

Arnell swiveled his chair sideways. "Anything you'd care to talk about?"

Daniel wondered how much he should say to someone he barely knew, but the man had been up front with him in every respect. He owed him the courtesy of an honest answer. Taking a long, steadying breath, he bent forward, hands clasped between his knees. "My wife and I separated a few months ago. Our teenage daughter is taking it pretty hard."

Brooding eyes met his, and a look of understanding passed between them. "Been there myself. Coaching is tough on a marriage. Takes a lot of work on both sides to keep things running smoothly."

Daniel reached for the Langston High School pamphlet he'd been browsing through and riffled the pages. "I'm afraid it's a lot more complicated than that."

Arnell's gruff voice grew soft with concern. "Only you can say when it's time to throw in the towel. But think long and hard about it, because that decision isn't easily undone."

He started to blurt out, "You think I don't know that?" Then he realized maybe he'd kept this interview appointment for the very reason that the job might just provide an easy way out of a hopeless situation. Yeah, he desperately wanted Natalie to come back to him and Lissa so they could get on with their lives.

But on whose terms? Arnell hit the nail on the head—marriage meant compromise. When it came right down to it, how much was Daniel really willing to give to make his marriage work? How much of its failure could he blame on himself?

"I guess I still have a lot to sort out," he said at last. "Sorry if I wasted your time."

"Never a waste of time shooting the breeze with another fine coach." Arnell leaned forward, his mouth flattened into an apologetic frown. "Unfortunately, the administration's on my case to hurry this thing along, so I'll need an answer pretty quick. I just learned yesterday that Coach Baker has pushed up his retirement to March 1. Health reasons, I understand. We need to name his replacement ASAP so we can work on a smooth transition for next fall."

He reached for the yellow legal pad on which he'd been taking notes and perused Daniel's résumé once more. "Don't mean to pressure you, Pearce, but everything I've seen and heard so far tells me you're the man."

Daniel rubbed a hand across his upper lip, slick with nervous perspiration. Another opportunity this good might never come his way again. His dream job finally lay within reach, and all he had to do was say yes.

He twisted his wedding band. His stomach churned with indecision. "How much time can you give me?"

Arnell's brow furrowed. "End of January. That's the best I can do."

Daniel nodded thoughtfully as he contemplated what might be the most difficult decision he'd ever faced. He could say yes today and probably admit defeat where his marriage was concerned.

Or he could risk everything to stay and fight for Natalie.

He'd never felt more confused.

God, help me! It was the only prayer he had left.

13

Natalie shoved away from her desk, every muscle in her neck and shoulders screaming. Her right wrist tingled with the ominous early-warning signs of carpal tunnel syndrome. The nagging headache reminded her she hadn't taken a lunch break. She used to look forward to Saturdays, kicking back with coffee and the newspaper, or swaying to her favorite music on the stereo while she captured on canvas the colors of a sunset over the mountains or a forest canopy of autumn leaves, or even leisurely afternoon walks around the town square, which usually ended at Carla's Confections. Lissa always ordered a huge banana split, while she and Daniel—

Natalie cupped her palms at the sides of her head and gave a shudder. Thoughts like those were dangerous. Thoughts like those were exactly why she kept herself so busy and why she now worked on Saturday.

Lately, though, even long hours and hard work didn't keep the thoughts at bay. Images of Daniel floated in and out of her consciousness with unnerving regularity.

It had to be the Christmas season stirring up all these old longings. They would pass. They had to. One more thing to talk out with Dr. Sirpless on her next visit.

She shook out her wrist before hitting the intercom button to summon Deannie.

Less than a minute later the overgrown teenybopper flounced into Natalie's office. "Present and accounted for, Your Highness." She fired off a crisp salute.

Natalie scooped up the last batch of proofs she'd printed out. "Don't forget: five proofreaders, with initials. Then phone the clients first thing Monday morning about approving the final copy."

Deannie gave her the thumbs-up sign. "Gotcha."

Natalie logged off the computer. "Okay, I'm shutting down and going home."

"I'll be right behind you, soon as I take care of this stuff. Have an absolutely fabulous weekend, okay?"

"Right." Sliding her arms into her coat, Natalie muttered, "If no more weird mistakes turn up, it most certainly will be fabulous."

In the rear parking lot, she settled behind the wheel of her car and sank back in exhaustion. By all appearances, Deannie still had enough energy for a hot date and partying all night with her friends. For Natalie, those days were long gone. Even before she'd become a certified workaholic, she could barely remember having the kind of stamina required to work all week and play all weekend.

Weekend. What a misnomer. A measly thirty-six hours at most, from clocking out Saturday evening until she had to show up for work on Monday morning. It hardly seemed worth taking a break. Besides, she could really use an extra work day to get ahead of the Christmas rush. But Jeff remained adamant that absolutely no one on their staff would work on Sundays, no matter how far behind they were.

Okay, she had to admit that a day away from work might actually be good for her. It couldn't hurt to relax a little and put the strain of the past week out of her mind. What that "something" might be, she had yet to determine. Of course, Sunday morning would find Jeff and his family—and just about everyone else in town—at church. Worship used to mean a lot to Natalie, too, before her mother had a stroke and her marriage began to collapse. For a long time after her mother's debilitating illness, she had tried to attend for her father's sake, if nothing else, but after the separation she couldn't bear the awkwardness of running into Daniel.

A horn blared behind her, and she realized she'd just sat through a green light. Gunning the engine, she sped through the intersection under a yellow light that turned red before the guy behind her could make it through. The sounds of his repeated blasts died away only after she turned at the next corner.

Yes, she definitely needed some downtime. No Mr. Craunauer, no Deannie, no accusatory looks from Jeff about her recent blunders and where their business was headed. No agonizing over her marriage or her daughter if she could help it. She'd run out of strength to cope with it all. The Christmas season closed in on her like a rapidly narrowing tunnel with barely a glimmer of light at the end. All she could think about was surviving this hectic, memory-laden holiday with at least a few shreds of her sanity intact.

Halfway home, she remembered her cupboard was bare and made a quick stop at the supermarket. Browsing the frozen-food section, she decided to pamper herself tonight with a microwave lasagna dinner and a prepackaged spinach salad with pecans and cranberries. She even splurged on a single-serving frozen key lime pie.

Dusk faded to darkness and a light snow had begun to fall by the time she pulled into her covered parking space next to the apartment building. She tucked her groceries under one arm and pushed the car door shut with her hip. The smell of wood smoke drifted from neighborhood fireplaces. She could see it rising against the low clouds, aglow with reflected city lights. Several of her neighbors had strung icicle lights along their balconies or rooflines. Others had draped twinkling multicolored lights around shrubs and trees. In the commons area, bright spotlights shone on a life-size Santa scene, complete with plastic reindeer, sleigh, and elves.

Everywhere she went, she couldn't escape Christmas. *Oh, Mom, this was your season. I miss you so much.*

For a blissful moment she gave in to a flood of memories, allowing them to transport her back through happy scenes of her childhood—all those special Christmas mornings with Mom and Dad and Hart. She tilted her head and opened her mouth, catching snowflakes and savoring their quickly vanishing tingle on her tongue. At that brief moment, she felt giddy, light, free—

"Mom, what are you doing?"

At the sound of Lissa's voice, Natalie jerked around, the blissful memories dissipating like smoke on the breeze. It took a moment before her vision cleared enough to see Lissa standing at the end of the sidewalk. Daniel waited just behind her, a stupid half-grin on his face.

Natalie's cheeks flamed. "I . . . I . . . What are you doing here?"

Daniel's grin changed to a look of confusion. "You weren't expecting us? Tomorrow *is* your Sunday to spend with Lissa—or do I have my weekends mixed up?"

Guilt tore through Natalie's chest like an ice cube swallowed whole. "Oh, Lissa, I was so busy at work that I completely forgot."

Her daughter's expression crumbled. "Let's go, Dad." She spun around and stomped toward Daniel's Bronco. "I told you Mom didn't really want me over this weekend."

"Wait." Natalie took mincing steps toward her daughter. "Lissa, it's not what you think. It's been a terrible week. Our plans just slipped my mind, that's all." She cast Lissa a pleading look. "And after the way things ended yesterday, I . . . well . . . I wasn't sure you'd even be speaking to me."

"It's always about you, isn't it?" Lissa lifted her chin, and Natalie could see how hard she worked to keep it from trembling. "Don't you think Dad has a life too? He might have a *date* or something tomorrow and need me out of his hair."

Daniel looked askance at his daughter and chuckled nervously. "She's kidding, of course. Seriously, if the timing is bad, we can reschedule for next weekend."

"No, please, it's okay." How had Natalie grown so busy and preoccupied that weekends with Lissa could be forgotten so easily? This was her *daughter*, for crying out loud. She stepped close enough to lay a hand on Lissa's crossed arms. "Honey, please stay. I was just going to make myself some supper. We can—" Glancing at her small bag of groceries, she realized she didn't have enough for two. She shifted the bag to her other arm. "Hey, you don't want to eat my cooking anyway. Why don't we go out for pizza or burgers or something?"

Lissa hesitated. Her eyes narrowed. "Dad too?"

Daniel shuffled his feet. "Uh, Lissa, I don't think that's fair to your mom."

Natalie bit down her sudden apprehension. She wouldn't for anything add another brick to the already monstrous wall between her and Lissa. "No, it's okay. We can all go together, if that's what you want." She hoped the darkness hid the tremor that rippled through her. "Just give me a minute to put these things in the fridge."

She rushed upstairs to her apartment, nearly dropping the keys in her fumbling attempt to get the door open. Kicking it closed behind her, she stood in the small entryway for three full seconds trying to figure out a way out of this mess. She took several slow breaths. *Just dinner. Right?*

She shoved the whole grocery bag into the freezer and scurried to the bathroom for a quick check of her makeup. A dab of powder to cut the shine on her nose, a coat of lipstick on her winter-chapped lips, a futile attempt to refresh her wilted hairstyle.

She stopped, suddenly, and frowned at her reflection. "Get a grip, woman. This is *not* a date. You don't have to impress anyone."

With a shudder, she grabbed her purse from the kitchen counter and started downstairs. In the parking lot, Daniel had warmed up the aging Bronco. Lissa sat in the back seat.

"Where to?" Daniel asked as Natalie took the front passenger seat. He looked as nervous as she felt.

She chewed her lip. Sitting this close to him, how was she supposed to concentrate on anything except maintaining her equilibrium? She could feel the squeak forming in her voice before she even opened her mouth. "Anything's fine. You choose."

Daniel drummed his fingers on the steering wheel. "There's the Saigon Buffet, or we could try that new place in Putnam— Madge's something-or-other."

"Madge's Taste of Home." Brightly lit. Quick service. Natalie jumped on the idea like a frog on a bug. "I heard it's pretty good. Let's go."

"Hey, wait." Lissa leaned between the seats. "I feel like Italian, don't you guys? Let's go to Adamo's."

"But, Liss," Daniel said, glancing over his shoulder, "you and I just ate there last—"

"Oh, so what? It's my favorite restaurant. What do you say, Mom?"

Natalie felt the blood drain from her face, while Lissa fairly glowed with anticipation. Adamo's, a small, family-owned restaurant halfway between Fawn Ridge and Putnam, used to be Natalie and Daniel's favorite spot . . . and no secret to their scheming daughter.

Daniel faced forward and shrugged. "It's up to you, Natalie."

"Well, if Lissa has her heart set on it."

After all, it was just dinner. *Just dinner*—that would be her mantra for the rest of the evening.

But sitting so close to Daniel again, she found herself engulfed by memories and had to suppress a shiver. Her glance took in the strong lines of his profile. Her nostrils filled with the achingly familiar smell of his favorite suede jacket. Unwillingly, she let her gaze drift to his sturdy right hand as it rested on the gear shift. How small a reach it would be to touch him, to rest her head against his shoulder, to breathe in the masculine scent of his cologne.

Oh, Daniel . . .

Suppressing a moan, she looked away. It was over between them. As much as she wanted things to be different, she had to face the truth. Her life remained in shambles, and until— if ever—she found her way back to wholeness, she was sure to bring only pain to the people she loved. Wedding vows or not, God couldn't possibly want them to hang on when all they did was hurt each other. Wouldn't it be better in the long run for Daniel to move on? Better for Lissa if her parents kept their distance from each other? Why should their problems wound her more than they had already?

Natalie tucked clenched fists firmly in her lap. She'd agreed to this "family" dinner far too hurriedly. *Lissa, sweetheart, please don't get the wrong idea.*

But the starry-eyed look she'd glimpsed in her daughter's eyes told her it was already too late. The best Natalie could hope for now was to remain pleasant but detached. Surely, Daniel would cooperate and not feed Lissa's fantasies. Later, when they could arrange some time alone, they'd have a serious discussion about how best to help their daughter accept the inevitable.

But all the rational thinking in the world could not prepare Natalie for the barrage of emotions that hit her the moment they stepped inside Adamo's. The romantic ambience enveloped her with all the subtlety of a sentimental Valentine's Day card. If not for the promises she had just made to herself on the drive over, she could almost believe the whole last year had never happened.

A mustachioed host recognized them immediately. With frequent nods and bows, he cheerily escorted them through the dining room. Weaving through the tables, they passed several acquaintances—Pastor Mayer and his family, Maeve Lindon from the bakery, even Alan, the speed-demon delivery driver from the print shop, who had a curly-haired blonde snuggled next to him in a shadowy booth. Considering the rural community they lived in, Natalie shouldn't have been surprised to run into people she knew, but it was one more thing she'd failed to take into account. She pasted on her most nonchalant smile and tried to ignore both their questioning stares and the nervous embarrassment curdling her stomach. She could only imagine the rumors that would fly around church tomorrow . . . and the office on Monday.

At a small table in a quiet corner, the host pulled out a chair for her, while Daniel played the gentleman for Lissa. A shaft of moonlight angled through the beveled-glass windows and mingled with the yellow-white glow of a small oil lamp in the center of the immaculate tablecloth.

"Your menus." With dramatic flourish, their server flipped open burgundy leather folders in front of each of them. "We also have a special tonight, Chef Valerio's rigatoni Siciliani, a sumptuous blend of shrimp, calamari, and crab in a savory marinara sauce. May I bring you something to drink while you decide?"

Natalie eyed the wine list, sorely tempted. "Just water for me, please. Lissa, do you want a soft drink?"

Lissa ordered a lemon-lime soda, and Daniel asked for a glass of iced tea. When the server returned with their drinks, Natalie still hadn't decided what to have. Everything here tasted wonderful. Remembering what she'd just stuffed into her freezer at home, she stifled a laugh. Frozen lasagna and prepackaged key lime pie—*pampering? Get a life, Natalie!*

"Have you made your selection, miss?" The server angled his raven head toward Lissa and shot her a rakish grin. Only then did Natalie take note of his youthful good looks. The kid couldn't be much more than twenty.

Yikes. With Lissa's hair clipped up behind one ear and dipping glamorously across the other eye—and especially in this lighting—she could easily pass for sixteen or even older.

"I'd like the manicotti." Lissa smiled at the server, a flirtatious sparkle in her eye. "With a small Greek salad and your crusty garlic bread."

Natalie tightened her grip on the menu and resisted the urge to kick her daughter in the shin. Add one more item to the long list of issues she already needed to cover with Daniel: *No dating for Lissa until she graduates from college!*

When the server finally tore his Valentino eyes off Lissa and turned to Natalie, she was still too flustered to think straight. She cleared her throat and buried her face in the menu. "You go ahead, Daniel."

He went with the chef's special, and Natalie finally settled on the lasagna Fabiana, a uniquely delicious creation by the restaurant owner's wife. That bland brick of Lean Cuisine could wait. Adamo's lasagna beat the frozen stuff by light-years.

"Excellent choices." The server gave Natalie a curt nod before angling another seductive gaze at Lissa. "I will return with your salads shortly."

Daniel lifted his tea glass and smiled at Natalie. "This was a good idea. Better than hamburgers, that's for sure." The tension around his eyes belied the light tone of his voice.

The business of ordering taken care of, Natalie found herself struggling to maintain her composure. It was hard enough making eye contact with the man across the table. Instead, she fiddled with the ornately folded napkin propped in the center of her place setting. "Haven't been here in ages, at least not for a meal."

"Lissa and I have come a few times." Daniel cleared his throat. He glanced around and toyed with his salad fork. "Not often, though."

"I helped design their new menus." The bright, boastful tone in Natalie's voice surprised her. She certainly hadn't intended to brag about it . . . just couldn't think of anything else to say.

"Really?" Daniel's attention returned to her, his eyes softening. "I'll have to take a closer look at one before we leave."

"Mom did a super job." A Cheshire-cat grin lit Lissa's face. "She is the most amazing graphic artist."

Daniel smiled across the table. "Indeed she is."

Natalie lowered her gaze as heat shot through her chest. It came as a shock that Lissa even knew of the work she'd done for Adamo's. Perhaps her daughter hadn't drifted as far out of touch as she feared. She had to find a way to spend more time with her—certainly after the holiday rush passed. And she'd have to reconsider inviting Lissa out to ride. Maybe tomorrow she could talk her into it.

An awkward silence ensued until their salads arrived. Natalie ate hers slowly and deliberately, hoping to forestall further conversation. It helped that Daniel didn't show much interest in talking either, which surprised her because he usually had plenty to say about the way she ran her life.

Okay, okay, she had to admit she'd done her fair share of ragging on him. Maybe the silence was a good sign, an indication they were both ready to cool it and start a new phase of their relationship. It would be so much easier if the end of their marriage didn't result in the permanent loss of the lively friendship they once treasured.

After dinner, feeling mellow and more content than she had in months, Natalie pushed away from the table and released a satisfied moan. "My goodness, I'm stuffed."

"Oh, Mom, you've *got* to have dessert." Lissa reached for the small dessert menu tucked beneath a vase of fragrant pink roses.

Natalie laid a hand on her stomach, which pressed painfully against the waistband of her slacks. "Not possible. I couldn't force down one more bite."

"At least have a cappuccino with me." Daniel signaled the server.

The flirting waiter was not to be deterred. Gaze locked with Lissa's, his accent heavy on the Italiano, he said, "But your dining experience would be grievously incomplete without at least a small serving of Adamo's world-famous tiramisu."

Natalie doubted the guy even knew what the word *grievously* meant. In fact, she seriously doubted he was even Italian. Maybe she should order dessert just to get the guy to go away and take his leering eyes off Lissa.

She slapped her hand on the table. "Okay, you talked us into it. But just one, with three forks."

It turned out to be the richest melt-in-your-mouth tiramisu Natalie had ever tasted—even better than she remembered. As they lingered over their decaf cappuccinos and a hot chocolate for Lissa, Natalie succumbed to another stream of memories—other evenings with Daniel . . . long-ago times of courtship and sharing dreams and heart-to-heart talks. Each moment shimmered in and out of focus like the frames of a treasured home movie.

In the flickering lamplight, she caught the hopeful sparkle in Lissa's blue eyes as her gaze danced back and forth between her parents. A sad emptiness crept into Natalie's heart, edging out the sweet recollections. She stiffened. She couldn't let this fantasy continue.

"It's late. We should be going." Crumpling her napkin beside her cup and saucer, she scanned the dining area for their server. When she caught his attention, she signaled for the bill and twisted around to retrieve her shoulder bag from the back of her chair.

"My treat." Daniel placed a restraining hand on her arm.

Warmth shot through her at his touch. She closed her mind to the sensation, the memories. "No, I insist. Separate checks, please." Nervously, she rummaged through her purse. "And I'll get Lissa's."

"Put your money away." Daniel cocked his hip to retrieve his wallet. "I said it's my treat."

"And I said no. I can pay my own way."

She should have known the pleasant evening was too good to last. After a record two hours of civility, they'd resorted to the inevitable arguing. Fingers taut with rage, she pulled out some cash and shoved it at Daniel. "Here, this should cover it."

As the server handed Daniel the bill, Mr. Adamo, the owner, sauntered over. "Good evening. So glad to see you and your family, Mrs. Pearce." He gave a slight bow. "I wanted to personally thank you for your delightfully creative talents in designing our new menu. Everyone agrees, it is absolutely exquisite."

Natalie shoved the anger to another part of her brain and gave Mr. Adamo a self-conscious smile. "I'm so glad you're happy with my work. It's always a pleasure doing business with you."

A thoughtful look came over the man's face. He chuckled softly. "The horse and rider, an amazing touch of inspiration for the watermark. How did you know?"

Natalie gave him a blank stare. "Horse and rider?"

"Yes. In the Old Country my family raised horses. We were very proud of our championship bloodlines. I was once a skilled rider myself and even came close to qualifying for the Olympics."

Lissa's jaw dropped. "That's wild. I had no idea."

Mr. Adamo lifted his hands and shrugged. "Of course, it was so long ago that I did not think anyone here even knew of it."

An eerie sense of doom tightened the muscles behind Natalie's skull. "May . . . may I see one of your menus again?"

"But of course." Mr. Adamo snatched one from the hands of a server on his way through the dining room. He held the burgundy folder to the light, opening it to show Natalie the inside cover.

Her mouth fell open in stunned shock. She couldn't believe she hadn't noticed it right away. On the other hand, she'd been entirely focused on making it through the evening with Daniel without losing what little composure she'd managed to cling to.

Now she saw it clearly: the profile of a dressage rider on his stately Hanoverian mount, a full-page maroon watermark on a parchment background.

"Striking, isn't it?" Mr. Adamo peered over her shoulder.

"Um-hmm." Natalie almost choked.

She knew with absolute certainty she'd used a grape-arbor graphic for the watermark, exactly as Mr. Adamo had requested. She wasn't sure she could survive until Monday to check her computer files. Either she had gone completely crazy, or someone had been breaking into her computer and redoing the copy before Jeff received it for printing.

But how? Not even Jeff or Deannie had password access to her computer. She'd developed a unique system for file security and never wrote down her passwords.

If she ruled out the likelihood of a computer break-in, losing her mind was the only other explanation, and the way she felt, it seemed a distinct possibility. At least this time the client was pleased with the "mistake."

Horses, paintbrushes, watercolors, her mother—the images intertwined in Natalie's mind like tangled Christmas-tree lights as Daniel drove to her apartment.

I've been working too hard—way too hard.

She made up her mind to shove the printing business and all the bizarre errors aside . . . at least for one day. Tomorrow she and Lissa would do something fun together. If Lissa wasn't interested in horseback riding, then they'd go to a movie or drive up the highway to the regional shopping mall. The outing would do them both good and give them a much-needed opportunity to reconnect.

Thoughts of riding brought to mind the therapeutic riding center and Natalie's indecision about donating Windy to the program. The idea of giving away her precious mare raised a lump in her throat, but she knew it was for the best. If she had trouble making time for her own daughter anymore, she certainly didn't have time for a horse.

At the sound of the telephone, Deannie muted the TV and glanced at the clock. Almost midnight. And she'd just gotten to the good part of a romantic movie. Who'd be calling so late? She drew her knees up under her purple fleece robe and reached for the phone.

When she recognized the familiar name on the Caller ID, an involuntary shiver coursed through her. "Hey, Lissa. It's late. What's up?"

"I think we're getting her attention." Natalie's daughter spoke just above a whisper.

Deannie gripped the phone. "It's about time. But I think she's getting suspicious of me. I can't afford to lose this job. How much longer do you think it's going to take?"

"Not long, I hope. A few more lucky breaks like tonight, and we should have her right where we want her."

Deannie sat forward, nerves tingling. "What happened?"

Lissa chuckled. "Remember the Adamo's menu?"

"Yeah. But I thought we'd blown that one." Deannie twisted a curl around her finger, remembering. Natalie had stayed home from work with the flu the day Deannie's uncle printed the menus. Alan delivered them to the restaurant before anyone at the office realized the copy had been changed. Deannie thought sure Mr. Adamo would eventually call to point out the mistake, but he never did.

"Well, she had dinner at Adamo's tonight," Lissa stated. "And you won't believe this, but she never even noticed the menu looked different until Mr. Adamo personally showed her the horse and rider. And get this." She allowed a dramatic pause. "He *thanked* her for her 'amazing touch of inspiration.'"

"*All right!* Was she totally undone?"

"She turned so white, I was afraid someone was going to have to carry her out."

"Yes!" Deannie released a high-pitched squeak and pounded her knee with a fist. "It worked after all!"

"Did you have any clue the Adamos were horse people? You're the one who suggested switching to a horse graphic."

"Actually, I did a bit of research." Deannie allowed a touch of self-satisfaction to creep into her voice. "You can find out an awful lot on the Web. I just looked up 'Adamo' and 'Italy,' and I came across this whole genealogical site with tons of information about their family history."

"Yeah, but that was risky, suggesting a graphic he might actually approve of."

Deannie sank luxuriously into the chair cushions. "That's part of the brilliance of the plan. She was thrown totally off balance, right? A lot worse than if he'd been mad about it."

"You are too clever, girl. Your uncle will beg you to join the business when he realizes what you can do."

"I only hope you're right." The familiar doubts dimmed her enthusiasm. She took a deep breath and forced herself to ignore them. "Okay, so what's our next move?"

"Just keep doing what we've been doing. You downloaded the latest file I sent you?"

"Yep, got it when I checked my email after work. Everything's ready for Monday morning." Deannie reached for the computer disk next to the phone.

"Great. But remember, one step at a time. Use the stuff only if she doesn't give you a choice."

"Gotcha."

"Good. Once Mom loses her job, she'll have to get back together with Dad."

14

The microwave beeped, and Lissa popped open the door, releasing the aroma of maple-cinnamon oatmeal into Natalie's kitchen. Lissa set the bowl on the counter and retrieved the milk carton from the refrigerator. "I think we should go to church, Mom."

Natalie's hand froze halfway to the coffeemaker. "Oh, honey . . . " Cringing inwardly, she set her cup under the spigot, pressed the start button, and let the gurgling sounds fill up the strained silence while she framed her excuse. "I've had such an exhausting week. I don't think I have the energy."

"Give me a break. Just last night you were trying to talk me into going horseback riding today." Lissa waltzed to the table, her voice taking on a mocking, sing-song lilt. "If you're too tired for church, you're too tired for riding."

Natalie sank into a birchwood chair across from her daughter and took a careful sip of the Irish cream-flavored brew. "You don't understand. Sometimes church seems . . . confining, in an obligatory sort of way. Horseback riding makes me feel free, alive, re-energized." Okay, so it sounded New Age-y. And very, very lame. She could tell by Lissa's classic eye roll that she wasn't buying it.

"Give it up, Mom. I bet you haven't been on a horse in months." Lissa took a bite of oatmeal. "And it's probably been almost as long since you've been to church."

"It's hard, Lissa." Natalie shook her head. "I just don't feel comfortable in church anymore."

"If you're worried about running into Dad, he's been going to early service for a long time now."

Daniel. Natalie's stomach did a flip-flop. Like she needed to be reminded of all the feelings the dinner at Adamo's had conjured up.

"And anyway, Mom, you've got to stop avoiding him. Didn't you have a good time last night? Wasn't it great, all of us being together like a family again?"

"Sure it was, but . . . oh, Lissa, you're not making this easy."

"Good." She wolfed down several more spoonfuls, all the while shooting dagger-sharp glances at her mother.

Natalie twisted sideways in the chair. If she didn't look at her daughter, maybe the accusations wouldn't sting so much. So much for the relaxing, enjoyable day she'd hoped for.

If she could only survive this holiday season, the worst would be over. Afterward she'd plunge headlong into whatever avenues of counseling Dr. Sirpless pursued, as many times a week as necessary to get her head on straight. Then, perhaps, she'd be strong enough to face the critical decisions that could permanently change her family's future.

In the meantime, she had an obstinate thirteen-year-old daughter to contend with—and *contend* seemed to be the operative word.

"All right," she said. "I'll make a deal with you. We'll go to church this morning if you'll go riding with me this afternoon."

Lissa fixed her mother with a cool stare. "Deal. And no backing out."

Natalie rose with feigned confidence and fired back a stern glance of her own. "And that works both ways."

An hour later, she and Lissa made their way down the center aisle of Fawn Ridge Fellowship Church as the first hymn began.

Her father looked up in surprise when she edged into the family pew to stand beside him. "Rosy-girl, so good to see you here."

"Don't make a big deal of it," she mouthed over the organ's reedy vibrato. "Lissa coerced me."

"Good for her." Natalie's father looked past her and gave his granddaughter a conspiratorial wink.

Natalie let her mind wander during the service. She could only imagine what must be going through Pastor Mayer's head as he glanced her way from the pulpit—first seeing her last night at Adamo's with Daniel, now seated in church like a dutiful parishioner.

FYI, Pastor, I am not with Daniel this morning, I hope you noticed.

Snatches of the pastor's Advent message filtered through her defensive thoughts . . . something about Joseph's tender concern for Mary and what a devoted husband he was. She glanced briefly toward her father and noticed the tears in his eyes. How he must miss Mom!

Swallowing her self-pity, she lightly touched his arm and smiled in sympathy. If ever an ideal marriage existed between two ordinary human beings, it had to be Bram and Belinda Morgan's.

Clad in a pair of ragged gray sweatpants and a red Putnam Panthers T-shirt, Daniel snuggled deeper into his recliner and unfolded the Sunday paper. As usual, he turned first to the sports section to check the weekend basketball stats.

But his mind wouldn't stay focused. This morning at church he'd successfully sidestepped the pastor's prying questions after seeing him and Natalie together at Adamo's. His simple response—"We're working on staying friends for Lissa's sake."—seemed to partially satisfy Pastor Mayer's caring concern. Then, on his way to the parking lot after the Sunday-school hour, he'd seen Natalie arrive with Lissa moments before the late service began. Knowing his presence would make her even more uptight than she already appeared, he had stayed out of sight.

Even so, it was good to see her at church. If only she'd let go of the guilt and allow a spark of God's forgiveness to warm her heart. Why couldn't she see how wrong it was for her to continue blaming herself for something that was no one's fault?

The phone rang. He picked up the cordless extension next to his chair.

"Hey, Daniel, it's Hart. You doing anything this afternoon?"

"Uh, no." The chipper sound of his brother-in-law's voice took him by surprise. They'd taken to each other like brothers soon after Natalie introduced them, but their friendship had been strained lately by the problems between Natalie and Daniel.

"I'm out at the farm and wondered if maybe you'd like to drop by."

"And . . . why would I want to do that?"

"Natalie and Lissa showed up to go riding." Hart snickered. "Lissa couldn't wait to tell everyone all about her parents' *date*."

A vein throbbed in Daniel's temple. He reached up to give it a one-finger massage. "It most definitely was *not* a date."

"Sure, whatever you say. I just thought you might want to strike while the iron is hot, if you get my drift." His tone became conspiratorial. "You could come up with a good excuse. Like maybe you have plans later and wanted to pick up Lissa early."

Matchmaking didn't flatter his normally very discreet brother-in-law, but he couldn't blame the man for trying. Daniel had rarely met a family with closer ties than the Morgan clan, and certainly not a brother more protective of his only sister. He'd never forget Hart's probing questions the first time he drove out to the Morgan farm to pick up Natalie for a date. Hart and Celia "just happened" to be there, ostensibly to drop off something Natalie's mother needed from town. While Bram and Belinda Morgan stood to one side and smiled knowingly, Hart somehow managed to extract Daniel's entire life history in the space of ten minutes.

He grimaced and switched the phone to his other ear. "Sorry, Hart, your idea won't fly. Lissa knows very well I have nothing better to do than waste my Sunday afternoons reading the paper and watching ESPN."

"Just come out, man. It's a beautiful day. I could saddle up a horse for you, and you could meet them on the trail. It would be a very casual thing, no pressure—"

Daniel laughed out loud. He rose abruptly and paced in front of the television. "Who are you kidding, bro? That sounds like nothing *but* pressure."

Not to mention he was a whole lot more comfortable on a basketball court than in the saddle. Though Natalie had often persuaded him to go trail riding with her, horses had always been her thing, not his. He remained a city boy, through and through. If not for the coaching position he'd been offered in

Putnam after finishing college in St. Louis, he might never even have met Natalie.

Hart gave a loud snort. "You're not making this easy."

"Neither are you."

"Yeah, but—" Hart suddenly coughed, and Daniel could hear someone else in the room with him. "Hey, Nat . . . uh, nobody. Just checking my voice mail." After a pause, he whispered into the phone, "Just think about it, Dan. They'll be out here all afternoon."

The line went dead.

～❧～

Natalie gave her brother a skeptical frown. She knew that look in his eyes too well; he was up to something. Probably some Christmas surprise she wasn't supposed to know about. It better not have anything to do with Daniel. She wished Lissa had never opened her mouth about dinner at Adamo's last night, and she hoped she'd made it clear that absolutely nothing had changed.

She set her booted foot on the edge of a kitchen chair to adjust the Velcro closures on her suede half-chaps. In her bent-over position, she felt the tell-tale strain on the backside of her riding tights. *Ugh.* Good thing nobody was standing behind her. Months of desk work and little exercise had resulted in sagging muscles and bulges in places she never knew she had. She stood and self-consciously tugged her oversized sweatshirt farther down around her hips.

Hart set the phone in the cradle and started toward the door. "Need help tacking up? Who's Lissa going to ride?"

And since when did Hart ever volunteer to help her tack her horse? "I thought I'd let her ride Windy, and I'll take Rocky. Dad said he could use the exercise." She shrugged off the suspicious murmurings humming through her thoughts. Bad enough she already suspected a conspiracy at the office. She sure didn't need to add her own family into the mix.

Hart shrugged into his jacket. "I hope you're not planning to take Rocky over any fences."

She bristled. Why did older brothers always feel like they had the right to tell you what to do? "Dad told me he's been a little sore in the stifle. I'll take it easy."

"I'm not worried about Rocky." Hart poked her in the ribs. "I was more concerned about you, considering how long it's been since you rode. I'd hate to make a rush trip to the ER."

Realizing he'd only been baiting her, she felt the resentment evaporate. She returned his poke with a playful slug on the shoulder. "You have no respect, big brother. You forget, while you were slaving over equine anatomy texts in vet school, Windy and I were winning blue ribbons all over the state."

They traded harmless barbs all the way out to the barn, where Lissa already had Windy secured in the crossties for grooming and tacking. "She looks great," Natalie told her daughter. She rubbed Windy's nose before ducking into the combination tack room/barn office to collect her riding gear.

Her father startled her as he emerged from the storage closet just inside the door. "Hey, sweetheart, I thought you were still in the house."

The nervous tone of his voice gave her the distinct impression he was hiding something, not to mention his abrupt slamming of the closet door—but not before she glimpsed a shimmer of silver peering out from behind some crates. Her conspiracy theories churned toward the surface again, at the same moment something stirred in her memory, a feeling of *déjà vu*.

Before she could sort it out, Dad grabbed her arm and propelled her over to the tiers of saddle racks. "I've been riding Rocky in this new Wintec lately—easier on his back than my heavy old Steuben. We've been working more basic dressage since his injury. Helps loosen him up. I doubt Rocky will ever be a jumper again."

Natalie forced her thoughts back to the ride. "That goes for me too. Nice, easy, flat dressage work sounds perfectly fine." She scanned the racks on the adjacent wall for the sturdy little half-Morgan/half-Arab's bridle.

Dad winked and started out the door. "Rocky's grazing in the south paddock. I'll bring him in."

While Dad and Hart tripped over themselves trying to help get Rocky saddled, Natalie could only shrug and get out of the way. She ran a hand along the horse's left rear leg, checking the knee joint for any heat or swelling. The old boy seemed fine, and soon Natalie and Lissa reined their mounts up the lane between the mares' pasture and the hayfield. The grasses lay brown and dormant, awaiting spring rains and warmer temperatures. Beyond the fields they approached a shallow stream, where Windy, in the lead, put on the brakes.

"Oh, great," Lissa called over her shoulder. "I forgot how she hates walking through water."

"Give her a light tap with the crop. Don't let her have her way, or we'll never get across."

Several not-so-gentle taps later, Windy was no closer to setting foot in the stream. She whinnied and backed and twisted and squirmed, the whites of her eyes showing and her ears pinned against her skull.

Natalie started forward. "Maybe if Rocky and I go first—"

"Stubborn old Appaloosa." Lissa gave the horse one good thwack.

With an explosion of motion, Windy made a running leap and sailed across the stream, and then galloped up the incline on the other side with no signs of stopping. Heart in her throat, adrenaline surging, Natalie urged Rocky across the stream in pursuit. "Lissa! Hang on!"

Heels down, sit deep, shoulders back, elbows in. In the course of microseconds, her mind processed all the commands she willed Lissa to remember, but she couldn't get the words out fast enough or loud enough for her daughter to hear. At least she hadn't gotten any argument from Lissa about wearing a riding helmet.

Then, amidst the pounding of horses' hooves on winter-hard ground, she heard the unmistakable ringing of Lissa's delighted laughter. She caught up to her daughter under the leafless branches of an oak tree, where they both reined safely to a halt.

"Wow, that was fun!" Lissa reached down to stroke Windy's brown-spotted withers. "What a ride, old girl!"

"Fun for you, maybe." Natalie took several panting breaths and tried to subdue the tremors coursing through her entire body. "You scared me half to death."

"Oh, Mom, get over it." The laughter in Lissa's eyes faded, and she turned her horse down the hill toward the woods.

"You could have been hurt." Her voice sounded hoarse from the remnants of fear. Natalie's heart still pounded as she followed her daughter across the meadow.

Lissa gave an exaggerated shrug. "And who told me to use the crop, huh?"

"And didn't I say a 'light tap,' *huh?*" Natalie swallowed down the lump in her throat. "I was coming to lead you across, if only you'd waited."

Lissa twisted sideways in her saddle until she was looking straight at Natalie. Her glare could have melted the polar icecap.

"If I wait around for you to fix things, nothing will ever happen." Tossing her blonde braid, she spurred Windy into a canter and headed toward the trail through the woods.

Natalie could do nothing but follow and hope Rocky's knees—and her backside—held up.

∗

Daniel shoved his gloved hands deeper into the pockets of his fleece jacket. The chilly December air nipped at him through the open barn door and gave him one more reason he wished he'd stayed home. He watched Hart saddle up a fat, shaggy brown horse that looked as if he'd much rather munch on a pile of hay or take a long snooze—anything but haul some city slicker in sweats and sneakers out on a trail ride.

"I can't believe I let you talk me into this."

Hart slanted him a crooked smile. "I didn't exactly twist your arm." He gave the cinch one last tug before finishing off a Western knot.

Daniel reached for the dusty white schooling helmet Hart had found for him and brushed off the top with his sleeve. "Yes, you did. You twisted pretty hard, actually."

"So sue me. Look, you know I don't like to stick my nose into other people's business," Hart said as he adjusted the stirrup length, "but you're family, and Christmas is coming, and I hate to see you left out in the cold."

"What are you trying to say, Hart?"

"I just felt really bad that you didn't come out for Nat's birthday dinner. You should have been there. You had a right to be there."

"No, I didn't." He turned the helmet in his hands and fingered the buckle. "Natalie wouldn't have wanted me there. That was reason enough to stay away."

Hart released a humorless chuckle. "Don't you get it, man? She *did* want you there. The whole family could see it in her eyes. It hurt her that you didn't come, and not just because you didn't bring Lissa."

His brother-in-law's words seared his heart. Natalie missed him? He'd never have guessed, especially considering the way last night ended. One more argument, one more ruined evening, one more lost chance to set things right.

"I had no idea," he said at last.

"I kind of figured." Hart gave a soft, sad chuckle. "But I'd have thought after your date last night, you might at least have a clue."

"How many ways do I have to say this? It *wasn't* a date."

"And Natalie agrees with you." Hart walked around the horse for another tack inspection. "But your daughter refuses to be convinced."

That kid. He'd have to straighten things out with her eventually. He couldn't let her continue living on false hope. Now, if he could only convince his brother-in-law. "You realize Natalie will figure out you put me up to this."

"Big deal. Besides, I did it as much for Dad as for you and Natalie." Hart's teasing grin faded. "You know what a tough Christmas this is going to be for him. It could be so much better if you and my sister would get back together."

"And you don't think that's what I want?"

"Then quit stalling and do something about it." Hart positioned himself at the sleepy-eyed horse's head, one hand on the reins. "Here, need a leg up?"

Daniel glared at his brother-in-law and uttered a defeated moan before gripping the saddle horn with his left hand. "I think I can make it. He's pretty short."

Setting one foot in the stirrup, he heaved himself off the ground and dropped into the scuffed, worn Western saddle with a thud. The horse gave a long, low rumble.

"Same to you." Daniel wriggled his rear into a more comfortable position. "Blame it on the guy holding your bridle."

Hart passed him the knotted leather reins. "You remember how to steer? Pokey's a neck-reiner. Shouldn't give you any problems."

"Pokey, huh? Hope he lives up to his name."

"Slow as molasses . . . except he can be a little spooky about sudden noises. Shouldn't be a problem on a nice afternoon like this, though." Hart frowned and rubbed his chin. "But if you're not home by dark, just hang on, okay?"

Daniel gripped the saddle horn reflexively. "Why, exactly?"

"Because if you're not back at the barn by suppertime, you'll see just how fast a hungry old cow pony can move."

"Gotcha." Unwilling to let go of the saddle horn, Daniel gave a clumsy thumbs-up sign with his reining hand. "Okay, now that you've finagled this little rendezvous, which way to Natalie and Lissa?"

Hart directed him out the rear barn door and down the lane towards the stream crossing. "They've been out awhile, so you'll probably run into them before long. If not, just follow the trail to the woods."

Pokey's slow, plodding gait soon banished the last of Daniel's nervousness. He barely even had to rein. The horse seemed perfectly content to wander at will along the well-traveled path. At the stream, Pokey didn't even lift his head, just splashed through the rippling water and up the other side as if he were sleepwalking.

"Atta boy." Daniel reached forward to pat the furry brown neck. "You take care of me, and I'll take care of you. I bet I can beg an apple or a carrot or two from Bram once we get back to the barn."

As they crested the hill, he glimpsed two riders trotting in his direction. Strands of blonde hair—the woman's short and wispy, the girl's a long, unraveling braid—had blown loose from beneath sleek black helmets. Daniel reined Pokey to a halt near a scraggly pine tree, and the pudgy gelding obeyed with a thankful grunt. Watching his wife and daughter approach, Daniel found himself struck silent by their grace and skill. Natalie's rising trot appeared as smooth and controlled as any pro he'd ever seen on TV's Olympics coverage. When Lissa swerved Windy to her left and sailed over a fallen log, she could have been a blonde Elizabeth Taylor from the classic movie *National Velvet*.

Lost in the moment, his heart bursting with love and pride, Daniel let out a spontaneous whoop. "All right, Lissa!"

In the same instant, Pokey shot his head up, pinned his ears, and sped off at a gallop. Panic froze Daniel's brain. Dropping the reins, he seized the saddle horn with both hands and held on for all he was worth. "Oh, no! Whoa, boy, *whoa!*"

"*Daniel!*" Natalie cried.

In his terror-filled stupor he saw Lissa canter up beside Natalie. "I don't believe it," he heard his daughter yell. "Is that *Dad?*"

Pokey raced straight toward the other horses, with Daniel's world flashing by like a video on fast-forward. As Pokey barreled between Rocky and Windy, Daniel gathered his senses enough to shout, "Help! What do I do?"

"Grab the reins, you idiot!" Natalie yelled.

He heard their horses' hooves thundering behind him—catching up quickly, he could only hope. Surely a fat little horse like Pokey couldn't run *that* fast . . . or that far.

Why hadn't he remembered Hart's warning about loud noises?

Reins . . . reins. They had to be down there somewhere. Releasing one hand from the saddle horn, he raked his fingers along the bushy mane until he found the leather knot. He grabbed it and yanked backward with all his strength.

Pokey's sudden stop almost threw him over the horse's head. The saddle horn jammed into his gut. He gasped in agony, the breath almost knocked from him.

"You stupid horse, you could have killed me!"

The now docile equine twitched his ears and leaned down to grab a mouthful of the bright green winter rye grass growing on the hillside.

"Way to go, Dad!" Lissa cantered over and halted beside him. "I haven't seen you ride like that in a long, long time."

"And I hope you never do again." Still struggling for air, he hauled in several deep breaths. His stomach felt like he'd been slugged with a baseball bat.

Natalie reached across to tousle Pokey's forelock. "What on earth are you doing out here, Daniel?"

"I, uh . . . " Embarrassment quickly swallowed up the bitter remnants of abject terror. Why, exactly, had Hart thought this was such a good idea? Making a complete fool of himself while risking life and limb certainly wasn't part of the original plan. He drew his shoulders up and gathered what dignity he had left. "It was a nice afternoon and I, uh, I just thought . . . "

Natalie's gaze narrowed. She sat straight in the saddle and rested her hands on the pommel. "You just thought what?"

Lissa nosed Windy up beside her mother on Rocky. "Obviously, he heard we were riding today and wanted to spend time with you." She beamed a triumphant smile toward Daniel. "Isn't that right, Dad?"

Natalie cast her daughter a withering look. "Lissa, please."

Daniel gulped. "Well, I . . . ."

"No use denying it, you two." Lissa let out a high-pitched giggle. "So have a nice ride, and I'll see you guys at the barn!" Thumping Windy with the riding crop, she raced down the hill toward the stream and disappeared from view.

The silence she left behind was deafening.

Daniel's breath whistled out through clenched teeth. "Uh, this is awkward."

Her gaze still fixed on the horizon, Natalie gave her head a small shake. "Poor Windy only thought she was in line for retirement. The old gal hasn't been ridden this hard since before . . . " Her voice trailed off. Tucking a strand of tangled hair beneath her helmet strap, she turned to Daniel with a knowing frown. "Hart put you up to this, didn't he?"

He rubbed the saddle horn imprint on his abdomen and figured there'd be an ugly purple bruise there by the time he got home. "What was your first clue?"

She nodded toward the drowsing brown horse. "You obviously didn't catch and saddle Pokey all on your own."

His pride stung. He squared his shoulders. "What makes you so sure?"

"Well, for one thing, you don't catch Pokey in the paddock unless you tempt him with at least three or four carrots. He may be fat and lazy, but he doesn't like to work and can scurry away from a halter and lead rope faster than you can say, 'Giddy-up.'"

"Okay, so Hart helped me . . . a little."

She smirked. "How about a lot?"

"I just stood there and watched. Does that make you feel better?"

The gentle softening around Natalie's eyes made the whole dreadful experience worthwhile. *Almost.* "Are you sure you're okay?" Tenderness laced her tone. "You still look a little pale."

"My entire life just passed before my eyes, but I'll live." He smiled hopefully and tried not to think about how stiff and sore he would be tomorrow.

Natalie nodded in understanding and turned Rocky toward home. Barely lifting his head from the grass, Pokey followed.

"I had kind of a different ending in mind, though," he said.

Natalie abruptly halted her horse and looked back at him. "What's that supposed to mean?"

His throat closed. "Nat, I miss you. Why can't we work things out?"

"Please, Daniel, don't start—"

"Why? Why do you keep pushing me away? Last night—"

"Last night was a mistake. Just like always, we couldn't keep from fighting. That's the story of our lives, and I'm sick of it." She drove her heels into Rocky's sides and cantered down the hill toward the stream crossing.

Daniel labored to get the stubborn Pokey moving faster, but the speed demon of ten minutes ago now seemed content with a slow, lumbering walk, pausing often to jerk the reins from Daniel's hand by diving for a clump of grass. By the time they reached the barn, Rocky had been brushed and turned out in the paddock. Natalie was nowhere to be seen.

Hart emerged from the tack room as Daniel dismounted. "So how'd it go, pardner?"

"It didn't." His leg muscles trembled as he tried to find his balance on solid ground again. His thighs felt like they'd been wrapped around an elephant.

Unfastening Pokey's bridle, Hart cast Daniel a regretful look. "I gathered that after Natalie got here a full half-hour ahead of you."

"Is she still around?" He fumbled with the clasp of his riding helmet.

"Uh, no. Said she had a few things to catch up on before work tomorrow."

"That figures. And Lissa?"

"In the house playing cribbage with Dad. Natalie thought Lissa could ride home with you and save you a trip to pick her up later in town." He hefted the saddle off Pokey's back and headed into the tack room.

"Well, that certainly keeps the afternoon from being a total waste." Disappointment clung to him like the sweat-muddied dirt beneath Pokey's saddle blanket. He followed Hart into the tack room and tossed the damp blanket onto an empty rack.

Hart clapped him on the shoulder. "Sorry, man. I really hoped after last night, you might find an opening."

"She's just not ready." He stared toward the house. "And I'm beginning to think she never will be."

⋘⋙

Natalie settled stiffly into her desk chair on Monday morning. Her "horse muscles" screamed at her in protest for months of neglect. Yesterday had been a good day, though. At least it started out that way. Riding with Lissa, she felt a closeness with her daughter that she hadn't experienced in . . . okay, if she were completely honest, probably not since the separation.

Natalie rotated her shoulders in each direction in preparation for another marathon computer session. Her thoughts wouldn't cooperate, however. Why did Daniel have to show up at the farm and give Lissa more false hope? When Natalie returned to the barn without Daniel, Lissa had barely spoken a word to her. The familiar look of disillusionment shone through accusing eyes brimming with unshed tears.

Without warning, Deannie appeared across the desk from Natalie, jolting her back to the present. "You have a sunburn."

"Do I?" Natalie barely glanced at Deannie and powered up the computer. Then, remembering the task she'd given her partner's niece on Saturday, she held her breath and glanced up furtively. "Please don't tell me you found more errors."

"Nope, not a one. Here are the proofs, with five sets of initials on each copy, just like you asked." Deannie plopped a stack of file folders on the desk.

Natalie closed her eyes in sweet relief.

"By the way, I heard you had dinner at Adamo's Saturday evening. How was it?"

Natalie's eyes flew open. She spent about two seconds wondering which of her acquaintances at Adamo's had informed Deannie she'd been there—Alan, the egotistical Top Gun delivery driver, no doubt—then another half-minute wondering why her dinner plans should interest anyone else in the first place. "Fine. Dinner was perfectly fine." She cocked an eyebrow and dared her assistant to say more.

"Oh." Deannie pushed out her lower lip. "That's it? Fine?"

"Look, Deannie." She placed both palms on her desktop and forced a calm she didn't feel. "I know you mean well, and I'm sorry if I'm not as friendly as I could be. It's just that I've got a job to do, and lately it hasn't been going very well."

"Yeah, I know." Deannie meandered over to the desk. She opened one of the folders she'd just returned and idly ran her finger along the proof copy. "Oh, my. What is this?" She bent over for a closer look.

Natalie followed the girl's gaze to the inside text of a custom Christmas card Natalie had designed for Andrew Pennington, a local attorney:

> *May your holidays be bright with promise,*
> *Your New Year full of hope.*
> *Blessings of the season,*
> *Awesome Painter, Attorney-at-Law*

Natalie's mouth dropped open. Her throat felt like she'd swallowed a fat, pigment-slathered paintbrush. "But—but you had five people initial—"

"Oops."

"I don't know what's going on around here, but I will find out." Natalie stood. Any second now, she'd be hyperventilating. Her stress level had just pegged into the red. She needed air. *Now.* She headed for the door.

"But what about the card?" Deannie blocked Natalie's way. "Mr. Painter's secretary—I mean, Mr. *Pennington's*—is probably on her way over here now."

Natalie squeezed her eyes shut, her only thought the effort it took to take the next breath. *In . . . out . . . in . . . out.* When a semblance of control returned, she steadied her gaze on her wide-eyed assistant. "Do you know anything about desktop publishing?"

"Um, a little. Why?"

"If I give you my password, can you open the file and fix it?" How hard could it be? All she had to do was correct two little words. Natalie could always change the password later.

"Oh, sure, you bet." With a grin, Deannie planted herself in Natalie's chair and poised her fingers over the computer keys. She looked up expectantly. "But . . . just in case . . . where can I find you if there are any more problems?"

Natalie didn't want to hear about any more problems—ever again. But this annoying little warning bell in the back of her mind clanged with unsettling urgency. Something told her the real problems hadn't even begun to surface. Before she could change her mind and eject Jeff Garner's charity project from her office—and her life—once and for all, she grabbed a pen and scribbled on a notepad. "Here. The Painter—*Pennington*—password and my cell number."

Without looking back, she reached for her purse, yanked her down-filled jacket off the coat tree, and marched out of the office.

～◎～

Belinda Morgan rested her hand in her husband's, quietly drawing strength from its solid feel. If only she could speak, tell him again how much she loved him. If only she could reach up and smooth his wrinkled brow and kiss away the worry lines on his forehead.

She'd lost track of how long she'd been here, confined in this bed of scratchy sheets over a lumpy mattress, trapped in a body that didn't pay any more mind to her than that contrary old nanny-goat Hart used to chase around the farm as a boy. She thought she recognized the brushed cotton gown she wore as one of her own. It smelled faintly of her favorite lemony laundry soap . . . but those stains—how did they get there?

I must get this off and wash it before . . . before . . .

Seemingly of its own volition, her head rocked back and forth against the flattened foam pillow.

"It's okay, darlin'." Bram stilled the motion with a touch of his hand. He held her face so her eyes looked directly into his. "I've been thinking. I want you to come home." His Adam's apple moved as he swallowed. "Home for Christmas."

Christmas? *Oh, Bram, is it Christmastime already? Why, sweetheart, there's so much to do. Have you cut the tree? Oh, please tell me I haven't missed Natalie Rose's birthday. And the nativity scene, the star . . .*

What was that awful moaning sound, and why did her husband look at her that way, as if he couldn't understand a word she said?

"Please, honey, lie still. Here, let me . . . " He plucked a tissue from the box on the bedside table and dabbed at the corner of her mouth.

Did you know Lissa visited me the other morning? She brought me watercolors. I'm so out of practice, though, made such a mess. Last time I held a paintbrush—oh, surely not more than a few days ago?

But no, no. So much time had passed, so many wasted months trapped in this bed, this prison, this *nightmare*. At least she'd finished Bram's and Natalie's gifts before her body mutinied. She'd planned to start on Hart's the very next week.

Oh, dear Lord, it can't be Christmas already! Please give me more time—

"It won't be easy, I know," her husband went on.

She tried to keep her tired eyes on him, drink him up like warm cocoa on a cold winter morning. How she adored the shock of gray hair falling across his forehead like an apostrophe, the barn smell she could never quite launder out of his frayed flannel shirts. She knew if she could peer far enough over the edge of the bed, she'd see his stained work boots and pick out the scrape across the right toe where Rocky had stomped on Bram's foot not two days after he'd bought those boots.

"But I've been asking around, and I've found a home-care nurse who's available." His voice cracked, and Belinda almost couldn't bear the sound of it. "Darlin', I just can't leave you here any longer."

⋘

When Natalie left the office, she had no particular destination in mind—she just drove, with her thoughts spinning out as fast as the tires on the pavement. She was *not* a person who made careless errors.

No, you're an incorrigible perfectionist. Nothing is ever good enough for you. Everything has to be perfect.

And where did I get that?

From her dear, stubborn—yes, *stubborn*—mother. No denying it any longer, or the anger it evoked, either. Mom was always a stickler for detail, a woman who held each of her children accountable, who always kept her promises.

Only there was one promise Mom couldn't keep—the Morgans' fiftieth perfect Christmas.

Rage welled up inside Natalie. Hot, writhing, suffocating rage at a world tilted so far out of balance that she felt she'd never find solid ground again. She slammed on the brakes and skidded to a stop on the gravel shoulder. Angry tears seared her cheeks.

"It's not fair, Mom! You promised!"

Crumpled over the steering wheel, she gave in fully to the fury, fear, and guilt. When the worst of the sobs subsided, she reached across the console to pull her cell phone from her purse. Her next appointment with Dr. Sirpless was still a few days away, but she needed to talk, needed to—

The sound of a knock on her window made her drop the phone. Sucking in a quick breath, she lifted her head in bewilderment. Her brother peered through the glass, his expression etched with worry. Hastily, she swiped at her wet, burning cheeks and then unlocked her door.

Hart pulled it open and leaned in. He touched a gloved hand to her face. "You okay?"

"Yes . . . no . . . " She shuddered. "Hart, I think I'm losing my mind."

"Hey, I always knew you were crazy." He laughed without humor and rested his knees on the doorframe. "Okay, Nat, talk to me."

In halting words she told him about the bizarre series of mistakes at work. "This may sound even crazier," she went on, "but I'm starting to wonder if God is trying to tell me something."

"Then maybe you should listen." An icy gust of wind whistled around the door, and Hart shivered. "Mind if we go somewhere warmer to talk? My next appointment isn't for another hour or so, and I'll bet Dad has the woodstove stoked."

She glanced at her surroundings and realized they were less than half a mile from the farm. Curling up under an afghan next to the warm glow of a fire sounded inviting. "Let's go," she said, reaching for the gearshift. She followed her brother's mud-stained pickup and parked behind it in their father's driveway.

They found Dad in the kitchen rinsing out the coffee carafe. He looked up from the sink in surprise. "Thought I heard someone drive up. Just got home, myself." He cast Natalie a concerned look as he set the carafe in the drainer. "What's wrong, Rosy-girl?"

She opened her mouth but could utter only a muted sob.

Hart answered for her, his tone sympathetic. "Nat's having a bad day." He took her coat and briskly rubbed her shoulders. "How about some hot chocolate to warm this girl up?"

"Coming right up." Dad brushed her forehead with a kiss on his way to fill the teakettle.

In the living room, Natalie and Hart scooted armchairs close to the woodstove. Sky, the hulking Great Dane, drowsed on the braided rug at their feet. A few minutes later Natalie heard the harmonic trilling of the teakettle, and shortly afterward Dad carried in two steaming mugs of hot chocolate.

"Just sit here and enjoy it." He hovered for a moment, lips pressed together, and then gave his hands a brisk rub and turned toward the kitchen. "Got some things to finish up. Be back in a few minutes."

Natalie gave a weak smile as she wrapped her hands around the huge ceramic mug decorated with laughing snowmen. It felt good to be coddled, to soak up the warmth of hearth and family. She hadn't felt so drained since those long, excruciating hours while she sat outside the ICU waiting for updates on her mother's condition.

She leaned her head back and let her gaze drift around the familiar room. Dad had turned on the tree lights for them, and their childhood Christmas stockings dangled from a narrow shelf above the stove. A few feet away, on an antique library table draped in forest-green velvet, the delicately painted life-like figurines of her mother's ceramic nativity scene portrayed the first Christmas.

Natalie's stomach twisted with fresh grief. The starry backdrop, usually in place until Mom painted the newest star early on Christmas morning, was missing.

Then she saw it, leaning on an easel in the alcove, a small area off the living room where Mom used to paint because of the excellent natural light.

Natalie's throat closed. "It looks like it's waiting for her."

Hart followed her gaze. He shook his head sadly. "Dad must have put it there. He just won't give up hope."

Their father ambled in from the kitchen, hands thrust into the pockets of his corduroy jeans. "Sore yet from yesterday?" He shot Natalie a knowing wink.

She rolled her eyes and smiled. "What do you think?"

Hart grinned. "Daniel said you were looking pretty fine out there."

The secondhand compliment swathed her in unexpected warmth. How Daniel even remembered how "fine" she looked after his little adventure on Pokey, she couldn't imagine. In her mind's eye she replayed the image of Daniel barreling toward her on the mangy old horse. He must have been watching them for a while before his ridiculous shout startled the poor animal.

She refused to think beyond those next few minutes to the point where Daniel had tried yet again to get past her defenses. To the point where she panicked under the pressure of his pleading gaze and tore off to the barn.

Dad patted her shoulder. "Always knew you couldn't stay away from the horses forever. Riding's in your blood."

Natalie shifted in the chair and rubbed her backside. "In my blood, and a few other places I don't care to mention."

Chuckling, Dad pulled over the ottoman and sat down. He extended his hands toward the heat radiating from the stove. "You may be a little achy for a few days, but getting back on a horse is like riding a bike. Even if it's been awhile, your body remembers. The muscles just have to be reminded."

"Right now," Natalie said with a grim laugh, "my muscles would rather forget."

Hart wadded up the Christmas napkin beneath his mug and tossed it at Natalie with a smirk. "Don't count on that happening for a few days."

The friendly banter faded to comfortable silence. Watching the glowing embers through the smoky glass, Natalie felt a languorous peace settling over her. She wished she could stay like this forever.

Dad's quiet voice edged its way into the stillness. "Rosy-girl, I was hoping to talk with you and Hart about something yesterday, but you both left before I had a chance."

Rosy-girl. Coming from Dad, the pet name sometimes comforted her—sometimes sent a warning chill through her. With effort she drew herself out of the dreamlike trance. "What is it, Dad?"

"I've been thinking." He reached down to stroke Sky's head, and the big dog looked up at him with soulful eyes. "I'd like to bring your mom home for Christmas."

His statement banished the last of Natalie's brain fog like a gust of winter wind. She sat forward. "Dad, are you serious?"

"I wanted to ask how you both felt about it first."

Hart braced his forearms on his knees. "If you think she can handle it that sure would be nice. It would mean a lot to the whole family to have her with us for Christmas Day."

"Actually," Dad began, clearing his throat, "I want her home to stay. I'm working on arrangements for a live-in caregiver."

Natalie laid her hand on his shirtsleeve, a tightness gripping her chest. "Oh, Dad, I want Mom home, too, but is it really a good idea? And would she even know she's here?"

But then she remembered the watercolors; her mother tried to paint. Could it really be possible, after all? Could Mom recover enough to be home with her family for the promised fiftieth Christmas?

Her father spoke again, but Natalie didn't hear him over the buzzing in her ears. She set her mug on the floor and tossed the afghan across the chair arm as she stood. In a daze she crossed the room to the Christmas tree. She found the little Appaloosa horse ornament and cradled it in her hand.

The muscles just have to be reminded.

She felt her father's hand at her elbow. "I need to know what both you and Hart honestly think about the idea. It would mean everything to me to have your mom home again, but I won't do it without your support."

A bright bubble of hope rose in Natalie's heart. She turned and wrapped her arms around her father, relishing the soft brush of flannel against her cheek. "I think it's a wonderful idea, Dad. Yes, let's bring Mom home, where she belongs."

15

Of course the path to statehood required significant sacrifice—"

A light tapping at Daniel's classroom door interrupted his history lesson.

"Hold that thought, class." He laid his lecture notes aside and strode to the door.

Mr. Lattimore, the assistant principal, stood in the corridor, his face grim. "Sorry to interrupt your class, Mr. Pearce, but you've had an urgent phone call." He held out a slip of paper.

With a nod of thanks, Daniel took the form and scanned it:

To: Daniel Pearce
From: Dr. Hartley Morgan
Message: Please call ASAP. Need to talk.

Hart's clinic phone number followed. Daniel pondered the cryptic message, his stomach tightening. Hart would never bother Daniel at school unless . . . . Had something happened with Belinda? With Natalie?

Mr. Lattimore stuffed his hands in his trouser pockets and rocked on his heels. "I can take over your class if this is something you need to handle."

Daniel nodded. He stepped inside the classroom and cleared his throat. "Small family emergency, kids. Mr. Lattimore's in charge until I get back." He ignored the collective groan. "Please take out your books and work on the questions at the end of chapter eleven. And be prepared for a quiz on this section tomorrow."

An even louder groan followed him out the door. He couldn't suppress a grin at the guilty pleasure it gave him, one of the few rewards for having to teach a subject he didn't feel much passion about just to keep his coaching job.

In the teachers' lounge he took a steadying breath before dialing Hart's number and then paced in the small room while waiting for the receptionist to get his brother-in-law on the line.

"That was fast." Hart sounded out of breath. "Didn't expect to hear from you till after school."

"Your message seemed urgent. Is it your mom?"

"Yeah . . . sort of." Hart paused. An ominous edge crept into his tone. "Any chance you could get away for lunch?"

Daniel looked at his watch—eleven-thirty—then raked a nervous hand across the back of his head. His fourth-period class ended in twenty-five minutes, and Mr. Lattimore had it covered. The school allowed only a half-hour lunch break, but he didn't think Lattimore would mind if he asked Carl to take his P.E. class that started right after lunch. "Yeah, I think I can arrange it, but it would help if you could meet me somewhere here in Putnam."

They decided on Casey's Diner as soon after twelve as both of them could get there. Daniel had already claimed a corner booth when Hart arrived. The lanky veterinarian shook off his khaki barn jacket and tossed it on the bench seat as he slid in across from Daniel.

"After yesterday's fiasco, I wasn't expecting to see you again so soon." Daniel absently rubbed the tender spot below his ribcage. "In fact, I was counting on it."

Hart cocked his head, looking appropriately sheepish. "Sorry things didn't go better."

"Yeah, me too." Daniel laced his fingers atop the laminated menu that lay open before him. "So what's up? I can't believe you'd drive all the way over to Putnam just to get on my case again about Natalie. Talk about beating a dead horse."

A waitress with frosted hair sauntered over and plopped down two glasses of ice water. "You gentlemen ready to order yet?" She plucked a chili-pepper-shaped pen from the pocket of her green apron and tapped it against an order pad.

Hart grabbed one of the menus tucked between the napkin holder and condiments. "What's good here, Dan?"

Daniel propped his menu against the edge of the table and scanned the entrees. "I like their chicken-fried steak," he began, but the way his stomach had been feeling lately, he sure didn't need anything that heavy. "Think I'll have the baked fish plate this time. And a glass of iced tea." He nodded to the waitress.

"Sounds good. Same for me." Hart jammed the menu back in its spot and knocked over a salt shaker.

"You're wound up tighter than a spring." Daniel lifted an eyebrow as he took a long drink of water. "All right, let's have it."

Hart dusted the spilled salt crystals into a small pile and covered it with a napkin. He pressed his fingertips together and closed his eyes for a moment. "Dad's bringing Mom home."

A million thoughts raced through Daniel's head. A jumble of emotions tangled in his gut, not the least of which was suspicion. He eyed his brother-in-law. "That should be good news. Why don't you look happy about it?"

"Because it's *not* good news." Hart snorted. "At least not the kind of 'good' Natalie is hoping for." He went on to explain about finding Natalie by the roadside earlier, the trip to the farm, and their conversation with Bram.

"After Natalie left, Dad and I talked awhile longer," Hart continued. "He didn't know how to tell Natalie, but the real reason he's bringing Mom home is because the doctor told him she probably won't last much longer."

Daniel's heart plummeted as his vague suspicions found substance. "How long?"

"Can't say. Weeks maybe. A couple months at most. Dad's praying for a miracle—we all are—but whatever happens, he wants Mom home for Christmas."

The waitress returned with their lunches. Daniel stared at his plate of parmesan-sprinkled flounder and wished he hadn't ordered it. His thoughts locked on Natalie . . . all her dashed hopes . . . the guilt she couldn't shake. If only she hadn't worked so hard to push him out of her life, maybe he could do something now to help.

Much as he loved Bram and Belinda, much as he hoped for both their sakes that Belinda could yet pull through, there was one miracle he wanted even more.

Dear God, I want my wife home for Christmas too.

Natalie shot a nervous glance toward the dashboard clock. How did it get to be twelve-fifteen already? Leaving her dad's, she'd needed time to sort out all her confused feelings about bringing Mom home and had been aimlessly driving the back roads, lost in thought. At least she hadn't gotten any panicked phone calls from Deannie—

"Oh, no." With one eye on the highway ahead, she groped along the floorboard where her cell phone had fallen earlier. She found it beneath the seat, but a quick look at the blank display confirmed she'd never turned it on. Cursing under her breath, she pushed the on button and waited for the phone to cycle through its ridiculously slow powering-up sequence. As soon as the signal bars lit up, she pressed the speed-dial code for her office. Deannie answered on the third ring.

"It's me." Natalie winced. "I hope you haven't been trying to call."

"Nope. Things are going smooth as glass . . . at least at the moment."

Natalie slowed behind a cattle trailer, wrinkling her nose at the manure smells flowing through the heater vent. "At the moment? What's that supposed to mean?" And why did Deannie always have to sound so cryptic?

"Oh, nothing." Papers rustled in the background. "Listen, there's no rush. I can hold down the fort. It's been awhile since my college course, but this computer design work is really coming back to me. You know, like riding a bike."

Like riding a bike. Her father's own words jolted Natalie like a slap. She could barely contain the excited screech aching to tear from her throat. The watercolor set! Lissa had the right idea after all.

The cattle truck turned off at the next intersection, and she pressed her foot to the gas pedal. She struggled to keep her tone light and natural. "Okay, Deannie, as long as you have things under control, I do have one more stop I'd like to make."

"No problem," the girl responded almost too quickly. "Take your time."

Natalie refused to waste any more brainpower scrutinizing Deannie's infuriating quirks. After saying good-bye she tossed the cell phone onto the passenger seat. It landed next to a brochure open to a small map and driving directions to Reach for the Stars Therapeutic Riding Academy. One decision she'd made after leaving Dad's was to contact the center right away about donating Windy. If her mother really was coming home, she had all the more reason to relieve herself—and Dad—of any unnecessary responsibilities. Mom had sacrificed so much for Natalie. Now, finally, Natalie might find both the courage and the opportunity to repay her.

Twenty minutes later, following the signs to Reach for the Stars, she turned onto a short gravel road bordered by white rail fences. Horses grazed in rolling pastures on either side. At the end of the road stood a massive gray barn-like building with navy-blue trim. Her tires bounced across a cattle guard as she drove through an open gate. She parked between a mud-spattered "dually" pickup and a Toyota sedan with a dented fender.

Grabbing her purse and the brochure, she got out and locked the car. A sign posted on the building indicated HORSE ENTRANCE to the right, with an arrow pointing to a broad sliding barn door. Human traffic was directed to the PEOPLE ENTRANCE, left and around the corner. With a quiet chuckle, Natalie headed left.

Gymnasium-style light fixtures cast a bluish glow throughout the cavernous interior, which sheltered a riding arena with bleacher seating along one side. The rest of the building housed rows of horse stalls, tack and feed rooms, and offices. A riding class appeared to be in progress at the near end of the arena as several onlookers watched from the bleachers.

Natalie breathed in the familiar smells of soft dirt, hay, and horse manure, and felt the day's tension literally fall from her shoulders.

She could think of nothing—nothing in the world—so calming as the aura surrounding a quiet, attentive horse. No wonder the riding school could claim such astounding results with their clients. Windy would make a perfect addition to their stable . . . provided, of course, they avoided water crossings.

Careful not to disturb the class, Natalie found the main office and timidly stepped inside.

A petite, auburn-haired woman stood near a filing cabinet paging through a file. She looked up and smiled. "Mrs. Dixon?"

"Er, no. My name is Natalie Pearce. I'm looking for"—she consulted the brochure—"Mona Kauffman."

"I'm Mona. What can I do for you?" She wore an oversized navy sweatshirt with the words REACH FOR THE STARS, arching over a silhouetted horse and rider heading toward a blazing star.

Natalie angled an envious glance at the woman's taut thigh muscles, accentuated by sleek gray riding breeches—a sight that only reminded Natalie how woefully out of shape she was. She adjusted the strap of her shoulder bag and strove for a nonchalant pose. "I called recently asking about donating a horse. I'm ready to make that decision, if you're interested." She went on to describe Windy's age, training, and personality.

Mona nodded thoughtfully. "She sounds like a good candidate, but, of course, we have our own series of tests she'd have to pass." She explained that a riding lesson at Reach for the Stars probably wasn't like anything Natalie had ever seen.

"Maybe you should take a look for yourself." Mona laid the file aside and led Natalie out of the office.

As they approached the arena, she got a closer view of the class of three young riders. A handler with halter and lead rope led each horse, and two assistants walked alongside to support the rider with a forearm bracing the thigh. The horses traveled at an easy walk in a twenty-meter circle around the instructor.

One child attempted to snap large plastic pop beads together. Another concentrated on stringing spools onto a shoelace. The third, Natalie guessed was a child with Down syndrome. As he rode, he practiced clipping and unclipping colorful clothespins to his horse's mane. With each successful attempt, he squealed gleefully, but the horse neither flinched at the tug of the clothespins nor showed any reaction to the child's ear-splitting laughter.

"As you can see," Mona explained, motioning toward the arena, "the horses we accept must be able to stand a lot of unusual commotion and activity going on around them—and on top of them," she added with a smile. "If your horse can meet those criteria—"

An older woman in faded jeans and Western boots came up and tapped Mona on the shoulder. "Sorry to interrupt," she said, "but Mr. Dixon is here for his evaluation."

Mona smiled apologetically at Natalie. "I'm afraid I have an appointment. This is Karen, our office assistant. If you'll give her your name and number, I'll phone you later about coming over to see your horse."

"Thank you, I'll do that."

Natalie watched as Mona dashed off to greet a plump woman pushing a gray-haired man in a wheelchair. The couple looked to be in their sixties, the woman wearing a hopeful, expectant look, her hands animated as she talked with Mona. Natalie turned her attention to the man in the wheelchair and found herself wondering how exactly Mona and the riding center could help him. There was something hauntingly familiar about the way he held his head cocked to one side and how only the right half of his mouth moved as he spoke.

Natalie's throat closed in recognition. *Mom.* She glanced again at the brochure. On the front was a color photograph of a child with leg braces and crutches reaching up to caress a horse's nose. She cast Karen a confused look. "I assumed you only worked with children."

"Oh, no, we have clients of all ages, and all types of disabilities, both physical and cognitive. Mr. Dixon is recovering from a stroke, and Mona's going to evaluate him to see if he's ready to start riding therapy. I don't understand everything about how it works, but I've seen the amazing changes that are possible after even a few short weeks in the program."

Karen's tone sparkled as she warmed to her subject. "You see, the motion of a horse's walking gait is almost identical to ours. When someone who can't walk sits on a horse, the *feeling* of walking goes all the way from his seat bones to his brain."

Natalie's brow furrowed. A chill prickled up her spine and down her limbs. "So someone like Mr. Dixon might possibly learn to walk again after a stroke?"

Karen nodded. "That's what we're hoping."

Natalie drove back toward Fawn Ridge in a daze. When she arrived at her next destination, she realized only a miracle had kept her from wrapping herself around a telephone pole or getting pulled over for speeding. She certainly had no memory of driving those long, straight miles of country roads. All she saw in her mind's eye was that little Christmas ornament, the one her mother had painted all those years ago.

Windy, cantering across a meadow.

And Mom on her back.

Okay, so maybe Mom would never ride Windy bareback across an open field. Maybe Mom would never do much more than string pop beads together while Windy walked in a slow circle around the arena at Reach for the Stars.

But it was something. Something to hope for. Something to pray for.

It didn't take long for the medicine smells and polished tile corridors of Hope Gardens Convalescent Center to draw her vision away from those "stars" and back down to the reality facing her on solid ground. Just walking in the front door of the place never failed to make her shudder. Hope Gardens wasn't such an unpleasant facility, she had to admit. A usually friendly and caring staff attended the residents, but budget problems and understaffing took their inevitable toll. The harried nurses could spend only so much time with each resident.

And, Natalie admitted sadly, places like this were often where the ill and elderly came to die.

She stifled a shiver. *All the more reason to get Mom back home where she belongs.*

"Mrs. Pearce, what a surprise." Mrs. Blaylock bustled from her office as Natalie passed the doorway. "Won't you come in for a moment?"

With barely subdued distaste, she backtracked and followed the large woman into her office. Mrs. Blaylock motioned Natalie toward one of the visitors' chairs as she took her seat behind the immaculate desk. Natalie sat stiffly, one eyebrow lifted in suspicion. She had trouble trusting anyone whose desk wasn't cluttered with files and paperwork.

"I've had several conversations with your father recently." Mrs. Blaylock ran thick fingers across the folds of her gray wool skirt. "I'm very concerned about his intention to remove your mother from our care."

"What could be better than being cared for in her own home by a full-time nurse?" If Mrs. Blalock thought she could convince Natalie to talk her father out of this plan, the old bat had another think coming. Natalie tugged off her winter gloves and tucked them into her handbag. "Who knows, maybe being in familiar surroundings will do my mother good."

Muscle memory. Like riding a bike. Lissa and the watercolor set. Reach for the Stars. When she considered all the strange happenings in her life recently, it seemed as though each one had been directing her inexorably toward this solution, this renewed reason to hope. Why hadn't she made these connections months ago?

"Besides," she began slowly, already anticipating Mrs. Blalock's negative response, "I've come across a new possibility for therapy."

The administrator spread her hands in a gesture of helplessness. Her condescending glare spoke volumes, which didn't stop her from speaking her mind anyway. "Mrs. Pearce, after all this time, I thought you'd accepted the doctors' prognosis. Why can't you let your mother live out her last days in peace?"

Natalie plucked one of Mrs. Blaylock's business cards from a gray faux-granite holder on the corner of the desk. She flicked the card between two fingers. "Hope Gardens, huh? What happened to the 'hope'?" Hot waves of determination flamed her neck and cheeks. She rose in a huff and marched out of the office.

She didn't slow her pace until she reached the door to her mother's room. One hand on the knob, the other clutching her throat, she suddenly didn't know if she could enter. Was she insane for continuing to hold out hope for Mom's recovery? Clearly Mr. Dixon's stroke hadn't been nearly as serious as her mother's. He was alert, could speak coherent, if halting, sentences.

And Mom on horseback? Had Natalie already forgotten Mom's discomfort around horses—even more so after that stormy night Windy was born? What kind of foolishness had made her believe putting Mom on a horse—even if they could convince her to try it—would miraculously bring her back to them?

Discouragement raked Natalie's nerves. She pressed her lips together and turned to leave.

"Nnnn. Nnnnnn." The moaning sounds came from beyond her mother's half-open door.

She stood there for an eternity, her feet refusing to move. The soft, insistent keening finally drew her to the door. She peered inside, her stomach convulsing at the sight of her mother's shrunken form. In her "good" hand she clutched a handful of twisted sheet and banged her fist repeatedly against the mattress.

"Nnnnn. Nnnaaaa." Her clouded gaze seemed directed straight at Natalie.

"Hi, Mom. Yes, it's me." On legs that felt like rubber, she ventured forward. How many months had she wasted by allowing her guilt and fear to keep her away?

The closer Natalie drew to the bed, the more her mother's agitation increased. The clenched hand moved rapidly and her mouth opened and closed as if she wanted desperately to say something. Then Natalie saw a single tear slip down her mother's cheek, mingling with the spittle that formed at the corner of her mouth.

Natalie's heart climbed into her throat, her own tears nearly blinding her. She reached for a tissue and tenderly wiped away the moisture on her mother's face. Her heart thrilled.

You're in there, aren't you, Mom? Some part of you is still fighting to come back to us.

Easing onto the edge of the bed, she untangled her mother's gnarled fist from the perspiration-dampened sheet and drew the fingers to her lips for a gentle kiss. "It's okay, Mom. You're coming home. I'll never leave you alone again."

16

*N*atalie never made it back to the office that day. Instead, she spent the afternoon walking along the sun-dappled pathways of Fawn Ridge's forested city park. Right or wrong, she'd made some vital decisions. First on the list, she'd cancel the lease on her apartment and move into the farmhouse with her parents. Then she'd dissolve her partnership with Jeff and resume part-time work from home as a freelance graphic designer. Doing so would allow her to continue supporting herself while spending as much time with Mom as possible and helping in her therapy and recovery.

Nothing else mattered now, nothing.

Her mind made up, she drove to the farm to tell Dad. She found him with lemon-scented soapsuds creeping up his arms as he washed his supper dishes in the kitchen sink.

He looked up with a surprised grin as she rushed over to give him a hug. "What are you doing here, Rosy-girl? Thought you were working late these days."

"After I left here this morning I could barely give work another thought." She hung her coat by the back door. "The idea of Mom coming home again—it's all I've been able to think about."

He remained silent as he rinsed the last plate, set it in the drainer, and dried his hands on an embroidered dish towel. "I bet you haven't even had supper yet, girl. Celia brought over one of her famous meatloaves earlier. There's plenty left."

Before she could refuse, he found the plastic container in the refrigerator, sliced a large hunk onto a plate, and set it in the microwave. "There's a bag of salad greens in the produce drawer. Help yourself. I'll fix you some iced tea."

Hunger was the last thing on her mind, but she went through the motions of eating anyway. She could tell from the way Dad fussed over her that he wouldn't be ready to hear her plans until he made sure she was well fed.

And she had to admit, food hadn't tasted this good in . . . okay, not since the other night at Adamo's, but she wouldn't let her mind go there. Savoring a bite of meatloaf, she tried to identify the mixture of flavors. Basil, maybe. An aromatic aftertaste of garlic and onion. And a sauce on top with a definite but not unpleasant kick. She'd have to give Celia a call later and ask her for the recipe.

Finally, pushing her empty plate aside, she told Dad everything she'd decided this afternoon.

He gave his head a decisive shake. "I don't want you turning your own life upside-down, Rosy. We'll manage just fine with the nurse living here. And your business—you and Jeff have worked so hard to build it. Besides, we don't know how long . . . " His work-roughened hand curled into a fist. He lowered his gaze to the floor.

"It doesn't matter how long Mom's recovery takes. I'm going to be with her every step of the way." Poor Dad. He had to be struggling as hard as Natalie to let himself believe there could still be hope. She reached across the table and laid her hand on his arm. "Dad, I need to do this. Let me."

He took her hand and pressed it between his two callused ones. "You're thinking with your heart, not your head, Rosy-girl. I don't want you doing something you'll regret."

"I already regret plenty," she replied over the ache in her chest. "I'm through hiding behind my work to avoid dealing with Mom's illness. Jeff and the printing business can get along without me." She gazed at him with pleading eyes. "Besides, Dad, I honestly think there's a chance we can have Mom back—*really* back with us."

He returned her earnest gaze with moisture-rimmed eyes. "I want that, too, more than you'll ever know. But—" He glanced down, his Adam's apple bobbing. When his eyes met hers again, they held such intense sadness that Natalie had to look away. Surely, Dad hadn't already given up? Not now, not with Mom coming home.

"It'll be okay, Dad, you'll see." She smiled through unshed tears.

He gave her hand a final squeeze and dragged his flannel shirtsleeve across his eyes. "But quitting your job, letting go of everything you've dreamed about and worked so hard for . . . it isn't what your mother would want. Most of all, she'd want you and Daniel—"

"One thing at a time, okay?" A knifelike pain sliced upward through her heart. "Please, Dad, I don't want to argue about this. Nothing you can say will change my mind."

Her chair scraped across the floor as she rose. She bent to give her father a quick hug. "It's been a long day, and I'm exhausted. Don't worry about me, okay? Let's concentrate on getting Mom better, and I promise, everything else will work out fine."

At the door, she slipped into her coat, fished her car keys out of her handbag, and then paused for one last glance at her father. How tired he looked, one elbow resting on the edge of the table, his gray head bowed. Throughout the past year, he'd been the family's pillar of strength, but the strain had etched deep crevices in his face.

And I didn't make things any easier.

Softly, she pulled the door closed behind her and stepped into the cold winter evening. A front had whisked away the clouds, leaving the sky a velvety blue-black mantle sprinkled with stars. She thought of the hope each one of those stars represented to the disabled clients at the therapeutic riding center.

She thought of her mother's starry backdrop for the nativity scene, waiting for the fiftieth star.

She thought of fifty perfect Christmases and all the love stored up and shining bright through the years her parents had been together.

Dear God, don't let Daniel give up on us yet. If you'll give him a little more patience, I promise I'll try again.

Yes, after Mom recovered, she would try to be the wife Daniel deserved. She would make this marriage work if it took the rest of her life.

And she prayed to God it would.

❧

On Wednesday afternoon, Daniel sat behind his desk and stared at the hastily scrawled note in front of him. Coach Arnell at Langston High had been leaving messages since Monday, hoping to hurry his decision about the assistant-coach position. He'd picked up the phone three times already, only to slam the receiver down before dialing. How could he make such a decision without discussing it with Natalie, especially after what Hart had told him over lunch a few days ago?

"Hey, Dad." Lissa sauntered into the office and dropped her bulging backpack on the nearest chair.

Daniel looked up with a start. "Is it that time already?"

"I didn't see the car out front, so I figured I'd find you here." She pushed a stack of papers aside and perched on the edge of the desk, blowing out a long puff of air that lifted her pale bangs off her forehead. "Can you believe Mr. O'Grady assigned three book reports over the holidays?"

"Mean ol' Mr. O'Grady." Daniel clicked his tongue and discreetly slid Coach Arnell's phone message into the top drawer. "So you'll have to read some mind-expanding books instead of spending all your time shopping, watching videos, and hanging out with Jody."

"Like you know anything." Lissa lifted her chin and glared at him.

"Watch it, young lady." The kid had gotten way too big for her britches lately, and it was only getting worse.

And yet they were talking. He sure didn't want to do anything to discourage her. He gave a laugh meant to sound casual, but it didn't. "So what do you have in mind for the holidays?"

Lissa dropped her gaze to pick at a hangnail. Her insolent expression melted as her lower lip began to tremble. "Spend time with Grandma, for one thing. I want to be there when Granddad brings her home Saturday." She peered at him through slitted eyes. "I think we *all* should be there."

He knew exactly what she meant. He didn't know how to reply. Instead, he pushed his chair out and reached for his Panthers jacket, draped over the corner of a glass case full of tarnished basketball trophies from years gone by—kind of like the way his heart felt these days. Faded memories, tainted hopes.

"Let's go home, kiddo. We'll talk about it later."

The short drive to their apartment passed in silence. Daniel couldn't imagine how to break it to his daughter that her grandmother was coming home to die. And according to recent conversations with Bram and Hart, neither of them had been able to tell Natalie, either. Someone had to, and soon, before the shock of realization devastated her completely. And if that happened, he might never win his wife back.

Dread sat like a lump of cold oatmeal in the pit of his stomach. He had to do *something*, before it was too late. "Hey, Liss, I just remembered an errand I need to run." He dropped his gym bag amid the clutter on the kitchen table. "Will you be okay for a little while?"

"Oh, please, Dad. I'm almost fourteen, for crying out loud." Lissa opened the refrigerator and grabbed a soft drink. "So what's up? Last-minute Christmas shopping? Don't forget my new laptop, PDA, digital camera . . . and how about one of those color printer/fax/scanner combo thingies?"

Daniel shook off his worry long enough to choke out a mocking laugh. "On a coach's salary? In your dreams." With a roll of his eyes, he locked the apartment door behind him and jogged to his car.

He let the engine idle while he hammered his frustrations against the steering wheel. Only one thing to do . . . *talk to Natalie*. Arriving in downtown Fawn Ridge, he pulled into a parking space in front of the print shop. Through the spray-on snow art decorating Natalie's office window, he could see her pecking away at her computer. Steeling himself, he went inside.

Deannie greeted him at the front counter. "Hey, Daniel, long time no see. How's it going?" She flicked a red curl off her shoulder and cast him a megawatt smile.

"Pretty good." He shrugged one shoulder. "I hoped to catch Natalie before she leaves."

"Oh, you know her. She'll be here till all hours of the night." Deannie glanced at her computer terminal and tapped some keys. "Go on back, why don't you? I know she'll be *so* glad you stopped by."

"Yeah, right," he said under his breath. He nodded his thanks and started down the corridor.

"Nat?" He tapped on her partially open door and peered inside.

She looked up, and for a split second he imagined he saw a hint of happy surprise in her eyes. "Daniel. What are you doing here?" Her expression quickly changed to worry. "Something hasn't happened with Lissa—"

"No, no, Lissa's fine." He waved a hand. "I just wanted . . . "

Suddenly he couldn't remember why he came or what he'd planned to say. His legs felt like two limp celery stalks, the way they got pale and rubbery if you left them in the produce drawer too long. He sidled across the office and planted himself in the chair opposite Natalie's desk.

She drummed her fingers on a file folder. "Not to rush you, but I've got a lot to finish up before the weekend, since Mom's coming home."

Daniel's senses returned with painful clarity. He took a bolstering breath. "That's what I came to talk to you about." He twisted his wedding ring and tried not to dwell on the fact that he hadn't seen Natalie wearing hers for months. "I know Lissa wants to stay out at the farm for the holidays so she can be near her grandmother, but—"

"That's a great idea." Natalie's expression brightened. "Mom would love it, and I would too." She bit her lip. "You wouldn't mind terribly, would you? You did take Lissa to your parents' for Thanksgiving."

"It's not that." He closed his eyes briefly, searching for the right words. "I just don't want Lissa to be hurt," he said finally. *I don't want you to be hurt, Natalie.*

"Lissa will be fine. She's been visiting Mom at the nursing home all along, even when . . . " She looked away, sadness crinkling the corners of her eyes. "Even when I couldn't bear to anymore."

She turned toward him, tears glistening on her lashes. He struggled to breathe against the stabbing pain under his heart. "It's going to be a good Christmas, Daniel, a *perfect* Christmas. Let Lissa come out to the farm. It'll be so good for Mom to have the family all together—"

Deannie popped into the office. "Sorry to interrupt, but Mrs. Nielsen's on the phone asking if it's too late to make a change in her daughter's wedding invitation. Can you talk to her?"

"Sure. I'm working on it now." Natalie reached for the phone. "Daniel, I've really got to take care of this. Can we talk later?"

"Uh, sure," he said, rising. Everything left unsaid boiled and churned in his belly. "But soon, okay? There's still a lot we need to—"

Natalie didn't give him a chance to finish. "Hi, Mrs. Nielsen. How can I help you?"

"You've got to forgive her." Deannie took Daniel's arm and ushered him to the front office. "Things have been so hectic lately. But it's sure to let up with Christmas almost here." She paused by the counter, her green eyes dancing. "Sounds like you're making some special plans for the holidays, huh?"

He arched a brow. What *was* this gal up to? And why should she be so interested in his Christmas plans? "Natalie's very excited about her mother coming home. She's—we're all—hoping for the best."

He said good-bye and left, feeling as if he'd been trampled in a full-court press. Between Natalie's blind optimism and Deannie's irrepressible . . . whatever it was . . . he'd never even had a chance to approach Natalie with the truth about her mother.

Perfect Christmas? Not much chance of that. Not when his wife faced what might be the most painful Christmas of her life.

❧

"It's fine, Mrs. Nielsen. I'm making the change as we speak," Natalie said into the phone as she typed. "I'll have Deannie give you a call in the morning, and you can come by to okay the proof before we go to press."

Nothing could ruffle her composure today, not with Mom coming home this weekend. Lissa would spend the Christmas holidays at the farm, and together they would help Mom begin painting therapy. It might be many more months before she'd be ready for a class at Reach for the Stars, but everything started with baby steps.

As if life could possibly get any better, Natalie breathed a sigh of relief that the rush of holiday advertising and pro-motional mailings would soon be over. She was on track to be completely caught up by Friday, thanks in large part to Deannie's help. For the first time since hiring Jeff's flighty, sometimes airhead niece, Natalie felt truly grateful to have Deannie around. She almost wished she could keep her as her assistant when she returned to freelancing.

A tiny twinge of anxiety crept in. She had yet to speak to Jeff about her intention to dissolve their partnership. She still hadn't found the right time or the right words—maybe this afternoon. Hard as it would be to break the news to him after all this partnership had done to boost her career, she couldn't put off the discussion much longer.

Deannie waltzed into the office. "Don't you just love Christmas?" Smiling smugly, she set an aromatic mug of spice tea and a massive frosted Christmas cookie on a poinsettia napkin in front of Natalie.

Natalie glanced up from her computer. "Wow! To what do I owe this special treatment?"

"Just spreading a little Christmas cheer. Mom sent over the spice tea mix, and Alan's girlfriend made the cookies."

Natalie raised a brow. "Alan has *a* girlfriend?" Emphasis on the singular. Half the phone calls that came into the shop were some girl or another asking for the hotshot delivery van driver. If his ego got any bigger, his head would explode.

"Well, he's supposedly got a steady date for all the holiday parties." Deannie released a moan that sounded almost envious before lifting her chin. "So . . . how are things with you?" She drew out the question with meaning.

"As in . . . ?" Natalie bit into the cookie, dropping yellow crumbs in her lap. She flicked them away with the back of her hand.

"Your family and stuff." Deannie ran her finger along the edge of the desk. "You know, *things.*"

Natalie closed her eyes for a moment, mild irritation mixing with idle curiosity. Deannie had this infernal penchant for maneuvering personal topics into the conversation—topics that were really none of her business. "You already know we're bringing my mother home on Saturday. My dad had a hospital bed delivered, and the live-in caregiver is moving in Friday to get things set up."

Deannie strolled to the window and gazed toward the brightly decorated tree across the street in the town square.

"It'll be so wonderful to have your family all together again for Christmas."

"Yes, it will." Natalie perused the wedding invitation layout on her computer screen while she sipped from her mug.

"And I know Lissa's going to be thrilled to have you and Daniel back together—"

Hot spiced tea seared Natalie's throat as she swallowed to keep from spewing it all over her desk. It took her several sputtering coughs to recover.

Deannie pivoted from the window. "Natalie, are you all right? Do you need the Heimlich maneuver or something?"

"I'm fine." Waving her assistant away, Natalie shook the crumbs off the Christmas napkin and patted her lips with it.

"Was it me? Did I say something that upset you?"

"Yes, as a matter of fact." She had thought nothing could shake her mountaintop exhilaration. *Leave it to Deannie.*

"Oh." Deannie's lips flattened. "You and Daniel. You're not getting back together, are you?"

Natalie stood, fingertips pressed so hard against the desktop, her knuckles throbbed. She nailed her assistant with a piercing glare. "Miss Garner, listen and listen good. The state of my marriage is not your concern, and I resent your off-handed comments and meddling."

"Well, somebody has to meddle." Deannie lifted her hands toward the ceiling, her face reddening to almost the same shade as her hair. "Because you're obviously too boneheaded to figure things out for yourself." Flinging her curls, she stormed out of the office.

Natalie sank into her chair and rubbed her temples furiously. She took back all her earlier magnanimous praise for Deannie. The girl was hopeless, utterly hopeless.

So much for a peaceful end to the Christmas rush. Muttering, she returned to the wedding invitation for one last review before printing out the proof copy.

Mr. and Mrs. Frederick Howard Nielsen
and
Mrs. David Carl Simms
request the honor of your presence
at the marriage of their . . .

The screen went black for a moment. Then, just as abruptly, it cleared. Shoulders relaxing, she resumed her review from the top . . . and gasped in stunned shock.

Mr. and Mrs. Abraham Eugene Morgan
request the honor of your presence
at the marriage of their daughter
Natalie Rose Morgan
to
Mr. Daniel James Pearce

She shoved away from her desk with such force that her chair slammed into the wall.

"Deannie!"

She thundered down the corridor. It had to be some kind of computer trick, and who else but Deannie could be responsible? "Deannie Garner, I want to talk to you. Immediately!"

Jeff stepped out of his office, blocking her path. "What's going on out here? Keep it down, will you? There could be customers out front."

"She's trying to sabotage me." Natalie stared at him incredulously, so shaken she could hardly catch her breath. Each word scraped her throat raw. "That has to be it. How else—"

Jeff grabbed her arm and steered her into his office. Pointing her toward a chair, he closed the door and seated himself on the edge of his desk. "Just chill out and tell me what this is all about."

She ignored the chair. Instead she paced the small space, one hand pressed to the back of her neck, the other clutching her heaving stomach. "I didn't want to believe it—I still don't have a clue how she did it—but I'm absolutely convinced Deannie is behind all those mistakes I've *supposedly* been making lately." She halted and locked her gaze with Jeff's. "*Why?* Why would she want to hurt me this way?"

"Deannie, sabotage your work? Do you realize how paranoid that sounds?"

She sucked in her breath, tried to rein in her stampeding emotions. "I'm sorry, Jeff. I know she's your niece." She lifted her shoulders helplessly as all the fight drained out of her. "I just can't think of any other explanation."

Jeff looked toward the ceiling and laughed softly. "Deannie's got her faults, I admit. She has an ambitious streak, but as for intentionally setting out to hurt you, or anyone else for that matter . . . " He gave a doubtful shrug.

"Listen," he went on, "you've been under a lot of stress lately—this whole year, in fact." He placed his hands gently on Natalie's shoulders. "Maybe you need some time off."

She suddenly forgot all about Deannie. She looked up at him with sorrowful eyes. "I haven't known how to tell you, but the truth is I need to ask you for a lot more than 'time off.'"

With difficulty she explained her plans to move into her parents' home and her desire to end the partnership. "Have our attorneys draw up the necessary paperwork, and you can buy me out for whatever amount you think is fair." Her voice cracked. "Especially considering how useless I've been to you lately."

"That's absolutely not true." Jeff blew out through pursed lips. "Fact is, I don't know where this business would be without you. Your artistic talent, your business know-how, your rapport with the advertising clients—I'd never be able to replace you."

She frowned and stared at the carpet. "Thanks for the vote of confidence, but I can't give the business the attention it deserves and still be there for my mom the way I need to. And eventually I'll return to freelancing part time, which means I could still accept projects from you like I used to."

Jeff shoved his hands into the pockets of his slacks. "I see you've made up your mind. But let's wait at least a couple of months before we finalize anything."

"As far as I'm concerned, the decision is final." Natalie raised her chin. "But if you'd feel better waiting, it's okay with me."

"I think it's the wise thing to do. For now, this discussion is just between you and me."

They agreed Natalie would take a few days off during Christmas week to get her mother settled in and then come in half-days for a week or two to wrap up any pending projects and pack her personal belongings. She thanked Jeff for his understanding and excused herself.

On the way to her office she glimpsed Deannie slipping quietly into the break room. *Had* Natalie become paranoid? Or was the girl really out to get her somehow? It did sound crazy now, after she'd calmed down. Warily, she walked behind her desk and gave the mouse a gentle push. The screensaver flickered and her "enter password" box appeared. She typed a few keys and the screen returned to the wedding invitation she'd been working on. With a thankful sigh, she saw everything appeared as it should.

17

I almost blew it." Phone receiver tucked between her chin and shoulder, Deannie deftly folded a tomato-and-green-pepper omelet sizzling in a buttered skillet.

"What do you mean, you almost blew it?" came Lissa's exasperated response. "Christmas is next Tuesday. We were supposed to have this plan totally wrapped up by then."

"Don't you think I know it?" Deannie frowned and rolled her eyes. She didn't know who frustrated her more—her pushy partner in crime or their hapless victim. "The whole problem is that your mom has a one-track mind. I got so upset with her, I lost my temper and almost gave myself away."

Lissa gasped. "What happened?"

Deannie explained about Daniel's unexpected visit to the office and overhearing the last part of their conversation. "It sounded like they were making up, like everyone would be together for Christmas. But when I brought up the subject later, she denied it." She slid the omelet onto a plate and cut off a steaming bite with the edge of a fork. "Ow! My tongue!"

"Are you *eating*? When we have so much at stake?"

"Hang on, okay?" Deannie blew several times, then grabbed an ice cube from the freezer and held it to the swelling blister on the tip of her tongue.

"Deannie!"

"Okay, okay. She was working on the Nielsen wedding invitation, and it gave me a brainstorm. I used the terminal at the front desk to hack into her computer—piece of cake, since we're on a network and you figured out how she comes up with all her passwords." She rolled her eyes. "For an artist your mother is *so* unimaginative! The first and last letters of the client's last name, plus the date the project came in—"

"So she's better with graphic design than computer passwords. Get over it. Now will you get to the point, please?"

"All right, already. After I hacked into her system, I changed the names on the wedding invitation to 'Natalie' and 'Daniel.' She totally freaked out."

Lissa burst out laughing. "Stroke of genius! That should have gotten her attention."

"No kidding. She went straight to Uncle Jeff's office, and they talked for a long time."

"About what? Did you hear any of it?"

"With everybody traipsing up and down the corridor, I didn't want to get caught with my ear to the door." The omelet had cooled now, and Deannie spoke between bites, leaning against the counter of her tiny apartment kitchen. "But she looked awfully relieved when she came out."

"Relieved?"

Deannie ran her tongue over her teeth as she replayed the scene in her mind's eye. "Yeah . . . like she'd come to some kind of decision."

Silence fell between them for several seconds. "Deannie, this could be important. You've got to find out what they talked about."

She tore a paper towel from the roll next to the sink and dabbed her mouth. "I suppose I could try to feel out Uncle Jeff about it, but I can hardly ever get him to talk shop with me." She bit her lip. "That's what really bugs me about this whole plan. My part of the deal was to get in good with my uncle so he'd be primed to make me his partner after *she's* out of the picture. So far he still thinks of me as his dumb, klutzy, no-account niece."

"Sorry, if you want your uncle's approval, you'll have to earn it yourself."

Eyes stinging, she slid her empty plate into the sink and ran water over it. "I just thought maybe . . . this time . . . "

"Hang in there. Maybe we can still both get what we want. I'm sure not ready to give up."

Deannie caught her reflection in the dark glass of the microwave door. She shook off a niggling twinge of guilt, gave her red curls a toss, and summoned up what determination she had left. "Neither am I."

⋘⋙

Dr. Sirpless crossed to her desk and picked up a steno pad and pen. A frown pulled one corner of her mouth downward as she took her usual chair at Natalie's left. "Sounds like you've had quite a week. Your mother coming home, deciding to end your business partnership . . . a lot of change for anyone to handle."

Natalie tapped her fingers on the navy velour armrest. She'd almost decided to cancel her Friday evening appointment, but anticipating an even busier few weeks as she moved out to the farm and helped with her mother's care, she might not have another chance to see Dr. Sirpless until well into the new year. It couldn't hurt to get a little professional perspective before she jumped off this cliff into the next phase of her life.

A shiver tightened her neck muscles. "I'm doing the right thing, aren't I?"

Dr. Sirpless gave a noncommittal smile and studied her notes. "Last time we met, you mentioned some unexplained errors at the print shop. What's happened with those? Have you cleared up the mystery?"

Natalie gave a short laugh. "Probably just me being paranoid."

"Why would you say that?"

She flicked a strand of hair off her face. She didn't feel like talking about work, not with Mom occupying all her thoughts. "It's not important anymore. Nothing matters now except getting my mother home and well again."

Dr. Sirpless laid her notebook and pen on the side table. "It's been nearly a year, Natalie. Are you sure that's a realistic expectation?"

"Dad thinks so."

"Does he? Are you sure there isn't another reason he wants to bring your mother home?"

"Of course there is. It's Christmas. Their fiftieth Christmas together."

"Natalie . . ."

A pulsing sensation began in the center of her stomach, a brittle tensing that spread outward through her limbs. "If you're trying to make me admit how ridiculous it is to hope for my mother's recovery after all these months, I get it. It's a long shot. But God can do anything, right?" Her voice broke. "It's Christmas."

❦

Saturday morning at the print shop turned out to be relatively quiet, a double blessing after the difficult session with

Dr. Sirpless last night. Just when Natalie felt she was making progress, finally digging out of her pit of discouragement, the doctor had to throw all these new angles at her—suggestions about unresolved anger, unrealistic expectations, misguided priorities.

At least the conversation had ended on a positive note. When Dr. Sirpless asked if Natalie had given any thought to restoring her marriage, she could truthfully answer that in the last couple of weeks she'd experienced a flicker of hope there too.

But one thing at a time. And today Natalie could only think about bringing Mom home. Jumpy with anticipation, she had to fight the compulsion to check her watch every five minutes while she reorganized her computer and client files. It was the least she could do to ease the transition for Jeff and whoever eventually replaced her.

Midmorning, she headed to the break room for a cup of coffee and a bagel. On the way, she passed Jeff's office and paused to glance in. Through the narrow glass beside the door she saw Deannie sitting across from him and almost didn't recognize the young woman. Deannie's normally confident posture had vanished, replaced by slumped shoulders and blotchy, tear-stained cheeks.

Natalie moved away from the door, her heart clenching. She'd finally convinced herself that her own jangled nerves had been the cause of the strange computer glitches. How selfish of her to blame Deannie, who obviously only wanted to make her uncle proud.

Besides, with Mom coming home, Natalie couldn't hold hard feelings against anyone. At noon she planned to meet Dad and Hart at Hope Gardens to pack up Mom's belongings. An ambulance would transport Mom to the farm, where the live-in nurse already had things ready.

Then on Sunday, after they had a chance to get Mom settled in, Daniel would bring Lissa out. Natalie floated down the corridor as she imagined spending the Christmas holidays with her family. With Mom soon on the road to recovery, and now the chance to reconnect with her daughter, her life finally seemed to be getting back on track. True happiness loomed on the horizon, almost within her grasp . . . except for the state of her marriage . . . except for Daniel.

She poured a mug of coffee and watched the steam rise. With all the angry words that had passed between them, was it even possible they could still reconcile? No question about it, getting back together would be the best Christmas gift they could give their daughter.

But it had to be right. They couldn't rush things. Daniel had so much to forgive her for, but would he? His recent efforts to get close to her again told her he surely must be willing, or at least intended to try. But could she ever fully accept his forgiveness, or anyone else's, until she found the strength to forgive herself?

A line from a psalm filtered into her thoughts: *For I know my transgressions, and my sin is always before me.* In her mind's eye, her sins loomed huge: failing her mother, shutting out her family, leaving her husband, neglecting her daughter.

She pressed a hand to her mouth and sank into the nearest chair. *Dear Lord, give me the courage to face my mistakes. Tell me there's still a chance to make things right.*

Deannie appeared in the doorway. "Oh, sorry. I, uh . . . " She turned to leave.

Natalie had never seen her assistant speechless before. Her heart twisted at the telltale redness encircling those usually perky green eyes. "It's okay. Sit down." She extended a hand toward the chair next to her. "I think we need to talk."

The girl wavered, twisting a curl around her finger. "What about?"

Natalie rose and strode to the counter. "Would you like a bagel? I'm toasting one for myself." She removed a plump cinnamon-raisin bagel from the wrapper.

"No, thanks."

Natalie took several calming breaths as she slipped the bagel into the slicer and drew a serrated knife through it. She dropped the halves into the toaster and carried her coffee to the table. Taking her seat, she searched for a way to breach the divide between them. "I'm so sorry if your uncle is upset with you for something I said to him."

Deannie clasped her hands together on the red Formica tabletop. When her eyes met Natalie's, they held a defiant look. "Uncle Jeff said you accused me of"—quickly she glanced away—"sabotaging you."

Something in the girl's voice and expression stirred Natalie's old suspicions. She narrowed her eyes. "Did you?"

"How could you suggest such a horrible, mean thing?" Deannie shook her hair back and crossed her arms. "Haven't I done a good job for you? Haven't I bailed you out when—when—"

The girl suddenly burst into tears. "Okay, okay! I may be sneaky and underhanded, but I'm a lousy liar." She stood abruptly and paced. "I already confessed to my uncle. Yes, I did it. All of it. Mr. Craunauer's Apple Cart flyer. The Moonbeams mailing. The wedding invitation you were working on the other day. There, are you satisfied?"

Natalie could only stare open-mouthed as shock waves pulsed through her. Yes, she'd suspected Deannie for a while, wanting to blame anyone but herself for the series of misprints. But even so, she had never quite believed the girl capable of this level of deception.

"Why?" Natalie asked. "Can you just tell me why?"

Deannie ripped a napkin from the dispenser and furiously wiped her eyes. Taking a shaky breath, she turned and leaned against the counter. "All I wanted was for my uncle to notice me, to give me a little credit for having some brains and talent. I kept thinking if I could make you look bad, and then be the one to catch your mistakes and fix them, Uncle Jeff would realize I could be an asset to his business. Then, if you left the company, maybe he'd make me his partner." Her jaw clenched as she continued in a hard voice. "Garner and Garner Printing and Advertising. Nice ring, huh?"

"Oh, Deannie." Natalie rose and took both the girl's hands in her own. "I'm sorry you felt driven to take such drastic steps. But I know your uncle loves you very much. Did you tell him what you've just told me?"

Deannie pulled her hands away and took a step sideways. "It only made him madder."

"Let me talk to him. Maybe—"

"No, you'll only make things worse. He already thinks I'm a complete failure. This really cinched it."

Natalie lifted a hand to smooth the tearful girl's curls. "Deannie Garner, you are *not* a failure. Anybody with the imagination and skill to break into my computer and make those changes . . . " She gave a cynical laugh and shook her head. "How you managed it is totally beyond me!" Sobering, she continued, "I'm certainly not condoning what you did. There's no getting around the fact that it was childish and irresponsible. But if you'd only apply your talents legitimately, I know your uncle would be proud to have you working with him."

Deannie sniffed noisily. "You're just saying that."

Natalie put a hand to the girl's chin, forcing eye contact. "I saw your work the other day when I let you fill in for me. You really do have an eye for graphic design."

"You honestly think so?" Deannie blinked rapidly as a fresh flood of tears poured down her cheeks. "Oh, Natalie, I'm so ashamed. Can you ever forgive me?"

Forgive you? How can I not, when I need forgiveness so badly myself?

"Of course I forgive you." She drew the girl into her embrace. "Let me talk to Jeff. I know we can get this whole mess straightened out."

❧

Deannie tugged a tissue from the box on her desk behind the front counter and blew her nose one more time. Natalie had gone immediately into Uncle Jeff's office, and though Deannie couldn't make out what they were saying, she could hear their raised voices through the walls. From the sound of things, Natalie must be letting her uncle have it pretty hard.

"You are such an idiot," Deannie chided herself. It was only at Lissa's persistent urging that she'd agreed to help break Natalie's confidence. If the plan succeeded, both Deannie and Lissa stood to benefit—the main reason Deannie had agreed to take part in the first place.

But she never expected to end up liking and respecting Natalie as much as she did right this moment.

Face it, Garner, you were a loser from day one. No wonder nobody, including your uncle, has any respect for you. The time had come to make some changes.

She steeled herself and lifted the telephone receiver, punching in Lissa's phone number. "Hi, it's me. I need to tell you something."

"Deannie? How many times have I told you not to call me? It's too risky."

"I know, but—"

"But what? Did something happen?"

"Yeah, something happened. I came to my senses. I can't do this anymore. Whatever you do from now on, you're on your own."

Lissa's voice rose shrilly. "You can't back out now!"

"Remember what you said yesterday about how it's up to me to prove myself to my uncle? I realized what I've been doing lately isn't the way to go about it."

"I know we've been sneaky, but you know what my mom's like. If you don't care about your own goals anymore, think about mine. How else am I going to get through to her?"

Deannie glanced over her shoulder. The door to her uncle's office remained closed; the discussion between him and Natalie continued. Even so, she turned her face toward the wall and lowered her voice as she spoke. "Lissa, I'm telling you, it's over. Your mom is in my uncle's office going to bat for me, in spite of everything I've done."

"Wha-what are you saying? You told her? She *knows*?"

"I never mentioned your name. No one has any clue anybody else is involved. And don't worry, I intend to keep it that way."

Deannie's head snapped around at the sound of a door opening. Her uncle and Natalie emerged from his office. "Gotta go now. All I can say is I wish you luck. If your mom ever does find out you were involved, you're going to need it." She dropped the receiver into its cradle as her uncle approached the front counter. Natalie had disappeared into her own office.

Deannie rested limp hands in her lap and looked sheepishly up at her uncle. "Am I totally fired?"

He folded his arms and appeared to examine a spot on the wall somewhere behind her head. "You should be, after those stunts you pulled. But Natalie has convinced me I should give you another chance."

A surge of sheer relief sent shivers up her spine. Her feet did a small tap dance under the desk. "Yes!"

Bracing his forearms on the counter, Uncle Jeff skewered her with his stare. "Young lady, what you did not only undermined a good and talented woman's self-confidence but also risked serious financial losses for this company. It's going to take me awhile to forget such irresponsibility."

Deannie bit her lip. "I promise, I've learned my lesson."

He shook his head. "Thing is, if you're as bright and creative as Natalie seems to think you are, you have the potential to become a valuable contributor to this company." His jaw tensed. Tiny creases formed in the soft skin under his eyes. "If I take a chance and promote you to graphic designer and customer liaison, can you assure me you'll channel those skills in the right direction?"

Deannie gulped. "What?"

His mouth stretched into a reluctant grin. "You heard me."

She flew from her chair, dashed around the counter, and wrapped him in a bear hug. "I'll make you so proud, you'll wonder what you ever did without me!"

Over her uncle's shoulder she glimpsed the block lettering on the glass door of the entrance. Mentally, she changed GARNER & PEARCE to GARNER & GARNER. She gave a squeal of delight. If she cleaned up her act and buckled down, her dream might still come true.

18

*L*issa perched on the edge of her bed and glared at the silent telephone. Panic knotted her stomach. "Deannie, you freakin' creep."

They had been so close to getting Mom out of the office and back home, the crucial first step in getting her and Dad back together. At least one part of the plan remained on track. Today Grandma would leave the nursing home and go home to the farm. Surely Granddad wouldn't have checked her out if she weren't improving.

Lissa relaxed slightly as she remembered the day she'd taken the watercolors to her grandmother. In that tiny second when she detected recognition in Grandma's eyes, in those moments as Grandma's pale, bony hand reached for the paintbrush, gripping it with determination, Lissa's whole world had tilted. If she hadn't already been late for school, she'd have stayed and helped her grandmother paint something—a tree, a flower, anything. If she could only revive in her grandmother's frail body the smallest memory of her awesome talent, the rest would follow. It *had to*.

And when Mom said Grandma had actually tried to paint on her own? Chills tingled up and down Lissa's arms.

Grandma would get better. She'd paint the new star for the manger scene. Mom would wake up to everything she'd been missing all these months and take Dad back. They'd be a family again. A real family.

A tear slipped down her cheek. As she reached for a tissue to blow her nose, guilt snaked up her spine. *Okay, Lord, I admit it. I did some horrible things. But you didn't seem to be doing anything. I'm sorry. I really want to trust you, but can you just give me some little sign?*

The slamming of the apartment door interrupted her prayer.

"Liss? You home?"

"In my room, Dad." She tossed the tissue in the wastebasket and followed thumping and rustling sounds to the kitchen, where she found her father putting away groceries.

"Here, catch." He tossed her a package of peanut butter cookies. "Early Christmas present."

"Oh wow." She faked a grin. "If this is a sample of what's to come, I can't wait till Christmas morning."

"You know what a big spender your dad is." With a laugh, he set a perspiring gallon jug of two-percent milk on the top shelf of the refrigerator.

Lissa slid her fingernail under the edge of the cellophane wrapper and tore open the cookie package. The tempting aroma of peanut butter filled the air. She shook out two golden-brown cookies and popped one in her mouth.

"Hey, don't spoil your lunch."

She wrinkled her nose as Dad set two cans of pork and beans by the stove. "If that's what we're having, I'll stick with cookies." Dusting crumbs off the front of her cable-knit sweater, she went to the cupboard for a glass. "How come we can't go with everybody to help move Grandma home?"

"Granddad didn't want too much commotion the first day. The move will be stressful enough." Her dad folded and flattened a brown paper grocery bag. He wore a thoughtful look as he reached into the next bag and set two boxes of cereal in the cupboard beside the stove.

Straightening, he turned to Lissa. "I, uh, heard something interesting this morning."

"Oh, yeah?" She retrieved the milk jug and filled her glass.

"I ran into Mrs. Garner at the market and she—"

"Deannie's mom?" Lissa stiffened. Her fumbling fingers would hardly work to screw the lid onto the milk jug.

"No, her aunt. Jeff's wife. She started rambling about what Jeff's going to do when your mom leaves the company." He shrugged, his brow wrinkled in confusion. "Did you have any idea she was even thinking about it?"

Lissa took a slow slip of milk and hoped Dad didn't notice how her hand trembled. *It was happening!* She let the cool liquid slide down her throat while she worked to control her excitement. "I knew Mom planned to take some time off from work over the holidays to help with Grandma." She looked askance at her father. "Mrs. Garner really said Mom's leaving the print shop?"

"Not in so many words, but she implied it's been a hot topic of discussion around their dinner table this week."

Lissa turned away and swept a hand across her cheek. "But Deannie never said . . . "

Her father stuffed the folded grocery sacks next to the trash can under the sink. "What about Deannie?"

"Oh, nothing." She forced a light tone and a smile. "I'll be in my room for a while."

Her thoughts were in a jumble as she trudged to the bedroom. Surely, Deannie would have said something if she'd known. After all, Mom's resignation had been their primary goal from the beginning. But if it were true, wouldn't Mom at least have mentioned it to her or Dad?

Pacing between the bed and dresser, she glanced at the clock. The red digital numbers read 11:48. Mom had probably left the office by now to meet Granddad and Uncle Hart at the nursing home.

But she had to know . . . and right away! She grabbed the phone and punched the number for the print shop.

Deannie answered on the second ring. "Garner and Gar—I mean, Garner and Pearce Printing and Advertising. May I help you?"

"Hey, it's me. And I caught that little slip, by the way."

"Lissa." Deannie released a nervous giggle. "What's up?"

"I just heard a rumor about my mom leaving the company." Her tone dripped sarcasm. "Want to fill me in here, *Miz* Garner?"

"Huh? Are you sure?" To Lissa's dismay, the surprise in Deannie's voice sounded genuine.

"My dad heard it from your aunt in the grocery store this morning. Yeah, I'd say my source is pretty reliable." She thrust her hip out and planted her fist on it. "Come on, Deannie, you've got to help me out here."

Deannie sputtered into the phone. "What am I supposed to do, just walk into Uncle Jeff's office and ask? Under the circumstances, can you imagine what that would sound like to him? Uh-uh, no way."

"Okay, if you won't ask him, I will. Transfer my call to your uncle."

"You're crazy," Deannie shot back, but a moment later Lissa heard several clicks as Deannie transferred the call.

"Jeff Garner," came the distracted greeting.

"Hi, Mr. Garner, it's Lissa Pearce." Her stomach knotted, but she forged ahead. "I . . . I'm so sorry to bother you, but I have to ask you about something."

"Hi, Lissa. How are you? Bet you're looking forward to having your grandmother home. I know your mom is sure excited about it."

"Yeah, we're all very happy." Lissa ran her fingers through her hair and then twisted the ends. "Mr. Garner, has my mom said anything to you about quitting her job?"

Silence fell. "You mean she hasn't told you?"

It's true! Lissa scrunched her eyes shut and clenched her fist in a tiny victory dance. She took several shallow breaths before replying. "Well, not officially. But I, um, heard she was thinking about it."

"Then I don't think it's my place to tell you anything more."

"That's okay. I understand." She thanked him and said good-bye. His hesitance didn't matter. She already had the answer she wanted.

She pumped her arms. *Yes, yes, yes!*

～☙～

Daniel dumped the pork and beans into a saucepan, retrieved a couple of hot dogs from the refrigerator, and sliced them into the beans. The smell reminded him of Boy Scouts and scorched meals over campfires. He pursed his lips. No wonder Lissa would rather eat cookies.

While the beans warmed, his thoughts returned to his conversation with Mrs. Garner at the supermarket. How many times had he questioned Natalie's decision to go into business with Jeff? She was an *artist*, for crying out loud. She shouldn't be sitting behind a desk pushing papers and getting eyestrain and carpal tunnel syndrome at a computer. But the idea that she'd alter her whole life—*again*—based on false assumptions galled him beyond belief. Even worse, facing her mother's inevitable death might only drive her deeper into withdrawal and denial.

He couldn't let that happen. Leaving the slice of buttered bread on the counter, he scribbled a note to Lissa on the back of the grocery receipt and tacked it under the Pete's Pizza refrigerator magnet—not their most efficient means of communication, but it served her right. He turned the burner off under the beans, yanked his jacket from a kitchen chair, and stormed out the door.

His Bronco still radiated warmth from his trip to the supermarket. Checking his watch, he figured if he hurried, he could arrive at Hope Gardens about the time everyone else did. Maybe he could pull Bram aside and convince him to be honest with Natalie before they moved her mother, before Natalie's hopes rose any higher—as if they weren't over the top already. He didn't blame Bram for wanting to bring his wife home to the farm for her last days, but Natalie deserved to go into the new arrangement with her eyes wide open.

As he approached the Hope Gardens turnoff, he caught sight of Hart's pickup and Natalie's silver Saturn parked behind an ambulance near the front entrance. Bolstering himself with a deep breath, he parked the Bronco nearby and marched inside.

He almost collided with a young, aqua-uniformed nurse carrying a food tray from the dining room. "May I help you, sir?"

"I'm Belinda Morgan's son-in-law. I'm looking for—"

"Oh, yes, they're preparing to transport her." She nodded in the direction of Belinda's room.

Daniel knew the way. As he rounded the corner, he saw the entourage emerging from Belinda's room. With Hart in the lead, two ambulance attendants guided the gurney on which his mother lay. Bram and Natalie followed.

"Hey, bro," Hart said, catching Daniel's eye with a look of surprise. "Didn't expect you."

As the group neared, Daniel's pulse quickened. He fell in step beside Hart. "I know," he said, "but I thought . . . " He glanced over his shoulder at Natalie but after a quick smile, she broke eye contact. Bram, his stoic face etched with weariness, cast him a knowing, almost apologetic look.

A flicker of something else shone in Bram Morgan's eyes, something that drew Daniel up short. He moved aside, leaning against the wall as the group passed. Poor old Bram hadn't given up hope either. To tell Natalie the truth would mean he'd have to admit it to himself, and the elderly, careworn man, obviously still deeply in love with his wife, simply could not do it.

Raking a hand through his hair, Daniel pushed away from the wall and started down the corridor, the ache of discouragement dogging every step. He pushed through the front doors into bright December sunlight in time to see an ambulance attendant close and latch the double doors at the back of the vehicle.

"Dan, you coming out to the house later?" Hart called as he walked around to the driver's side of his pickup.

"No, I'll stay out of your way for now." He paused on the sidewalk, his shoulders caving around the lump of defeat settling in his chest. The hurried trip to Hope Gardens had been a mistake—a waste of time, hope, and energy. Hands stuffed in his jacket pockets, he trudged toward the parking lot.

As he passed Natalie's car, she looked up from unlocking her door and offered a tentative smile. He'd fully intended to let things drop, to go on his way and try once more to trust that somehow the God he'd always believed in would work things out. But, suddenly, he couldn't help himself. He stopped, straightened his shoulders a little, and smiled at the slender, blonde beauty who was still his wife—for how much longer he would not hazard a guess. He didn't even attempt to disguise the look of love in his eyes.

"It was nice of you to come by." She glanced down shyly. "I didn't expect you'd be here, although I guess I should have known. You were always so good about visiting Mom even after we . . . "

Only the width of the car separated them, a mere hunk of gleaming, metallic-silver-painted steel. He could leap it if he had to. To get close to the woman he loved, he could easily lift that car and toss it across the parking lot.

Instead, he left his hands where they were, safely tucked away, and nonchalantly walked around the front of the car. "I, uh . . . " He was close enough to reach out and touch her if he wanted to and take her into his arms in one quick motion.

He rammed his hands even farther into the depths of his pockets. His fingers closed around the cool satin lining. "Nat," he said hoarsely, "I'm worried about you."

She gave a breezy laugh, and her keys jangled. "Don't be. Everything's fine."

"You don't know . . . "

She looked up with searching eyes. "What's wrong now? Is it something else with Lissa?"

"No. It's . . . I . . . " His vocal cords felt like someone had poured rubber cement down his throat. What was it about being close to her lately that turned him into a blithering idiot? Why couldn't he simply tell her what scared him so? Better yet, why couldn't he sweep her into his arms and shield her with his love from the inevitable pain and sorrow she would soon face?

Natalie's lips twisted with annoyance. She shrugged her purse strap higher on her shoulder and fumbled for the door handle. "For heaven's sake, Daniel, every time you get that tone in your voice, I'm certain something horrible has happened to our daughter. I wish you wouldn't worry me like this." She yanked open her door, another barrier between them.

He set his hands atop the doorframe and held it firmly. Gathering his wits, he blurted, "Are you quitting your job at the print shop?"

This time Natalie resorted to stammering. "I, uh . . . Where did you hear that?"

"From Sue Garner."

"Jeff's wife?" She laughed nervously.

"Well? Is it true?"

She looked past him as engine sounds started up. From behind him he heard Hart's voice. "We're heading out, Nat. See you at the farm."

Daniel glanced over his shoulder to see the ambulance pull out, followed by Hart's pickup.

"I really have to go." Natalie tossed her purse into the front passenger seat. She moved to sit behind the wheel, but Daniel caught her by the wrist.

"Wait." His heart hammered. He couldn't let her leave like this, couldn't let another chance to break through to her slip from his grasp. "Natalie, can't you just once be honest with me about what's going on in your life? Have things gotten so bad between us that we can't talk at all?"

She stared at his hand gripping her arm until, embarrassed, he released it. He noticed her breathing had become shallow and rapid, mirroring his.

She blinked furiously, avoiding his gaze. "I'm not intentionally keeping anything from you. But I can only deal with one thing at a time. Yes, I've asked Jeff to look into buying me out of the partnership. Later I'll freelance from home like I used to."

"Home. You mean the farm." It was not a question. He felt the stab of disappointment all the way to his spine.

"I'm canceling my apartment lease as of December 31. I'll start moving out right after Christmas." She brightened. "Lissa can help me. It'll be fun. Now, I really must get going. Mom will be waiting."

Before Daniel could utter another word, she slammed the car door and whipped out of the drive and onto the main road. The silver sedan sped from view around the next curve.

⊷⊷

Natalie knew she flirted with danger, accelerating past the speed limit on the rural two-lane highway, but Daniel's nearness had unnerved her. She glanced in the rearview mirror, fearing—and yet ridiculously hoping—Daniel might have followed. She had the road to herself, however, and with a deep, shuddering breath she relaxed the pressure on the gas pedal.

Slowing the car only made her realize how severely her hands were shaking. In fact, she trembled all over. She'd be useless to her mother if she ended up in the hospital—or worse, the morgue—if in her recklessness she wrapped the car around a utility pole or rolled it in a culvert. With effort, she calmed her breathing and tried to halt this absurd fit of trembling. In her mind's eye she could still picture Daniel's strangely worried expression and the unmistakable look of love in his eyes.

He still loves me. She felt more certain of it than ever.

Heat rose in her face. *Daniel, I love you too.*

Her own thoughts turned on her, bombarding her with Dr. Sirpless's implied questions from last night. *When are you going to face reality, Natalie? Admit what you know is true. Stop running. Stop hiding from the people you love.*

"Dear God, I'm trying," she said aloud, her eyes brimming. With all her heart she wanted to put her family back together. But she couldn't, not until she made amends for her failure to be there for her mother when she needed her most.

What about Daniel and Lissa? Don't they need you too?

The unspoken question cut her to the marrow, but she could only handle one load of guilt at a time. *I'm sorry. I'm sorry.* She hammered a fist against the steering wheel. Would there ever come a time when she could finally stop apologizing?

Releasing a tremulous breath, she opened the console and found a tissue to dry her eyes. The elation of seeing Mom leave that dreary nursing home had evaporated. The peace Natalie so longed for—the renewed spirit she'd felt certain would be hers now that Mom was coming home—still eluded her. All the way to the farm she sensed some vital grain of understanding lingered just beyond her mind's grasp, something she should know already, something with the power to make all the difference in her life.

And as she turned into the gravel driveway and parked alongside Hart's pickup, she realized Daniel knew and had tried to tell her, but she hadn't wanted to hear it.

19

$\mathcal{E}$arly Sunday morning, Natalie hurried downstairs to her mother's room, anxious to see how she had passed her first night at home. It would have seemed more right if they could have moved Mom straight into the upstairs bedroom she'd shared with Dad, but until she grew stronger, it would be easier on everyone taking care of her to have her in the hospital bed in the downstairs guestroom.

Natalie tapped on the partially closed door and tiptoed inside. "How's it going, Carolyn?"

The private nurse, a dark-haired woman in her late-forties, sat on the edge of Mom's bed with a bowl of Cream of Wheat. She smiled over her shoulder. "Hi, Mrs. Pearce. We're just having breakfast."

"Please, call me Natalie." She moved closer and extended her hand toward the bowl. "Would you mind if I take over?"

Carolyn offered a hesitant frown. "Are you sure? She had a small choking episode during supper last night."

A warning twinge pinched Natalie's stomach. "Does that happen often?"

"It isn't unusual." The unspoken addendum—*at this stage*—showed in the lift of the nurse's brow. "We just have to be careful."

"Of course." Maybe if Natalie had joined the stroke support group with her father, she'd know more about this aspect of patient care.

"Nnnn. Nnnaaaa." With jerky motions, Mom rolled her head toward Natalie.

"Yes, Mom, I'm here. This looks delicious. Sprinkled with cinnamon, just like you used to make for Hart and me, remember?" With a nod of assurance to the nurse, Natalie took the woman's place on the side of the bed and offered her mother a spoonful of the warm, milk-thinned cereal. A few white, grainy droplets trickled from the paralyzed side of her mother's mouth, and Natalie gently caught them with the spoon.

"I'm so glad to have you home, and just in time for Christmas," she said brightly as she offered her mother another bite. Wrinkled lips clamped down on the spoon. Disappointment clamped down on Natalie's heart. "Oh, Mom, don't—"

Cream of wheat dribbled onto the snowflake-bedecked paper napkin spread across her mother's chest. The shrunken woman gave a sputtering cough and turned her head away.

"Maybe you'd better let me," Carolyn quietly suggested.

Ignoring her, Natalie set the bowl on the nightstand and scooted closer against her mother's side. Tightness squeezed her chest as she pressed her mother's limp hands between her own. "You've got to eat to get stronger for Christmas—the fiftieth perfect Christmas you promised Dad." She spoke over the silent tears clogging her throat. "You do remember, don't you, Mom?"

Crepe-paper eyelids fluttered and closed. Her mother's breathing slowed as her head relaxed into the pillow.

A knot of alarm swelled under Natalie's heart. "Mom?"

"She's just very tired." Carolyn placed a hand on Natalie's shoulder. "The move and all . . . it's taken a toll on her strength."

Natalie shot the woman an anxious glance. "You don't think it was too much for her, that we shouldn't have brought her home yet."

The nurse smiled with compassion. "As long as the patient's health permits, it's almost always the best thing to return loved ones to their own home." Her voice dropped to a whisper as she added, "For the time remaining."

Bristling irritation corkscrewed up Natalie's spine. "You must have misunderstood. Mom came home so that we could be closer to her and help her get well."

Carolyn folded her hands at her waist and took a step back. "Yes, of course."

"So only positive talk from now on, okay?" Giving a firm nod, Natalie rose and crossed to the window. A powdered-sugar dusting of snow covered the winter-brown grass in the pastures. Rocky, the stocky bay gelding, followed Dad from the barn as he trundled out a wheelbarrow full of hay. Windy trotted close behind, and Natalie already missed her beloved Appaloosa mare. After Christmas, Mona Kauffman from Reach for the Stars would come out with a horse trailer to take Windy to her new home. At least Mona had said Natalie could visit her there anytime.

Once more, she recalled her strange experience the night of her birthday, when the little Appaloosa Christmas ornament had almost shattered, and the amazing vision of her mother riding free and happy across the pasture on Windy's back. It had seemed so *real*. Like a sign. A reason to hope again. If only they could get Mom well enough—and brave enough—by springtime, maybe they could convince her to try riding therapy. Maybe they'd even let Mom ride Windy.

Hugging herself against the chill that penetrated the windowpane, she turned toward Carolyn. "Have you heard of the therapeutic horseback riding program near Putnam?"

"My niece volunteers there. They do marvelous things for their clients." The nurse looked from Natalie to her mother and back again. She said nothing, but the dark expression in her eyes conveyed her doubts.

"Seeing Mom like she is now, it may seem like a long shot. But I—" Natalie stopped herself, fearing the pragmatic nurse would only scoff at talk of visions and signs. Instead, she nodded firmly and said, "I just know she's going to be all right." She turned back to the window, lost in thought.

Later, Natalie offered to sit with her mother while Carolyn took a short break. In the quiet room, she tried to turn her thoughts toward prayer but couldn't seem to get past the barrier of her emotions. Finally Mom stirred. Noticing a Bible on the bedside table, Natalie found a small devotion booklet tucked inside. "How about I read to you, Mom?"

Her mother wiggled two fingers as if asking Natalie to hold her hand. Natalie squeezed gently, feeling the warmth against her palm. Mom gave a soft cough and angled a glance toward the Bible in Natalie's lap.

Natalie released her mother's hand and opened the devotion booklet. The day's reading was from John 14, where Jesus told his disciples, "In my Father's house are many rooms; if it were not so, I would have told you. I am going there to prepare a place for you. And if I go and prepare a place for you, I will come back and take you to be with me that you also may be where I am."

Words that should have brought comfort only chilled Natalie. Again, she had the sense of some truth lurking just out of reach. She slid her gaze from the page to her mother's serene profile. Another weak cough resonated from Mom's throat. The midmorning shadows gave her skin a bluish cast.

Footsteps sounded on the stairway, and Natalie fumbled for the tissue she'd stuffed in her jeans pocket. She wiped the moisture from her eyes a moment before her father appeared in the doorway, looking dapper in his gray Western-cut Sunday suit, polished black boots, and string tie. He glanced at the Bible in Natalie's lap and smiled his approval. "Reading to your mom, sweetie? I know she appreciates it."

Then his gaze swept over her. Disappointment clouded his face. "I was hoping you'd go to church with me, Rosy-girl."

Natalie shifted self-consciously in her scruffy jeans and sweatshirt. "I'd rather spend this time with Mom. Maybe next Sunday."

"Sure." Dad went to the bedside and bent to give his wife a tender kiss on the cheek. Her eyelids lifted heavily in response. "Mornin', angel. Sleep well?"

Carolyn returned just then, a steaming mug of coffee in one hand and a knitting bag in the other. She set her things by the narrow recliner that had been delivered with the hospital bed. "She was a bit restless last night, but I know she's glad to be home."

"Good. That's good." Dad's Adam's apple vibrated as he stroked Mom's arm. "Belinda, honey, you won't mind if I leave you for a bit to go to church, will you?"

Mom's drowsy gaze cleared momentarily. One corner of her mouth curled in the beginnings of a smile.

"I've got so much to be thankful for," Dad continued, "especially having you with me again. And everybody in our Sunday-school class will be asking about you—can't let them down. I'll come straight home after the service, I promise."

Mom blinked twice and then her chest rose and fell in gentle sleep. Natalie smoothed a strand of her mother's gray hair. "She looks happier already, don't you think, Dad?"

"I reckon so." He gave a loud sniff before he kissed Mom again and strode out of the room. A few minutes later the back door closed with a thud.

Mom slept off and on the rest of the morning, while Natalie prepared Hart's old room for Lissa's arrival. That chore done, she stood at the foot of Mom's bed, arms folded across her ribs. The *click-click* of Carolyn's knitting needles played counterpoint to Mom's soft, snuffling breath, the only sounds in the sunlit room.

A sense of urgency prickled Natalie's insides. She'd so hoped for a stronger response from her mother, a clearer indication that coming home would spark the rapid recovery the whole family had been praying for. She tried to reassure herself that Mom just needed to regain her strength after being moved from the convalescent home.

But Christmas would be upon them in only two days. What if Mom didn't come around enough to be able to paint the fiftieth star? Lissa was right—that one simple act meant everything. Even if it took Dad, Hart, and Natalie to help Mom sit up and hold the paintbrush, she had to paint that star.

Carolyn began to hum softly, one of those catchy arrangements of a Christmas carol Natalie had heard playing endlessly on Deannie's radio at the print shop. An idea burst into her troubled thoughts. She spun around and hurried to the living room, where she selected a couple of Mom's favorite Christmas CDs from the storage carousel. She slid them into the stereo and hit the play button. In a moment the majestic chords of "Angels We Have Heard on High" poured from the speakers. She played with the volume knob until she found a level she thought could be comfortably heard down the hall in her mother's room. Surely, the Christmas music would lift Mom's spirits and help her find her way back to them.

And a little Christmas tree for the bedroom, that's what Mom needed. Somewhere in the attic Natalie's father had stored the small artificial tree she had decorated for her own room as a young girl, and there were plenty of extra lights and ornaments.

Half an hour later she had retrieved the dark-green, dust-covered plastic storage bag and emptied the misshapen tree and all its parts onto the kitchen floor. The stand had become so rickety that only duct tape held it together, but she could disguise the sticky gray layers by using one of Mom's extra Christmas tablecloths for a tree skirt. She wedged the metal tree trunk into the stand and then straightened and realigned the crushed branches. Wear and tear over the years had left them rather sparse, but lights and ornaments would fill in the gaps. In the hall closet she found the leftover decorations and soon had the little tree looking presentable.

With a ceremonial flourish, she carried it into her mother's room. "Carolyn, can you help me? I want to set this on the dresser where Mom can see it when she wakes up."

The nurse offered a cheery smile as she set aside her knitting. "I'm enjoying the Christmas music too." She moved a lamp and a stack of magazines to make room for the tree and helped Natalie arrange the brightly colored tablecloth around the base and find an outlet for the light cord.

"Do you think Mom can hear the music?" Natalie paused at the foot of the bed and gazed uneasily at her mother's sleeping form.

"I'm sure she can." Carolyn touched Natalie's arm. "Your mother may not be able to express it, but I know she's grateful to be in her own home again, with her family around her."

When are you going to face the truth, Natalie? That annoying little voice in her head refused to be silenced. She squeezed her fists until her nails dug into her palms and turned toward the brown-haired nurse, keeping her voice low. "You honestly don't think she's going to get better, do you?"

Carolyn's shoulders sagged. She signaled Natalie to join her in the hallway. "I could give you my professional opinion. I could tell you what her doctor has written in her chart. But I'm fairly certain that isn't what you want to hear."

"Probably not." Natalie inhaled a shivery breath and leaned against the doorframe. "But it's Christmas, right? Miracles happen."

The nurse offered her a sad smile. "Yes. Sometimes they do."

Daniel sat next to his daughter at the 8:30 church service, but his thoughts were anything but worshipful. He barely mumbled the words to the hymns, and when the pastor finished his sermon, Daniel knew he'd be hard pressed to recite any of the central points. He couldn't help but notice his daughter seemed equally preoccupied.

While the ushers collected the offering, he gave in fully to his wandering thoughts. Getting up early on Sunday morning was not his favorite thing to do, especially after a full week of school, usually with late nights and long weekends devoted to practices and games. But after Natalie left him, he couldn't bear the awkwardness of running into her at their usual eleven o'clock service. Lissa had put up a fuss, but Daniel insisted she'd have to settle for seeing her mother and the rest of the family during the Sunday-school hour.

Today, however, Lissa had talked him out of staying for Sunday school. The fidgeting girl simply couldn't wait to get back to the apartment to finish packing for her stay at the farm. Not that Daniel felt much like sitting through the adult singles class this morning. He'd never quite felt he belonged there, but he wasn't exactly half a couple any longer, either.

Leaving the sanctuary, they met Lissa's grandfather on his way to the senior adults' class. Lissa raced over and hugged him and asked how soon she could come out to the farm.

"Anytime you're ready, Grandma will be waiting." Bram gave his granddaughter a hug back and a smile that carried more sadness than joy.

Daniel wondered at seeing his father-in-law at church this morning and said so when Hart, Celia, and the twins arrived moments later.

"You know Dad," Hart said as they stood talking in the parking lot. "He'd have to be on his deathbed to miss Sunday services." He cringed at his own choice of words.

"Dad, can we go now?" Lissa tugged on his coat sleeve. "I need to finish packing."

"In a minute," he snapped, instantly regretting how the curt response must have sounded to Hart and his family. Willing a calm he didn't feel, he aimed his key remote at the Bronco and pressed the unlock button. Lissa flounced past him, climbed into the vehicle, and cast him a hurry-up glare through the tinted glass. He pretended not to notice, saying to Hart, "I just hope your dad uses his worship time to pray about how to help Natalie face the truth about her mother."

Hart glanced toward Celia. As if reading his mind, she ushered their lanky twin sons toward the church building. Then Hart shot Daniel a scathing look. "Lay off him, okay? You're so focused on Natalie, you're not seeing the big picture. Can't you see Dad is grieving? Don't you care what this whole thing is doing to him?"

"Of course I care. But it isn't doing anyone any good to deny the truth." Daniel glanced over his shoulder at his daughter, her arched eyebrows screaming her impatience.

"Lissa's expectations are even higher than Natalie's, if that's possible. I really dread taking her out there this afternoon."

Hart kicked at a loose stone near the curb. "You just came from worship, right?"

"You know I did." Daniel shot his brother-in-law a confused look.

"And you wouldn't be here if you didn't believe in Almighty God."

His irritation grew. "Of course not."

"Then act like you believe. Quit trying to take matters into your own hands and let God do his thing. Who knows? He might surprise us all." Hart narrowed his eyes at Daniel as if daring him to respond. A moment later he stalked away, leaving Daniel stewing over the truth of his brother-in-law's words.

On the way home, he stopped at a gas station to fill the tank and run the Bronco through the automatic car wash. The delay only added more fuel to Lissa's seething impatience. They picked up a fast-food brunch of poached eggs and sliced ham on English muffins and returned to the apartment, where Lissa immediately wolfed down her meal and began hauling enough luggage to the door for a whole army of teenagers.

"Dad, come *on*," she urged from the top step.

He dragged himself out of his recliner and played packhorse, helping Lissa lug her things down to the car. Rolling Lissa's massive wheeled suitcase, he looked up to see her heave an overstuffed duffel bag into the Bronco. By the time he reached the car, she'd already run back for the last two bags and tossed them inside. Scowling by the open tailgate, she tapped her booted toe.

"All right already." He hefted the suitcase and wedged it into the slot Lissa had saved for it in the back of the Bronco.

Getting in behind the wheel, he shut his eyes for a moment. Hart's words in the church parking lot still rang in his ears, and the truth stung. When had he gone from passive forbearance to pushing everyone to handle things his way? What made him suddenly think he had all the answers?

❧

Silent night, holy night! . . . The beloved words of Belinda Morgan's favorite Christmas carol enveloped her like comforting arms. Even more lovely, she breathed in the blessed smells of home. Under her hand she recognized the feel of a favorite cotton quilt, one her own mother had made, worn soft from years of use.

She sensed a presence nearby but could not find the strength to open her eyes. A gentle hand brushed her cheek, adjusted her pillow, and tucked the quilt around her tired frame.

Natalie? Did she speak her daughter's name, or only think it? Nothing about her body seemed to work right anymore. She felt her useless head begin to rock, as it seemed to do so often of its own volition. Again, the gentle touch to still it.

"It's all right, Belinda. Just rest quietly."

She should know the voice by now. Such a kind, gentle voice. Oh, yes, the nice lady named Carolyn, the nurse who did all the things for Belinda that she could no longer do for herself. She wished she could thank the woman for her tender ministrations.

"How's she doing?"

Oh, Natalie, there you are. Come and sit near me, my darling girl. We must talk.

"Still sleeping."

"You'll call me if she should wake up?"

"Of course."

But I am awake, can't you see? Natalie, please hear me.

There was so much she needed to make her daughter understand . . . so much left unsaid between them.

Oh, my dearest Natalie, this wasn't your fault, it was mine. I'd known for weeks that something wasn't right, but I didn't want to worry any of you—didn't want to admit it to myself. You mustn't blame yourself any longer. Your husband needs you. Lissa needs you. The whole family is counting on you now, more than you realize.

She felt her hand go into spasms. She clutched the quilt, grasping, clawing, reaching out in a desperate attempt to break out of this frightful state of *not being.*

All is calm, all is bright . . .

Another raspy cough strained her tired chest muscles. She must be calm, save what strength she had left. *Lord, I'm not quite ready to come home to you. Much as I long to, I have unfinished business here.*

She could almost hear the soft whisper of his reply. *Don't worry, Belinda. When the time comes, you will have the strength you need.*

As Natalie put away the leftovers from lunch, she heard a car in the driveway. She glimpsed Daniel's Bronco and hurried to greet her daughter at the door. "You're early," she said, giving Lissa a hug. "I didn't expect you until later."

"How's Grandma doing?" Without waiting for an answer she squirmed out of her mother's embrace and hurried toward the hallway.

"Hi to you too," Natalie mumbled.

"Sorry, but Lissa couldn't wait any longer." Daniel stood outside the screened porch next to a massive pile of luggage, shifting his weight from one foot to the other. His breath formed clouds in the December air.

An awkward silence stretched between them. Natalie shivered as the cold edged its way inside. "Um, do you want to come in and warm up? I can stir up some hot chocolate."

He looked uncertain, a kind of puppy-dog loneliness in his eyes that tugged at her heart. Still, she hoped he'd say no. Memories of yesterday's encounter outside the nursing home played in her mind, and she almost feared the nearness of him. Worse, she didn't want to risk their falling into the inevitable argument, especially with Christmas only a couple of days away and Mom right down the hall. She'd made up her mind to make this as pleasant and hope-filled a Christmas for their daughter—for the whole family—as she possibly could.

She came out of her brief mental fog to realize Daniel had opened the screen door and started inside with two of Lissa's bags. He propped them against the side of the refrigerator. "Sure, I'll stick around. Never been able to turn down your hot chocolate."

"Okay, great!" Could she sound any more like a lovesick teenybopper? She cleared her throat and shifted her voice to a lower register. "I'll get it started while you bring in the rest of Lissa's things."

As she set the teakettle to boil, she looked at the growing stack of luggage and wondered where in the world Lissa planned to put it all. Hart's old room was the smallest bedroom in the house.

Several minutes later, she sat across from Daniel at the oak table, marshmallows melting into a creamy froth in their steaming mugs. She blew gently and took a careful sip.

"How did your mom handle the move home?" Daniel asked.

She averted her eyes from his strong hands wrapped around the mug and the manly, curling hairs peeking from beneath the cuffs of his blue corduroy shirt. "She's been tired—not eating much." She glanced toward the hallway, where sounds of Lissa's cheery chatter echoed. "But she's getting lots of rest, and I know she'll come around. It's almost Christmas," she went on with a laugh that belied her doubts, "and when have you known my mother not to celebrate Christmas to its fullest?"

Daniel chuckled softly. "Never."

"I've already been thinking about how she can paint the fiftieth star for the nativity scene. On Christmas morning we'll prop the backdrop beside her on the bed, and I'll help her hold the brush and guide her hand." She smiled, her eyes misting, her heart clenching. "And that way she'll be able to keep her promise to Dad."

"Fifty perfect Christmases. Can you believe it?" Daniel stared into his hot chocolate. His voice grew thick with emotion. "Dear God, I wish . . . "

She stifled a tremor. "What? What do you wish, Daniel?"

He chewed his lip but did not meet her eyes. "Seeing how happy your parents have always been, I had dreams of you and me celebrating our fiftieth anniversary someday."

The bitter taste of guilt rose in Natalie's throat. "And obviously I ruined it for us." Too late to stop it, she heard the cynicism in her voice.

Apparently, Daniel heard it too. He snorted. "Heaven knows I did *my* best."

Suddenly all rational thought flew from her mind, and raging self-pity flooded in. "Your *best?* You call moving to Putnam with Lissa and leaving me when I needed you the most, your *best?*"

"Leaving *you?*" His voice rose. He leaned forward, forearms pressed against the tabletop, hands fisted until his knuckles turned white. "I think you've got it backwards. You left me, remember?"

Her body tensed in response. She returned his angry glare. "I did not leave you. You made me move out."

"As I recall, I told you that if you didn't want to be a wife and mother anymore, you'd better find another place to live, because *somebody* had to make a home for Lissa."

Natalie trembled with rage and fought to keep from screaming her reply. The words came out in a strained, ragged whisper. "You never once tried to understand what I was going through, never—"

"Like you ever cared about my feelings, what I wanted." He thrust himself backward and crossed his arms, the violent motion shaking the table and sloshing hot chocolate across the pinecone-print placemats.

"Coaching, that's all you ever think about." She twisted sideways in her chair, hardly able to bear the sight of him. "One more scouting trip, one more win, one more chance to be picked up by a big-city high school."

Daniel's jaw clenched. He sat forward again and drummed his fingers. "I was going to wait until things settled down after Christmas, but since you brought it up . . . I've had a job offer, a good one. It'll mean moving—"

She swung around to face him, her fury now laced with alarm. "Don't even think about taking Lissa with you. I'll sue for custody. I'll—"

Carolyn stepped into the kitchen. Her expression, though calm, held an urgency that abruptly silenced Natalie. "Mrs. Pearce, you'd better come quickly."

20

Natalie sprang from the chair, talons of dread clawing at her throat. She rushed past Carolyn, barely hearing the nurse's request that Daniel call Natalie's father in from the barn and get word to Hart.

She slowed as she entered the bedroom. Her gaze took in the scene, and time seemed to stop. To her left, the lights on the misshapen miniature Christmas tree twinkled in merry oblivion, the dresser mirror reflecting the colorful display. A patchwork quilt outlined the shape of her mother's thin legs. The amber glow of the bedside lamp cast highlights on the woman's silver hair.

Lissa sat close to her grandmother, clutching the thin, age-spotted hands. "Grandma, hold on. You've got to," she pleaded through her tears. "You *promised*."

Carolyn touched Natalie's arm and drew her aside. Keeping her voice low, she explained, "Your mother is running a temperature, and her breath sounds are diminished. After her choking incident yesterday, I'm afraid it might be aspiration pneumonia. I've called her doctor and started oxygen."

"Pneumonia?" The word wedged in Natalie's throat like a block of ice. She glimpsed the plastic tubing attached to a portable oxygen tank beside the bed. Her mother's chest rose and fell in ragged, shallow breaths. "Can't you do something else? What did the doctor say?"

"We'll start her on antibiotics and try to bring the fever down. I've raised the head of the bed to ease her breathing. Beyond that, it's a matter of keeping her comfortable."

Mom's head lay weakly against the pillow. Perspiration dotted her temples. Her eyelids drooped heavily . . . and yet, as Natalie drew close, Mom's eyes seemed to focus clearly on her. Natalie placed one hand on Lissa's heaving shoulder and rested the other on her mother's bony arm. "It's okay, Mom. I'm here. I'll take care of you."

Her mother's gaze filled with determination. The urgency spilled over into a choking cough and a fruitless attempt to speak. "Nnnaaaa. Luuuhh."

Shaking her head, Natalie smoothed a hand across her mother's brow. "I can't understand you, Mom. Don't try to talk. Just rest."

Her mother's mouth and throat labored, evidence of her frustration. "Luuuhh," she tried again and sputtered mean-inglessly before another coughing spell wracked her body.

Natalie sensed her father's presence beside her and glanced toward him with a helpless frown. The musky-sweet scent of hay and horses permeated his work-stained barn jacket. He pulled off his soiled leather gloves and stuffed them into a pocket.

Carolyn appeared at the foot of the bed. "I'm sorry for alarming you, but I thought you'd want the family together in case . . . "

"Yes, thank you," Dad said. "Do"—he swallowed with dif-ficulty—"do you think it's close?"

Carolyn shook her head. "There's no way to know."

Natalie edged away, her own breath catching in her throat. This could not be happening. Not now—the day before Christmas Eve! There were promises to keep, a star to paint.

Fifty perfect Christmases, Mom, you promised!

The bedcovers rustled, and the raspy voice murmured again, "Luuuhh." Her gaze locked with Natalie's. "Nnaaa. Luuuhh."

"Mom," Lissa urged through her sobs, "listen to Grandma. She's trying to tell you something. I know it's important."

Natalie moved her head slowly from side to side. Her limbs felt leaden, her mind numb. "I . . . I don't understand."

It was more than her mother's garbled words she couldn't make sense of. She no longer understood anything. All her restored hopes, and now this?

God, how could you!

Natalie's father knelt at the bedside, pressing his wife's face between his hands, drawing her attention to him. "We're listening, darling. Take your time."

Natalie watched through the mist of her tears as a strange and beautiful clarity came over Mom's face. With an effort drawn from her deepest being, she spoke: "T . . . tell Nnnatalie . . . nnnnot her fault . . . ffforgive . . . lllearn . . . to love."

Her clear, determined gaze fixed on Natalie. She drew in several gasping breaths, and her eyes fell shut.

❧

Daniel paced the hallway between Belinda's open bedroom door and the kitchen. With each trip, he glanced out the kitchen window in hopes of seeing Hart's pickup drive up. Pausing at the bedroom door, he saw his mother-in-law's frail body writhe in a series of raking coughs. She was already so weak. How would she ever survive this new assault?

A long, aching sigh scraped through his chest. He longed to help somehow, but Natalie had made it abundantly clear that she found his presence more an intrusion than a comfort. No reason to expect today to be any different, especially after the argument they'd just been having.

And Lissa. What could he possibly say to reassure his daughter, after all her hoping and praying and childlike tenacity?

His moment of anguish was interrupted by the rumble of tires on gravel. Tearing his gaze away from his sobbing wife, Daniel strode to the kitchen to meet his brother-in-law.

Hart burst through the door, eyes wide with panic. "Mom—how is she?"

Daniel laid a firm hand on Hart's arm, halting his headlong dash toward the hallway. "It doesn't look good. I'm sorry."

Shoulders sagging, Hart let his head drop forward as he expelled a shuddering breath. He rested one hand on the back of a chair and took a moment to compose himself. "Are Dad and Nat with her?" At Daniel's nod, he hurried from the kitchen.

Daniel hated feeling so helpless, so useless, so . . . in the way. He collapsed into the nearest chair and pressed his palms against his eyes. Tears would have been a welcome relief, no matter if some of his coaching colleagues might think them weak and unmanly, but at this moment Daniel felt only chilling numbness.

"Daddy?"

Lissa's shaky voice and tentative touch on his arm caught him by surprise. When he looked up into his daughter's tear-streaked face, his heart wrenched. He opened his arms to her and she collapsed onto his lap, burying her damp cheek against his neck.

"It's okay, sweetie." He tenderly stroked her hair.

"Why, Daddy? Why'd Grandma have to get sick like this? She's supposed to get better. I've prayed and prayed for her to get better."

"We all have, honey."

What was he supposed to say? That even though Grandma was dying, she'd be going to a better place? That time heals all sorrows? Platitudes never brought the comfort they were intended for. And they certainly wouldn't dry a little girl's tears. For now, holding her would have to suffice.

Trembling, Lissa lifted her head. "Oh, Daddy," she said, tears falling afresh, "I've messed things up so bad."

He crooked a finger under her chin, not sure what to make of this unexpected confession. "Lissa, what are you talking about?"

"It's so bad, I can't even tell you. You'll hate me." She buried her face deeper into the crook of his neck.

More confused than ever, Daniel kissed the top of his daughter's head. "I have no idea what this is all about, but I guarantee you, nothing could ever make me hate you, sweetheart. Come on, you can talk to me."

Her sobs grew louder, the wetness soaking through his shirt. He stretched one arm across the table to grab a napkin from the ceramic dispenser. Coaxing her to sit up and blow her nose, he willed himself to remain silent and wait, even as his mind raced in search of possible explanations. He couldn't for the life of him imagine what Lissa would have to feel guilty about, least of all concerning her grandmother. More than any of the rest of them, she had faithfully visited her grandmother at the convalescent home, talked to her as if she understood every word, prayed every night for her recovery.

Lissa wiped at the tears still streaming down her cheeks. "Everything I did—it was all for you and Mom. And now

Grandma could die, and I'm so scared for her, and I'd miss her so much, but . . . "

She clenched her fist around the soggy napkin. "But what scares me even more is that if Grandma dies now, Mom will never forgive herself, and she'll go back to working even harder, and she'll never make up with you, and you guys will get divorced for sure, and—"

"Hold on, hold on." Daniel pressed his daughter's face between his palms and tried to keep his voice level. "Lissa, honey, what exactly did you do?"

She closed her eyes for a moment and sucked in a quivering gulp of air. The revelation that followed left Daniel staring open-mouthed at his shamefaced child. Sinking deeper into the hard wooden chair, he felt the spindle-back press into his spine as Lissa told him how she'd schemed with Deannie.

"I thought if Mom didn't give all her time to working, she'd start thinking about how much she missed us and would want to make up with you. But I also wanted to help Grandma. I didn't know if she really could get better, but then after I brought Grandma the paint set, Mom seemed to think so, too, and if Grandma did get well, it would be even better because then Mom wouldn't have any reason to feel guilty anymore, and then you two could get back together and . . . and then we could be a family again."

She sighed as she ran out of steam. Her blue eyes shone. "But if Grandma doesn't get better . . . oh, Daddy, what are we going to do?"

Daniel slowly shook his head, still trying to comprehend what he'd just heard. "First of all," he began, "I want you to understand that whatever you've done, you are absolutely not responsible for whether Mom and I get back together." He tugged on a lock of her hair. "The problem is, Liss, no matter how good your intentions are, manipulating other people's lives and emotions is never the answer. It only makes things even harder to unravel in the end."

He cringed inwardly. *Look who's talking, fella.* He'd sure done his share of manipulating this past year. Maybe a good chunk of it was the passive-aggressive kind, but he couldn't deny the many ways he'd tried to manipulate Natalie into seeing things his way.

"But can you? Unravel things, I mean?" The plaintive note in her voice tore at his heart.

"We can sure try. But it's going to take some time. We all have a lot of healing to do." Again, he extended his arms and enfolded his daughter in his embrace. "And eventually you're going to have to tell your mother everything you've just told me."

"I know," she said into his tear-soaked collar.

He held her close, half listening to the muted sounds coming from down the hall and wishing he could hold and comfort Natalie like this. Her hopes for a "perfect Christmas"—maybe even her hopes of ever forgiving herself—could vanish forever if Belinda didn't pull through this crisis. He hated to admit how right Lissa might be, that any chance he and Natalie had of getting back together would die as well.

Lissa gulped and peered up at him. "What happens now? Will they take Grandma back to the hospital?"

"I'm not sure. Probably they'll try to take care of her here." Hard to explain to a scared little girl that in a case like Belinda's, extreme lifesaving measures usually weren't taken. His thoughts ventured again to Natalie and what this must be doing to her. He tried to think of ways he might help, errands or phone calls he could handle for the family.

On the other hand, considering Natalie's current state of mind, she'd probably see anything he did as interfering. *Tell it like it is, Pearce. Manipulating.* Yeah. Maybe he'd best stay out of the way for now.

He worried about Lissa too—the shock of witnessing her grandmother in such distress, coupled with remorse over the problems her scheming had caused. "Your mom and Granddad and Uncle Hart will be very preoccupied today," he began carefully. "It might be a good idea if you and I went home to the apartment for a while. We can check later—"

From behind him he heard a startled intake of breath, then Natalie's bruised retort. "You're not taking Lissa anywhere. I want her here with me, with my family."

Daniel turned and faced his wife, realizing he'd once again said the wrong thing. "I just thought—"

"You just thought you'd deprive me of one more person I love. No. Go if you want to, but Lissa stays. I need her." Her tone vibrated with desperation.

"Natalie, please." He lowered his voice. "You don't realize the effect all this is having on our daughter."

Hart appeared in the doorway beside Natalie. "Listen, Daniel, we're all pretty rattled about Mom. And Lissa's not a little kid anymore. If Natalie wants her here, let her stay."

"I'm only trying to think about what's best for everyone." Frustration burned behind his eyes. He turned to his daughter. "Liss, it's up to you."

Avoiding eye contact, she whispered, "I'll . . . I'll be okay, Dad. I can handle it."

Outnumbered, he raised his hands in surrender. "Fine. I'll get out of your way. But please let me know if there's anything I can do."

"Thanks." Hart placed a protective arm around Natalie's shoulder. "I know you meant well, Dan. We'll keep you posted about Mom."

Daniel lifted his suede jacket from the hook by the door. Shrugging it on, he walked over to Lissa and gave her a hug. "Hang in there, kiddo. If you need anything, call me. And remember what we talked about."

"I know," she answered shakily.

His heart ripping in two, he left.

❧

Christmas morning dawned with blazing glory, a golden sunrise more fitting for Easter Sunday than for the nativity. Shafts of sunlight sliced through the east windows of the farmhouse, a jarring, glaring light that seemed to mock Natalie's despair. Her mother, now unaware of her surroundings, had barely survived two grueling days and nights of coughing spasms. With each passing hour she grew more frail.

Natalie sat alone in the living room, a chair pulled close to the library table where the nativity scene stood in silent tableau. She'd spent the rest of Sunday and most of Christmas Eve at her mother's bedside, pleading with God for a miracle and yet increasingly convinced it would never come. She'd tried to catch an hour or two of sleep last night, but her tormented thoughts wouldn't subside. Giving up, she'd wandered the dark house until she found herself in the living room. She settled into the overstuffed chair and kept vigil there through the hushed early-morning hours, staring into the darkness, wondering, doubting, remembering.

As the harsh light of morning fell upon her mother's starry backdrop, still propped against the easel in the alcove, an angry sob caught in her throat. Her mother would not paint a new star this Christmas; the fifty-year-old promise would be broken. She fought the urge to take an ax to the thin piece of painted plywood and toss the fragments into the wood stove, then watch it go up in flames along with all her shattered hopes.

Her father appeared in the doorway. She'd heard him go out to the barn earlier, as he always did at dawn to check the horses and begin his daily chores. His whiskered cheeks crinkled into a sad smile. "Mornin', Rosy-girl. Merry Christmas."

Natalie pressed her palms against the arms of the chair, starting to rise. "Dad, don't—"

As he motioned for her to remain seated, she noticed that under one arm he carried a large, flat package wrapped in bright silver Christmas paper, a fluffy red bow tacked in the center. He placed the gift tenderly in her lap. "For you, from your mother."

"What—?"

"Open it." Dad pulled over the ottoman and sat in front of her, his bony, blue-jeaned knees protruding at awkward angles as he watched her expectantly.

Natalie stared at the package, tight bands of dread and disbelief closing around her throat. It took her several moments to find the courage, but finally, her fingers trembling with anticipation, she plucked off the bow and tore at the paper. As it parted, her gaze fell upon a gilt-framed oil painting, her mother's delicate but unmistakable signature across the lower right-hand corner.

The subject of the painting caused Natalie to suck in her breath in bittersweet agony. Her own image, bearing a wistful, almost dreamlike expression, filled the larger portion of the picture. The eyes looked upward with unmasked affection toward two other faces—Daniel's and Lissa's. Mom had crafted the painting in such a way that the three portraits were distinctly individual yet seamlessly interconnected. Natalie's sandy-blonde hair flowed into Lissa's silvery-yellow tresses, which blended with Daniel's darker waves. Natalie's head seemed to rest gently upon Daniel's shoulder.

She pressed a fist to her lips, unable to speak. In a sudden flash of memory she remembered the dream she'd had the night before Lissa hitched a ride to the convalescent home to take her grandmother the watercolor set. Daniel and Lissa had been in her dream, and starlight shining on something she couldn't make out, some kind of package.

And then she remembered that day in the barn, seeing something shiny in the tack room closet before Dad quickly blocked her view and closed the door. The gift had been there all along, waiting for her, waiting for this day, this moment.

Again, she had an unsettling impression that some vital truth lurked just beyond her understanding. Daniel knew, and . . . Mom knew.

"Forgive. Learn to love," Mom had urged.

"Isn't it something?" Her father shifted the portrait so it caught the now softening morning light. "Your mother's last painting. She finished it just days before her stroke, said she wanted to save it for your family Christmas present. She'd planned to do one of Hart and Celia and the boys, but—" A ragged moan tore from his chest. "She so wanted this Christmas to be special, our fiftieth Christmas together. But now . . . Oh, Rosy-girl, what will I ever do without her? What will I do when she's finally gone?"

For the first time since Mom's stroke, Natalie witnessed her father completely break down. His shoulders rocked with loud, painful sobs, and she could do nothing but set the painting aside and wrap him in her arms.

"Oh, my Belinda," he mourned, "oh, my darling Belinda."

She longed to be able to comfort her father, but her own grief and guilt seared with the intensity of a blazing ceramics kiln.

Forgive. Learn to love. The words repeated over and over in her mind until she thought she would go crazy from trying to understand.

"Mom?" Lissa's fragile voice cut through her silent, angry questions. Wrapped in an afghan, the girl stood at Natalie's side with sleep-tousled hair and tear-stained cheeks. "Is Granddad okay?"

Natalie rubbed her father's back and tried to lace her tone with the reassurance she knew her daughter needed. "Yeah, honey. It's just . . . with Grandma so sick, it's going to be a really tough Christmas."

Natalie's father, his tears spent, gave a final shudder and sat up. He dragged a sleeve across his face. Weakly, he smiled at Natalie, then looked up at his granddaughter. "Your old granddad's a mess this morning, huh?"

"Me, too, Granddad. I can't stop worrying about Grandma."

"Me, neither." He scooted over to make room for her next to him on the ottoman and tucked her under his arm. Their knees brushed Natalie's.

"I had this really weird dream," Lissa said, a tremor in her voice. "Grandma was in heaven, and she was so happy. God took her far out to the very edges of the universe. Then he gave her a set of oil paints in the most beautiful colors ever created. 'I've decided we need a few more stars out this way,' he told her, 'and I want you to paint them.'" Lissa cocked her head. "Isn't that the most wonderful thing you could imagine for Grandma, all better and painting stars for God?"

Natalie gazed at her daughter, glimpsing in her shining eyes an inexpressible mixture of hope and love. Her own heart seemed to shatter. "Yes," she answered, her voice raspy, "yes, it is."

A peaceful stillness enveloped Natalie, a gentle letting go—no, more of a letting *in*. Deep in the farthest recesses of her mind a new awareness filled her, a golden, glimmering silence.

Silence? No coughing, no strained breathing coming from the guest room.

"Oh, God—Mom?" Natalie stumbled past her father and daughter and tore down the hall. She grabbed the door facing and skidded into the bedroom, her heart hammering. "Carolyn? Is she . . ."

The nurse stood at the bedside, holding her stethoscope against Natalie's mother's chest. She looked toward Natalie and offered a gentle smile. "The fever's broken, and her lungs sound clear. She's sleeping comfortably."

Natalie collapsed against the footboard, a sob catching in her throat. She felt her father's arm go around her shoulder, his whiskery cheek brush hers. She found his hand and squeezed. "She made it to Christmas Day, Daddy. She kept her promise."

"She sure did, honey. God is good."

As she stood watching her mother sleep, that elusive truth Natalie had been avoiding crept forward, growing and gathering strength, crystallizing in her understanding like the pure, bright ring of the tiny glass bell Dad had hung on the tree the night of her birthday.

She knew now what she had to do. It would be a perfect Christmas after all.

21

*D*aniel had just climbed out of the shower when the phone rang. A towel wrapped around his waist and water dripping onto the carpet, he snatched up the receiver at his bedside. "Hello?"

"Hi, it's me."

At the sound of her voice, his jaw dropped. His grip on the towel faltered, and he almost dropped that too. "Natalie?"

"Daniel, I'm so sorry for how I treated you after . . . after Mom got so sick."

"It's okay, I understand. How is she?" He was almost afraid to ask. "Any change?"

"The worst is over. She's resting quietly—no more coughing or fever."

"That's great news." He cleared his throat. "And you? Are you doing okay?"

"Hanging in there. It's been a rough couple of days, but now that Mom's past the crisis, Dad and Lissa and I are getting dressed for the Christmas church service. I'm . . . I'm calling to invite you to spend the day with us."

He noted something different in her tone, a lightness, a freshness he hadn't heard in almost a year. His pulse quickened.

"Can you meet us at church," she asked tentatively, "then come over for dinner?"

He scrubbed a hand through his wet hair and mentally scrambled to take in this unexpected development. "Are you sure? I mean, I didn't expect anyone would be going."

She sighed. "Mom would never want us to skip church on Christmas morning. And . . . "

He could sense the struggle in her hesitation. His stomach muscles tensed. His grip tightened on the receiver.

"And it wouldn't be the same if we didn't go together—you and me and Lissa, as a family." Her tone softened even more. "I don't think I could bear it if the three of us missed even a single Christmas together."

He sank onto the edge of the bed and replied throatily, "Thanks, Nat. I'll be there."

✷

An hour later he met Natalie, Lissa, and Bram on the front steps of the church beneath the tall, white bell tower as Christmas chimes rang out across the rooftops. With Lissa between them, Daniel and Natalie followed Bram down the aisle to where Hart and Celia and the boys were holding places for them in the Morgans' usual pew. The eight of them completely filled one row, except for the place Belinda Morgan would have taken. They did not spread out to absorb her space but sat shoulder to shoulder, each drawing strength and hope from the other.

Glancing at his wife's serene profile over the fair head of their daughter, Daniel felt more certain than ever that something had changed in Natalie. Her impenetrable shell seemed to have cracked, and instead of crumbling with despair as he so feared, she seemed somehow stronger, more alive, more at peace than he'd ever known her to be in all the years they'd been married.

At the conclusion of the service, the pastor requested special prayers for Belinda Morgan and family. "Our dear sister in Christ survived a serious setback over the weekend, but I understand she is much improved this morning, a true blessing on this glorious Christmas Day." The pastor gave a soft chuckle. "And we all know how much Belinda loves Christmas."

Natalie's chin lifted almost imperceptibly, and Daniel glimpsed her sniff back a tear. He ached to reach around Lissa and place a reassuring hand on Natalie's shoulder, but something told him to wait.

At the closing hymn, "Joy to the World," the whole church resounded in voice and song. The last chords faded, and Daniel watched in admiration as the woman he loved graciously accepted expressions of concern from the family's many friends. Deannie Garner, looking as quiet and reserved as he'd ever seen her, walked over to their pew and gave Natalie a tear-filled embrace.

Natalie's annoyance with the girl had been no secret, but clearly something had changed there too. Had they managed to settle their differences during Natalie's last few days at the print shop, or had their flighty former babysitter finally grown up? Seeing Jeff Garner walk over, Daniel couldn't help but notice the open affection and pride in Jeff's eyes when he rested his arm on his niece's shoulder. Apparently, something had changed for the better in that relationship as well.

The family slowly made their way down the aisle amidst the many well-wishers. Among them were Miss Fellowes, who owned Moonbeams Bookstore, and Hart's veterinary clinic receptionist and her family. Even the grumpy Mr. Craunauer from The Apple Cart awaited his turn to offer words of encouragement to Natalie and the family.

"How you holding up, man?"

Daniel recognized the voice of his friend Carl Moreno and turned to greet him. "Better than a couple of days ago," he answered shakily, gripping Carl's hand. "Your family having a good Christmas?"

"Oh, yeah. Got the usual feast at my folks' house later." Carl coaxed Daniel aside. "You and Natalie, you back together . . . or is it just, you know, temporary because of Christmas and all?"

"Wish I could answer that. But I'm hopeful."

"I'm pulling for you."

"Thanks. That means a lot."

Carl returned to his family, and the congregants gradually moved from the church foyer into the cold but brilliant noon sunlight.

"So good to see all of you here together," Pastor Mayer said as the Pearces and Morgans approached him on the front steps. He gave Bram Morgan a warm embrace. "When I visited with you yesterday, things were looking pretty grim. I certainly didn't expect to see you at worship this morning."

"Natalie insisted." Bram gave his daughter a weary smile. "So here we are, right where Belinda would expect us to be."

A lump formed in Daniel's throat when his daughter spoke up. "It's my grandparents' fiftieth Christmas together," Lissa said. "I prayed so hard for Grandma to have Christmas with us, and I knew Jesus wouldn't let us down."

The pastor lightly touched her cheek and smiled knowingly. "He never does, sweetie. We may not always understand his ways, but he never, ever lets us down."

When Natalie returned to the farm with her family, the tempting aroma of roasting turkey greeted them as they stepped through the kitchen door. Until two days ago, she had been planning this dinner with great anticipation, a celebration of her mother's return to them and the fulfillment of a promise kept. When the crisis hit, she'd all but given up hope—hope of ever receiving her mother's forgiveness, hope of restoring her marriage, hope in the power of God.

Dad tossed his felt Western hat onto the coat rack. "I'll go check on your mother and let Carolyn know we're home."

"I'll go with you, Grandpa." Lissa kicked the back door closed with the heel of her suede boot.

Natalie strode to the stove and pulled open the oven door. "Give Mom a kiss for me. I'll be in as soon as I check on dinner."

Seeing Dad and Lissa's expectant faces, she knew she'd done the right thing by going through with her plans. Early that morning she'd peeled the potatoes, mixed the stuffing, and started the turkey roasting. After giving the turkey a quick basting, she tied one of her mother's aprons over her green wool jumper and set the potatoes on the stove. As she set the timer on the coffeemaker, Hart and his family arrived, the twins making a boisterous entrance through the kitchen door.

"Careful," Hart chided, one of Celia's pies balanced on each hand. "You boys make me drop one of these and you'll be eating Cheerios for dessert." The twins made way, and he slid the pies onto the counter.

Celia draped her coat and shoulder bag over a hook near the door. "How can I help?" she asked, pulling an apron from a drawer.

Natalie stirred the potatoes. "Would you like to make the gravy? You're the only person I know whose gravy rivals Mom's."

"That's quite a compliment." Biting her lip, Celia turned to the pantry for the flour canister.

"How about me?" Hart asked as he washed and dried his hands at the kitchen sink.

Laughter bubbled up in Natalie's throat. "You know what your job is."

"Mash the potatoes. How could I forget? It's the only cooking function my family trusts me with." Taking the spoon from Natalie, he stirred and tested the potatoes for doneness. "I'm an expert after all these years."

"Kurt and Kevin," Natalie instructed, "you guys can set the table." She and Dad had already added the extra leaf, brought in more chairs, and covered the scarred oak table with Mom's favorite Christmas tablecloth, the one with the festive red border of poinsettias. "You know where Grandma's Christmas china is and the silver."

The gangly blond boys nodded in unison and strode to the corner-style china cupboard.

Daniel stepped closer, his hands stuffed self-consciously into the pockets of his suit pants. "I don't have a job yet."

Natalie blew a strand of hair from her forehead. "Would you get the casserole dish from the fridge and stick it in the microwave?" She glanced at the clock over the stove. "Ten minutes on high should do it. Then you can open the sparkling cider."

She set a pan of rolls in the oven and set the timer before pausing for a deep breath. Had she forgotten anything?

Lissa trotted into the kitchen, her face beaming. "Grandma's eyes opened for a minute. I think she's waking up."

Natalie's heart lifted. She cast a harried glance around the kitchen, torn between the myriad dinner preparations and a sudden need to go to her mother.

"Go on," Celia urged with a cheery wink. "The rest of us can get dinner on the table."

She smiled her thanks, tossed her apron across a chair, and hurried with Lissa to her mother's room. Her father sat next to the bed and tenderly stroked Mom's hand. She stepped closer and touched his shoulder. "How's she doing, Dad?"

He smiled up at her, his eyes moist. "Still dozing. But feel her face. No trace of fever. And Carolyn says her lungs sound clear."

Lissa squeezed Natalie's waist. "It's a miracle, Mom."

"Yeah, I guess it is." A wave of emotion swelled, awe and humility and gratitude so powerful that Natalie feared her knees would buckle. She nudged her father's arm. "Daddy, would you mind if I spent a few moments alone with Mom?"

He glanced up with a questioning smile, then rose and nodded. "Lissa, let's you and I go see if we can help with dinner. Carolyn, want to join us?"

The door closed behind them, and Natalie sank into the chair her father had vacated. She pressed her mother's hand between her own and leaned close. "Hi, Mom. Can you hear me?"

Her mother's eyes fluttered open. The blue-gray gaze shifted toward Natalie, and a single tear slid down Mom's pale cheek.

"I just wanted to tell you, I understand now. I know what you were trying to tell me."

Several blinks. Another tear. A semblance of a crooked smile curled her mother's lips before her eyes drifted shut again.

Natalie rested her forehead upon the soft cotton quilt, soon wet with her own tears. *Gracious God, thank you for letting my mother see one more Christmas. Thank you for giving me the chance to show her how very much I love her, how much I love all my family.*

Rising, she pressed her lips to the wisp of silver hair curling at her mother's temple. One very important Christmas tradition had yet to be fulfilled, and she felt sure Mom wouldn't mind delegating the task this year.

In the kitchen Natalie found Lissa fiddling with a poinsettia-shaped napkin ring. A tingle of anticipation racing up her spine, she drew her daughter toward the hallway. "Come with me. I need your talents for something special."

The living room lay in afternoon shadows, illuminated by only the twinkling Christmas-tree lights and the glow from the wood stove. Natalie quietly closed the door to the kitchen, and the clatter of dishes and cooking utensils faded.

Lissa paused in front of the nativity scene, her eyebrows quirked in a questioning frown. "So what are we doing?"

With a secretive smile, Natalie crossed in front of her bewildered daughter and into the alcove. She rummaged through her mother's paint supplies and handed Lissa a thin sable brush. "How would you like to paint a star?"

⌘

The pungent smell of oil paint tickled Lissa's nose as she bent over the starry backdrop. She dipped the brush into a swirl of white and yellow paint, then bit her lip, her hand poised in midair.

"Mom, I can't. This is Grandma's job."

Mom tucked an errant strand of Lissa's hair behind her ear. "Grandma's still pretty tired from being sick. And she's already kept the biggest promise to Granddad, don't you think?"

Lissa quirked a smile. "Yeah, she made it to their fiftieth Christmas. But still . . . "

"I know, painting the star is Grandma's tradition. But traditions are for sharing, and I don't think Grandma will mind at all passing the job to her artistic and very determined granddaughter. After all, you're the one who reminded everyone how important this Christmas is."

Though Mom tried to sound cheery, Lissa couldn't miss the tremor in her voice. She fought extra hard not to cry herself while her heart overflowed with a confusing mixture of love and sorrow and pride.

Mom studied the backdrop. "Look, here's a good spot, right near the center. Make it a nice fat one, okay?"

Tentatively, Lissa touched the paint-coated brush to the midnight-blue backdrop in the spot Mom had indicated. With delicate strokes she fashioned an elongated star of palest yellow, then highlighted it with a light touch of shimmering teal blue. She sat back and blew out her pent-up breath.

"Beautiful," Mom whispered.

"I don't know." Lissa frowned and shook her head. "It's not as good as Grandma's stars."

Her mother's lips brushed the top of her hair. "It's perfect. Your grandmother will be so proud of you."

Lissa shivered with happiness. She reached for her grandmother's stained paint rag and wiped the excess paint off the brush before swirling it in a jar of brush cleaner. "Grandma's proud of you, too, Mom."

Her mother cast a bemused smile. "I know she is. For a long time I'd forgotten, but I'm finally beginning to believe it again." After another inspection of the newest star, she nodded with satisfaction. She lifted the backdrop from the easel and set it reverently in its place behind the nativity scene.

Lissa joined her next to the library table, silently intertwining her fingers with her mother's. Her gaze fell upon the ceramic baby Jesus, sleeping in the manger between the kneeling figures of Mary and Joseph. "I guess Jesus is the only kid in the universe who never goofed up and did something stupid."

"I bet Mary and Joseph would disagree." Mom released a gentle laugh. "I can just imagine how worried they were the time they searched and searched for him, only to find him talking with the teachers in the temple."

Lissa's stomach tightened. "Like you and Dad worried when I ran away and hid in Granddad's barn?"

"Exactly." Mom fixed her with a sad-eyed stare and squeezed her hand. "I worried, yes, but more for selfish reasons, because I didn't think I could handle one more problem. I was hurting so badly myself that I didn't even try to understand the pain you were going through after your dad and I separated."

Lissa curled her tongue over her upper lip. "I didn't try very hard to understand how you were feeling, either. You were so upset about Grandma, but I just wanted to find a way to get you and Dad back together. Mom, I . . . " She drew in a shaky breath, afraid to meet her mother's eyes. "I have to tell you something."

"Lissa, you know you can tell me anything, don't you?" Mom gulped suddenly, her lips flattened into an embarrassed frown. "Okay, maybe you *don't* know that. I haven't been very easy to talk to for quite a while now." She led Lissa to the chair and ottoman, where they sat facing each other. She clasped Lissa's hands. "But I'm listening now. What is it, sweetie?"

Taking courage from her mother's reassurance, Lissa inhaled deeply and poured out the same story she'd confessed to her father two days ago. Only when she finished did she lift her eyes to meet her mother's stunned gaze. "Are you mad? Will you ever forgive me?"

Long moments of silence passed while Lissa tried to read the expressions flitting across her mother's face. Everything she'd expected was there—shock, disbelief, confusion, regret. Then, finally, understanding.

Mom squeezed her hand. "Remember what Grandma told me the day she got so sick?"

Lissa spoke softly as the remembered terror of that afternoon ripped a wider hole in her heart. "She said it wasn't your fault. She told you to forgive and learn to love."

"It's taken me until this morning for those words to sink in. Grandma never once blamed me for not being there to help her the day she had her stroke. But I wouldn't listen to the truth—about what happened to her, about what forgiveness means, about how much you and your dad needed me." Her voice became breathy. "About how much I needed your dad and you. I didn't believe I deserved to be loved, so I pulled away from everyone I cared about most."

Lissa sniffled. "I kind of feel that way, too, after what I did to you."

"Then it's time we both learned that's *not* what families are all about." With misty eyes Mom glanced toward the nativity scene. "God gave his most precious gift to us by creating a special family. I'm sure it was so Jesus could learn firsthand about loving and forgiving." Her eyes twinkled. "Even when we really, *really* goof up."

"I think I get it." A pleasant warmth spread under Lissa's heart. "Family should mean we don't ever have to wonder if we're good enough or if we're forgiven. Our family loves us no matter what."

She paused, a hitch in her breath. "Mom, does this mean . . ." She almost couldn't get the words out. "Does this mean you and Dad will try to work things out?"

"I hope— "

Before her mother could finish her answer, a knock sounded on the closed living-room door. Uncle Hart's voice came from the other side. "Hey, you two, I don't know what kind of Christmas surprise you're cooking up, but dinner's on the table. Better come now or we'll start without you."

"Goodness, I lost all track of time." Lissa's mother started for the door, then glanced over her shoulder with a conspiratorial grin. "Not a word to anyone about the star, okay?"

Lissa gave a firm nod, another rush of pride swelling her heart. As she rose from the ottoman, her toe caught on something propped against the side of the chair. When she bent down to see what she'd hit, her gaze fell on the most amazing oil portrait she had ever seen.

"Oh!" The image of her family so marvelously interconnected filled her with new hope. She lifted her eyes heavenward. "Thank you, Jesus, thank you!"

‿✷

Natalie sighed with contentment and folded her napkin beside her empty plate. The sight of her family gathered together sent a shiver of delight through her limbs.

Daniel raised his glass of sparkling cider. "A toast to the chef."

"Hear, hear!" chimed the family.

Natalie smiled her thanks, not trusting herself to speak.

"And that was the best pumpkin pie I ever tasted." Hart leaned sideways to give his wife a hug.

Celia poked his ribs. "You mash a mean potato, yourself, Dr. Morgan."

"Why, thank you, ma'am." He pushed his chair away from the table and patted his full stomach.

Natalie glanced down the table at her father. He had eaten his Christmas dinner in silence, occasionally looking toward the empty chair at the opposite end where Mom should have been. At Natalie's suggestion they had set an empty place in honor of Belinda Morgan. Throughout the meal it had been a comforting yet poignant reminder of the special joy she always took in this holiday.

"Well," Hart began, "time to make use of my only other culinary talent—doing the dishes." He started to rise.

"Dishes can wait," Natalie said. "Dad, what would you say about us moving the rest of our Christmas celebration to Mom's room?" She stood and reached for his hand, a flutter of excitement tickling her insides.

It took him a moment to draw his gaze from Mom's empty chair and focus on Natalie. He looked up at her and smiled. "I think she'd like that."

"Everyone come help." Natalie's glance took in the whole family as she gave her father's hand a tug. She led them into the living room and started gathering up the gifts from under the tree. "Kevin and Kurt, would you take Joseph, Mary, and Baby Jesus from the nativity scene and set them on the dresser in Grandma's room? And Lissa," she added with a wink, "you can carry the backdrop."

Balancing an armful of gifts, she nodded to Celia to collect a few more. "Dad, Hart, and Daniel, maybe you could grab some extra chairs."

Before long, the guest room hummed with Christmas cheer. Natalie assured Carolyn they would keep their celebration low-key, but watching them arrange the gifts and nativity scene had already brought an unmistakable sparkle to Mom's eyes. The tilt of her lopsided smile made Natalie's heart sing.

When everyone had gathered, including Sky, the huge Great Dane, Natalie crossed to the dresser and adjusted the star-studded backdrop, making sure to center it just so behind the ceramic figurines of Mary, Joseph, and Jesus.

"Remember how Mom would get up before dawn to paint the star each Christmas morning?" She paused as she situated herself on the foot of her mother's bed. Admiring the starry scene through misty eyes, she went on, "When I was a kid, the first thing I'd do—even before looking for my presents under the tree—was to see if I could pick out the newest star."

Hart gave a soft laugh. "Yeah, me too. It used to be a competition to see which one of us would find it first."

"Think you can spot the new star today?" Natalie glanced at Lissa and winked.

"What—how—" Hart's brow furrowed as he looked from Natalie to their mother to the painting.

"I see it," Dad said, his voice barely audible. He lifted a hand and pointed. "There, the yellowish one near the center."

Hart moved closer and grinned appreciatively. Hoarsely he said, "Nice work, Rosy."

"Actually, Lissa painted the star. I didn't think Mom would mind passing the torch this year." She angled her mother a smile and glimpsed a grateful tear sliding down the wrinkled cheek.

No more words were spoken. None were needed. Stiffly, Natalie's father rose and moved his chair next to the scrawny Christmas tree and the pile of gifts in front of the dresser. Following his usual custom, he selected gifts one by one, read the tag, and handed the gift to the recipient. They took turns opening their presents and expressing thanks, and when all the packages were unwrapped, Natalie stood to begin the task of gathering up the torn paper and bows.

"Hang on, sis." Hart rose and nudged her back to her place on the end of the bed. "Everybody stay put. I'll be right back."

Kevin rubbed his hands together and elbowed Kurt. "I *knew* there had to be more presents. Santa forgot our new iPhones."

"In your dreams, boys." Celia tousled her nearest son's hair.

Before Natalie could ask if her father knew what Hart was up to, he returned with a small gold-wrapped box and a tall red Christmas bag. He set the packages at Dad's feet. "These are from Mom. She had me hide them in the clinic storage room nearly a year ago, and the secret's been burning a hole in my brain."

"What in the world?" Dad spread open the top of the bag to peer inside.

"Wait, I think you're supposed to open the little box first." Hart grinned at Mom, leaned over, and folded his arms across the back of Dad's chair.

Natalie's heart gave a thud. Her mother had been one busy lady before the stroke. Once again, Natalie wondered if Mom had suspected she wasn't well, but this time the thought made her cherish her mother's stubborn determination even more. And she realized something else, that perhaps in her mother's desperate attempt to speak two days ago, she had also been asking forgiveness for herself.

Dad balanced the gold box on one thigh and fiddled with the red-and-gold metallic ribbon until it fell away. When he lifted the lid, Natalie could just see the top of a Christmas ornament nestled in a soft bed of sparkly tissue paper. Her father crooked his work-roughened fingers around the tiny metal hook and lifted out the ornament. As it caught the twinkling tree lights, a collective sigh filled the quiet room.

Happy Golden Christmas, read the finely painted white script. A shiny gold background shone through the hand-painted lacy filigree decorating the rest of the ornament.

Dad made a choking sound, part laughter and part tears. Natalie hurried to his side and wrapped her arms around his neck. "Daddy, it's beautiful."

"There's one more gift." Hart patted his father's shoulder. "Open the bag, Dad."

While Dad reached inside the bag, Natalie took the ornament and found a prominent spot for it on the little Christmas tree. She turned in time to see tissue-paper wrapping fall away from another poignant painting—Mom and Dad, just as they appeared forty-nine years ago in their wedding photograph.

Daniel came and stood beside her, his hand creeping into hers. "I never realized how much you resemble your mother."

Her throat hurt too much to speak. She could only lean into him with a happy shiver.

The Christmas music playing on the living-room stereo faded to silence. Dad stood and lovingly set the wedding portrait in his chair. Moisture seeping from his eyes, he paused to admire the painting and then bent over the bed to give his wife a long, sweet kiss. "Thank you, my sweet Belinda, thank you." Straightening, he draped his arm around Natalie's other side and cast her a grateful smile. "And thank you, too, Rosy-girl. You made this a day we'll all cherish forever."

Snuggled between the two men she loved most in this world, Natalie wished time would stop. She stretched up to kiss her father's crinkly cheek. "It's Mom who made this a day to remember. She really outdid herself this Christmas, didn't she?"

"In spite of everything." Dad pressed his head to Natalie's. Releasing her, he returned to the bed to stroke his wife's face. Adoring eyes beamed up at him. "I reckon it's about time for evening chores, darlin'. You rest easy for a bit, and I'll sit and read to you soon as I'm done."

"I'll help with the horses, Granddad." Lissa hurried to follow her grandfather out, Sky trotting behind. "Back soon, Grandma."

Hart, Celia, and the boys went to the kitchen to begin the cleanup there, while Daniel stayed behind to help Natalie restore order to her mother's room. While she gathered the opened gifts, Daniel started carrying out the extra chairs. She caught up with him in the living room as he returned one of the straight-backed chairs to its place beside the library table.

He stooped to reach behind the easy chair where Natalie had been sitting earlier with her father. "What's this?"

Natalie glanced over to see him retrieve the portrait her mother had painted of them. Her heart skipped a beat as she watched Daniel's eyes grow wide. His lips parted in an awe-struck grin.

"This is beautiful," he breathed. "I thought the painting of your mom and dad was awesome. But this one's absolutely incredible. Why didn't you show it to me sooner?"

"Dad brought it to me early this morning. Then everything got so busy with church and dinner and all, I didn't think about it again." She timidly stepped closer, admiring the painting over his shoulder. Her glance fell to Daniel's extended arms, the cuffs of his white dress shirt rolled up. She noticed for the first time that he still wore his wedding band, and she self-consciously touched the naked ring finger of her left hand.

"Did you notice?" she asked softly, brushing her shoulder against his. "We haven't argued once today."

"Yeah. It's been nice." As natural as breathing he slid his arm around her and drew her close, his cheek pressing against her hair.

"I can't make any promises," she whispered, thinking of all the hurt that had passed between them, thinking of her mother and father and fifty years of time-tested love. She knew Mom and Dad had their share of rocky times, too, and loud, lengthy quarrels that sent Natalie and Hart scurrying for cover in the barn. But somehow their love had survived, even flourished. *What's their secret?* Natalie wondered, even as her own arm curled around Daniel's waist, feeling its tautness and warmth.

"I don't have to take that job," Daniel began. "We could wait and see—"

"Not now." She pressed a finger to his lips. "Just hold me."

Forgive yourself. Forgive each other. Her mother's voice rang through her thoughts, the message now crystal-clear. *Nobody's perfect—only God. And he's the best forgiver of all.*

She tilted her head to gaze into Daniel's eyes, and the love reflected there rocked her to the core. His strong arm supported her, and moments later she found herself locked securely in both his arms.

And loving every minute of it.

"I love you, Natalie," he whispered as his lips brushed hers.

"I love you too. I always will," she answered, and welcomed the warm, lingering kiss.

✑

Belinda Morgan let her gaze drift around the now quiet room. Fifty perfect Christmases. Maybe not perfect by the world's standards—was anything this side of heaven? How many times had she overcooked the turkey or purchased a gift the wrong size or color? How many Christmases were interrupted by an ice storm or a horse with colic? How many holidays had been marred by family squabbles, the flu, unexpected repair bills, or just someone's bad mood?

But today, surrounded by her family, witnessing the joy in her husband's eyes as he held their special "Golden Christmas" ornament, seeing Natalie smiling and once again in Daniel's arms where she belonged, Hart and his family . . .

She wriggled her head deeper into the billowy softness of her pillow and closed her eyes. *Thank you, Jesus. Happy birthday and Merry Christmas.*

Discussion Questions

1. Natalie Pearce is the central character in *One Imperfect Christmas*. How would you describe Natalie to a friend? What are her most notable strengths and weaknesses? In what ways do you identify with Natalie? How are you different?

2. Natalie's mother always made Christmas an extra-special time of year for the family. In what ways do you think such traditions helped shape Natalie's character and values? What is your favorite Christmas memory? Do you have special family traditions?

3. When Natalie's mother is incapacitated, Natalie blames herself. Given the circumstances, do you think she could or should have done anything differently? How would you distinguish between self-care and selfishness? Which was it for Natalie? Have you ever experienced similar guilt and wished you could change the past?

4. Natalie's guilt causes her to withdraw from her husband and daughter. Why do you think Natalie found it so hard to open up about what she was going through? Could her family have done more to help her face her feelings?

5. Daniel, Natalie's husband, struggles to balance career aspirations with his family's needs and desires. Do you think it would be unfair of him to uproot his family in order to advance his coaching career? How can a married couple determine whose needs take priority when family or career pulls them in opposite directions?

6. Why do you think it's sometimes difficult for a Christian to admit to the reality of depression? Whom do you find it easier to talk to during difficult times? A family member? Friend? Pastor? Counselor? How could you encourage someone who is hurting to share the burden?

7. In small communities like Fawn Ridge and Putnam, it's hard to be "invisible." In what ways do you think such a close-knit community helped or hindered Natalie and Daniel? Describe life in your community. How well do you know your neighbors? Could you count on them in a crisis? Could they count on you?

8. At times Natalie felt it would almost be better if her mother died rather than continue as an invalid. Can you identify with such feelings? Is it possible to find value in human suffering, for the

sufferer as well as for those who love and care for the person? Have you known someone whose suffering helped you grow in some way?

9. Natalie's daughter Lissa refuses to accept the end of her parents' marriage. Do you think she goes too far to keep them together? How would you describe Natalie and Daniel as parents? What have they done right? How have they failed? Do parents' mistakes say anything one way or the other about how much they love their children?

10. Deannie, Natalie's assistant, has her own motives for interfering in Natalie's life. Why do you think she became such a willing accomplice in Lissa's plans? Was her Uncle Jeff too forgiving or patient with her? Describe a time when you gave someone a second (or third or fourth) chance. Did it work out? Why or why not?

11. During one of her counseling sessions, Natalie finds herself calling her mother stubborn. Is she right? What kind of mother do you think Belinda Morgan was?

12. What legacy do you think Belinda most wants to leave to her family? What legacy do you want to leave to your loved ones?

13. We tend to think of Christmas as a time for miracles and often create unrealistic expectations for the holiday. Why do you think that is? What was the real Christmas miracle for Natalie? What would constitute a "perfect" Christmas for you?

∽ ∽ ∽

Want to learn more about author
Myra Johnson and check out other great
fiction from Abingdon Press?

Sign up for our fiction newsletter at
www.AbingdonPress.com
to read interviews with your favorite authors, find
tips for starting a reading group, and stay posted on what
new titles are on the horizon. It's the place to connect with
other fiction readers or to post a comment about this book.

Be sure to visit Myra online!

www.myrajohnson.com
www.myra.typepad.com

12/12

CPSIA information can be obtained at www.ICGtesting.com
Printed in the USA
BVOW072253311012

304382BV00001B/8/P

9 781426 700705